T0363549

Wanderers No More

A NOVEL

MICHELLE SAFTICH

ODYSSEY
BOOKS

Published by Odyssey Books in 2017

Copyright © Michelle Saftich 2017

All rights reserved. No part of this book may be reproduced or transmitted by any person or entity, including internet search engines or retailers, in any form or by any means, electronic or mechanical, including photocopying (except under the statutory exceptions provisions of the *Australian Copyright Act* 1968), recording, scanning or by any information storage and retrieval system without the prior written permission of the publisher.

www.odysseybooks.com.au

A Cataloguing-in-Publication entry is available from the National Library of Australia

ISBN: 978-1-925652-06-2 (pbk)
ISBN: 978-1-925652-07-9 (ebook)

This is a work of historical fiction, inspired by real-life persons and events. Names, characters and incidents have been changed for dramatic purposes. All characters and events in this story—even those based on real people and happenings—are entirely fictional.

Cover image from Alamy

For my father, Mauro, and in memory of his family.

*Also, for my husband, Rene, and sons Louis and Jimi
who inspire me to write about family and love.*

Chapter one

15 September 1950
Newcastle, Australia

The ship, now that it had its destination in sight, was groaning and lunging against the waves, eager to put an end to what would be its final run as a carrier from Europe to Australia. The industrial port was used to seeing vessels loaded with coal heading out between its heads, passing the lighthouse that watched them go. But this ship, the *Amarapoora*, was coming in and it was not carrying a cargo extracted from underground seams, but from a continent that had been left reeling from a long and devastating war.

It was a transportation that came with hopes, fears and mixed expectations. On board this 8,000-plus tonne former hospital ship were six hundred and thirty-four migrants, who had been collected from the Italian port of Genoa. They had been forty-six days at sea, longer than expected, for the ship had been hampered by mechanical problems. Most had boarded holding the hands of their loved ones and little else.

One of those passengers was a brown-eyed boy of six, travelling with his Italian family.

Each morning on the ship, Martino Saforo awoke to the scent of sweat, sea salt and stale air. But no more. This was the last day stuffiness would greet him at dawn. For today, he was to go ashore. Land! He couldn't wait for his feet to be upon it and he was even more excited to cast his eyes over this big, faraway land.

Pulling on a shirt and clambering over his brother, who

shared his bunk, he leapt down, tugged on tight shoes, and scampered out of the women's hold.

The outside air was cool after the heat below, and his skinny legs struggled up steps to the deck. Clinging tightly to the rail, he reached the top and looked about.

'Papa!'

His father, Ettore, dressed in a loose-fitting white shirt, brown trousers and brown hat, turned and smiled, his eyes shining, and Martino darted towards him. Within seconds he felt hands scooping him up and planting him upon broad shoulders. Being careful not to knock the hat, he clung to his father's sturdy neck, somehow without choking him. High and secure, he was now assured a good view of their docking.

It wasn't long before he saw his mother, Contessa, flustered and anxious, and his strong-looking Nonna haul themselves up on deck. Behind them were his two older brothers Taddeo and Nardo, his older sister Marietta and the youngest of them all, Isabella, just four.

'We're here,' he called to them and they spied him at once, his head sprouting above the milling passengers, who were fast gathering for their imminent arrival.

'Take this,' Nonna said on reaching him and placed a bread roll in his hand. 'You ran off before breakfast.'

Martino wolfed down the roll, chewing without tasting. He could always count on Nonna to see that he was fed. But for once his mind was not occupied by hunger, but by the excitement of what lay ahead.

Their ship had passed through the heads and was cutting its way into port. Australia! How long had his family been talking about coming here? Everything was going to get better now. Here, there was work. And he knew that with his father working, they would be able to afford nicer food, buy new things and, one day, buy a house. He had seen apartments and houses, trampled through their yards, peered through windows, wondering what it must be like to have a place of your own. But he had only ever known the life of a refugee: bedding down on the floor of noisy and crowded camps and queuing for food and showers.

His family's house had been bombed during the war, when his mother had held him as a baby in her arms. Friends had taken them in at first, but then came the four years of refugee camps.

His parents had often talked about their house. Nonna too, especially Nonna, as she loved to remember the past and tell stories of the wonderful times that had happened there, before the war; always she liked to remember their life before the war. He wished he could have seen their two-storey house. The bomb had left nothing but a hole in the ground, apparently. He had not seen the crater, the street, or the neighbourhood where he was born. Their Italian city of Fiume was taken by Yugoslavia, and he had been told it was not safe for them to return. He wondered if he ever would set foot there.

'Papa, what's the time? Are we getting off soon?' he asked, starting to get impatient.

'I don't know, Martino. I don't have my watch.'

Martino was instantly annoyed at himself for asking. Of course, his father didn't know the time. A few weeks ago, he had traded his watch for fruit when their ship had stopped off the coast of Yemen. Martino had been surprised to see men with dark skins in small boats paddle up beside the vast ship, waving their wares, and even more stunned to see his father unbuckle his round-faced watch with leather strap, offering it in exchange for a bunch of bananas and a few oranges. Even though such foods were scarce in war-torn Italy, he knew how much his father had treasured that watch. Appreciating the high price paid, he made sure he savoured his banana and sucked dry a piece of orange, tearing its flesh from the peel.

Their only other stop had been at Colombo, Sri Lanka, where Martino was delighted to see men with even darker skins and women in dazzling, light dresses of various colours. The world was starting to open up to him and he was curious ... what would Australia be like?

The deck was now crammed with people, craning their necks for glimpses of the city of Newcastle. He, too, had his eyes pinned on the passing shoreline and could see rows of large tin-topped wooden sheds, stacks of shipping containers, coal-filled carts and long, ugly warehouses.

Raised in a portside town, he was used to seeing the grotty side of a working harbour, and he was keen to see beyond it to the city. Surely, not long now. The ship was hardly moving and was so close ...

Suddenly, there was a raucous cheer from the passengers. Martino laughed at the sheer joy exploding around him. The ship had docked, finally. Looking below, he saw men in suits bunched together on the quay, forming an official welcoming party.

'We're here,' his father's voice boomed, and he felt strong hands swing him down from his vantage.

Passengers were already starting to shuffle towards the steps. His father grabbed hold of his hand, and with his free hand picked up their only suitcase.

'Come on. It's time,' he said.

He looked behind him to see Nonna holding Isabella's hand, and Taddeo, Nardo and Marietta walking with his mother. They moved along with the throng and eventually Martino saw that he was on the threshold of the steps that he had struggled up earlier.

'You go first,' his father said at his ear. Soon they were on the lower deck, then stumbling across a wooden ramp, their pathway outside to a congested quay.

'I won't miss that cordial,' Martino said to his brother, Nardo, who had appeared beside him.

'Me neither. You'd think they'd make another colour!'

'Come on, keep going,' their father urged.

They joined the end of a queue stretching from the customs office. Martino looked about for his family's friends who had travelled with them on the ship, but couldn't see them for the crowd extending in front of them and behind. Queues were familiar to him and he began to daydream as he so often did when stuck in one. A long time later, their documentation was sorted and stamped. As they walked through a gate, Martino glanced up at his mother and father. They seemed uptight, their backs straight, their chins high, but their eyes were sparkling with an emotion he rarely saw—happiness. He watched them look at each other, sharing the moment, and he understood.

They had arrived. They had got all the family there.

'Come on. Buses are waiting,' his father told them.

They walked briskly away from the port towards the inner city, coming into a street where there were well-dressed, ordinary townsfolk going about their daily business. Martino saw some glance over, their eyes quickly raking them up and down. A few gave a friendly nod or a smile, one man even waved, but there were others gazing at his family and the other arriving passengers with stony eyes, pressed lips, a couple of shaking heads ... Martino turned to his father, wondering if he could see the looks they were attracting. What was it? Were they doing something wrong?

Before he could ask his father about it, a young woman with short, wavy hair poking out from beneath a bell-shaped hat loomed close and pressed something cool and round into his hand.

'Here's a gift! Welcome to our country,' she said, speaking in English. Her smile was warm and genuine.

Martino blinked. What was she doing talking to him? What had she given him? A coin!

'Grazie,' he heard his father say on his behalf. He watched as the elegant woman glanced up at his father and, for some reason, started blushing and shifting uncomfortably. With a quick smile, she dashed off, moving towards another child.

Martino stared at his palm in awe. There sat a large, brown coin; on one side was the profile of a man's face, on the other side was an animal … a kangaroo!

'Let me see,' his brothers and sisters were instantly shouting.

'Keep moving,' their father commanded. 'We have to catch the bus.'

Martino shoved the coin in his pocket and hurried to catch up to his father. 'Why did that woman give me a coin?'

'She was being friendly. Welcoming you.'

'Is it much money?'

'No.'

'Who is the man on it?'

'The King of England.'

'Really? Australia has England's king on its money?'

'Yes. It was very nice of her.'

'It was! Why did she look at you strangely?'

'Did she?'

'Yes.'

'Martino, you ask too many questions. Just be happy a pretty lady gave you an Australian coin. You are lucky. Now, here's the bus.'

Standing in the aisle of the bus, Martino handed the coin to Taddeo, who at age thirteen was the eldest. He was the fairest of them too, not only in appearance but in his nature. He would ensure everyone had a chance to see it.

Ten-year-old Nardo peered enviously over Taddeo's shoulder. 'Why did Martino get a coin?' he muttered. 'I want one.'

'Your turn,' Taddeo said to Nardo, handing it to him. Nardo held it for a painfully long time, earning loud complaints from his sisters. At last, he passed it on to eight-year-old Marietta, and then to a pouting Isabella. When it returned to Martino, he was beaming with pride. The woman had given him a coin! Not his older brothers, who always got everything first, or his sweet-faced sisters, who were constantly being spoilt. Him! How happy he was. Perhaps Australia was going to be a lucky place for him.

The bus was roaring up streets, which were alive with morning activity. Martino saw rows of shops, selling clothes, medicines, meats, fresh bread. Above the shops were flat awnings, shading the footpaths. Above the awnings, the buildings rose for another storey, or several more; their brick or stone facades featured arched or rectangular windows, or signs made of large, cut-out letters. There were many shoppers keeping to the shade. The women looked nice, with full skirts, lovely hats, bright-coloured handbags, and matching shoes. He admired groups of them gathered on the street corners at kerbs, waiting for shiny motorcars to pass before crossing.

The clean and ordered city made for a wonderful sight after weeks of gazing at nothing but the sea. He also noticed that here, nothing seemed broken from the war. There were no boarded-up shops or windows, blocks of rubble or tanks rolling down the road. But soon the delightful shops and skirts and signs fell behind, and the bus took turns and ventured up streets into quieter areas. Houses appeared, impressive ones, solid looking, made of dark brick. They sat behind fences, side by side, on blocks that grew larger as they travelled further out.

It didn't seem long before Martino was no longer gazing at houses and cottages and wondering what they looked like inside, but instead was seeing broad expanses of countryside with the odd, lonely farmhouse. Now there was less to catch the eye, less to capture his imagination. Grassy fields, hills and farms stretched out in all directions. It was only when he saw a field of sheep that his eyes widened with interest again. He and his brothers found themselves laughing at the animals, so many of them, standing idle, with their narrow, dull-eyed faces and woolly coats.

Their amusement was short-lived. The sheep farms stretched on and on, providing a view of not much more than green grasses beneath four-legged, white blots. Where were they going? Was his father expected to be a shepherd? Where were all the houses, the schools, the coffee houses? Almost as soon as he had the thought, a row of cottages appeared. He noticed a church, a shop, and then the bus was travelling up the main street of a country town. At last, it veered to the kerb and grinded to an abrupt halt.

'It's a train station,' he heard his mother say to Nonna.

Martino hopped off the bus and glanced behind to see four similar buses also offloading passengers. As the footpath filled to overflowing, he suddenly heard: 'Martino, Martino!'

Through the crushing throng, he spied his best friend from Italy, Gian, straining against his mother's hand in an effort to reach him. Within seconds, he was surrounded by not only Gian's family but other friends from Italy too. Martino saw his father's friend, Edrico, and his wife Tazia, and their sour-faced son Monte, as well as the warm and friendly Coletta family—Lisa, Cappi, Lena and her husband Rico, and their daughters.

Constant companions in the refugee camps in Italy and on the ship out, the family groups were now overjoyed to find each other for the first time in their new country and there was a lot of talking all at once, no one listening to anyone else. Martino smiled, loving the security of being amongst familiar faces and having Gian by his side. He quickly showed his friend the Australian coin.

'Where did you get that?' Gian gasped. 'Did you find it?'

'No, a lady gave it to me.'

'Why?'

He shrugged. 'Maybe she thinks Italian boys are nice or something.'

'If only she knew!' he laughed.

'I think we need to go to the platform,' Nonna bellowed over the chaos. When the tall and staunch Nonna spoke, people listened. All the Italians in their group instantly started making their way inside the station. Martino felt his father take hold of his hand, and he was glad of it, for the crowd was thick. They gathered together on the platform, keeping close so as not to be separated.

'Well, we're here,' Martino heard his father say to his friends.

'Looks like they've plenty of room for us,' Edrico remarked. Short and almost completely bald, he kept his hat on and rocked on his heels to improve his height for a few seconds at a time.

'That's for sure,' his father said. 'We've seen nothing but open space since we left Newcastle.'

'And sheep!' Martino piped up, earning smiles from the men around him.

'A lot of sheep,' Roberto agreed. Roberto was a large-framed man, but was looking too thin for his size.

'Will we be living on a farm?' Martino asked.

'Who knows ... it depends on where they want us to work,' his father replied.

'They have space for us. Now I hope they have jobs,' Roberto commented. Anxious in nature, he was always quick to voice the fears that everyone else nursed. His wife Bianca gave him a sympathetic look as she tucked a pin into her coiled blond hair.

'Of course they have jobs, Papa,' Gian cut in. 'Someone has to get all that wool off the sheep.'

'Shearing! Hell! What would we know about that?' Roberto exploded, and there were smiles all round.

'As long as we get paid,' Edrico said, so seriously that the smiles turned to laughter. A banker before the war, money was often his greatest motivation.

Their chatter ended there, as a steam train rounded the bend and hissed to a noisy stop. Martino could hardly stand still. He and Gian loved trains! He couldn't wait to ride on an Australian one.

The train proved less exciting than he had hoped; it just traversed more countryside. After the train, they were put on a truck and taken just outside a small town called Greta. The truck made a turn off a dusty road and soon Martino saw that they were passing through a white gate and up a long driveway. On either side of the drive, he saw row after row of army barrack-style buildings. Was it an army camp? On the left were brown timber huts on stumps and on the other side were arched, steel sheds that looked like long tin cans cut in half.

He saw children jumping rope, a girl wobbling on one leg as she played hopscotch, and a group crouched down, flicking marbles. There were women standing around, some with babies on their hips, conversing in groups and men walking along the roadside, carrying boxes on their shoulders.

The engine was cut.

Martino watched his mother rise from her seat. She was wearing a long grey dress with a square neckline. The dress hung limply on her slender form. Her hair was a frizzy revolt of dark waves.

'Another camp,' she said, her voice thick with disappointment.

Martino was just as downcast. For some reason, he had thought they would be given their own place in Australia—like an apartment or a small cottage, something like a real home. But it seemed that wasn't to be, at least for a while yet. They had come from a refugee camp and they were being delivered to another one, a huge one.

'It will be okay, Mama,' Martino said, reaching for her hand. She took it and held on tight.

'Of course, it will be,' she said, proffering him a smile.

Other trucks stopped behind them and migrants were jumping off and amassing near the camp headquarters.

'Come on, then,' Martino heard his father say softly, his voice sounding husky. 'Let's go.'

A blue, red and white flag was hanging high on a pole at the administration building, where four official-looking men dressed in suits were waiting. Once the trucks had emptied out and everyone had assembled, one of them, an Italian interpreter, finally addressed the weary crowd.

'Welcome to Greta Migrant Camp. Welcome to Australia,' he said with a ready smile. 'We hope you find work and settle here happily. Firstly, let me advise you that you will be joining more than eight thousand people already housed in this camp. To begin, you must be registered and assigned to your accommodation. So we will start that process directly. Some housekeeping matters: meals are served in a common mess hall. The camp is divided into two sections, and in each section you will find a recreation hall, a chapel and a cinema hall. We hold social events, so there is some entertainment, and we try to organise bus trips into Greta. We are now close to capacity and have been setting up tents to ensure you are all accommodated. But for now, please queue here for registration at this building. More information will come later. No doubt you have many questions, and we have officers who can answer them in due course. But for now, we know you have travelled far and many of you are families with young children, so we don't want to keep you waiting any longer. We'll begin the necessary paperwork. Thank you.'

They were back in a queue, waiting for more forms to be signed and stamped and for an issue of clothing, linen, towels and a small allowance to be handed out. The sun was high in the sky when Martino, carrying some of the towels they had been given, walked with his family to their lodgings. They came to a door, one of many running along a shiny steel shed. His mother stepped forward and opened it.

'It's clean,' she murmured.

'And dry,' Nonna added.

Martino peered inside and saw six stretcher beds, a small cupboard, a window and little else. As he went to go inside, a wall of hot air met him and he hesitated. Nardo pushed him from behind and he stumbled in.

Achingly tired, Martino dropped the towels and flung himself down on a stretcher. His brothers and sisters did the same, keen to lie down.

'Children! Careful! These are not bunks,' his mother alerted them.

'I hope I don't break it,' his father remarked, assessing the narrow stretcher as he put down their suitcase and the bag of issued clothing.

'How long will we be here?' Nonna asked softly. Martino was unsettled to see that tears were pooling in her eyes.

'It's okay, Nonna. It won't be long, will it, Papa?' Martino asked.

'I don't know,' he shrugged. 'They didn't say. Soon, I hope. You heard the man, they are almost full here. They will have to give us jobs and move us soon. This is only temporary.'

'You always say it is temporary, but then it becomes years,' Taddeo said, sighing.

'It won't be years! Will it?' Martino found himself fearing the answer. He was exhausted from all the travel, from ship to bus to train to truck and was sitting on the same stretcher as Nardo, knowing that, as usual, they would have to share the same bed.

'No, definitely not,' his mother assured him. 'We will get a house, one day. We will ...'

'Not only that,' his father cut in. 'Tell me, what do you want to be when you grow up?'

'A soccer player—a great one,' Nardo replied instantly.

His father threw his head back with appreciative laughter. 'Good one. What about you Taddeo?'

'Me?' Taddeo grew serious and ran a hand through his fair hair. 'I want to help people. Maybe be a policeman or fireman or something like that.'

'I want to be a soccer player too!' Martino cried out.

'You're just copying your brother,' his father responded.

'No, I'm not. I can't help it if we want the same thing.'

'I want to be a ballerina,' Isabella stated.

'I want to sew,' Marietta said. 'I'll make ballet costumes for you, Bella,' she added and the sisters smiled at each other.

'All right. Well, in Australia, these things are possible. Here, you have a chance. In Italy, there are no jobs—they are all taken.'

Martino was not so sure. The Australian camp did not look like the place where dreams could come true. He gazed out the window and saw only the glaring steel sheeting of the neighbouring hut.

'First we must bring to life our most important dream. We must all work together to get a new house. Yes?' his mother was saying in earnest.

'That's right,' his father chimed in. His voice rose in volume. 'Any money we earn, we all put in the kitty for a deposit on a house. Together, we will save money so that we never have to live in a camp again. What do you say?'

'Yes, Papa,' Martino murmured, echoing his brothers and sisters. 'How long will that take?' A few weeks, months, years … he did not know, and it seemed his parents didn't know either.

'It will happen,' his father said simply.

It was hard to share his belief, and yet Martino found reason to hope. His hand went searching in his pocket, where his fingers found and grasped his Australian coin.

'Yes, here we will be lucky,' he said, only to receive a sharp blow from Nardo's elbow. The pain immediately made him feel less fortunate. He glanced sideways at his brother, who was looking at him as though he were crazy.

'Now, I'm going to find a barber. My hair needs a cut,' his father told them. 'I will be back in an hour.' He patted his eldest boy on the arm on the way out and Taddeo gave him a half smile.

Martino wandered to the doorway to watch his father walk along the steel barracks, his head bowed, hat tilted forward, and he could tell by his heavy stride that he was not as confident as he sounded. He was surprised to find himself feeling sorry for his father.

Then he felt his mother prodding at his shoulder.

'All right now, go outside and play. Explore if you like, but come back in an hour. Your Nonna and I will go see what the toilets are like. Isabella, you can come with us.'

Although he was tired, Martino listened to his mother and went outside. At least it was good to have solid ground underfoot again. He followed Nardo and Taddeo, who took the lead, Marietta hurrying to keep up with them. As soon as they rounded the first bend, they came across his friend Gian, his sisters Daniela and Francesca and his brother Elmo.

Martino stared at Daniela. Almost a teenager, she was one of the prettiest girls he had ever seen. Even now, with her fair, wispy hair pulled up into a messy ponytail, she looked like a princess from a storybook. But she only had eyes for his brother, Taddeo.

'How's your room?' she asked Taddeo with a friendly smile.

'Small and hot with stretcher beds,' Taddeo replied.

'We have real beds.'

'What, with a mattress but not on the floor?' Martino was stunned.

Daniela and Francesca nodded and giggled.

'How lucky.' He pouted.

'Gian says you got a coin,' Daniela said, comforting him. 'That's pretty lucky.'

'Yes, with a kangaroo.' He whipped out the coin and showed it around proudly. 'Gian, want to go searching for a real one?'

'A real kangaroo? Sure!'

'Anyone want to join us? We're going bush.'

'No, you're not,' Daniela said protectively. 'There are snakes out there!'

'We'll fight them off,' Gian shouted, and began running away, but Francesca, who was fast on her feet and impossible to outrun, charged after him and pulled him back.

'Come on, please let us go. We want to find a kangaroo,' Martino begged.

'No, you'll just get bitten by something horrible. You have to stay with us.'

'To do what?' Martino wanted to know.

'How about we check out the kitchens?' Daniela suggested.

'Great idea,' Francesca said, and Marietta nodded, her ringlets bouncing around her face.

'That's boring! Who cares about kitchens?' Gian said, sulking.

'The girls can do that. Let's see what other kids are doing for fun around here,' Nardo put to the boys. 'We might find a ball.'

Martino smiled—soccer!

Martino was happy to be on a ball hunt and joined the boys in strolling aimlessly around the camp, looking for other kids. As he rounded the huts, he heard languages he didn't know, just as he had on the ship. So many people from so many different countries, all here for a new life, he thought. He wondered what would happen to them all.

The grounds were spacious and Martino's mood brightened as he realised that the camp was going to make for a much better play area than the crowded ship. Suddenly, a group of boys playing cowboys and indians raced past, and he longed to run with them. So, intent was he on their game that he almost crashed into Elmo, who had stopped walking.

'How come the ground is black?' he queried, pointing to a large, grassless area backing on to the bushland.

A boy, making the sound of an indian, overheard the question and shouted back in Italian: 'They burn the grass to keep out the snakes and spiders.'

'You mean there really are snakes around here?' Martino was shocked.

'I see a ball,' Elmo shouted.

Sure enough, opposite the burnt-out strip, in a wide clearing on the bend, there were five boys kicking a ball back and forth to each other. Instantly, Martino's feet were itching for a kick. It had been seven weeks since he had felt the touch of a ball.

'You stay here. I'll go ask them if we can play,' Elmo said.

'I'll come with you,' Gian offered and the two broke into a trot, leaving the three brothers to hang back and wait. As soon as they were out of earshot, Taddeo turned to Nardo.

'So, what's the deal with Monte?' the older brother asked.

'What do you mean?' Nardo was on edge and rolled some stones with his big toe. Martino looked at them, wondering what was going on. What had he missed?

'You were staring at each other in the truck, all the way here,' Taddeo began.

'We were?'

'Yes, like two people who want to kill each other.'

'It's his problem.'

'You shouldn't have hit him,' Taddeo pointed out.

'You know why I did,' Nardo said, glancing at Martino.

Martino knew too. Back in Italy, Monte had persuaded him and his friend Gian to catch a train. The train had taken them miles away and they had become lost in the big city of Milan.

They were lucky to be found in time. Any later and their families would have missed the ship to Australia … Remembering it made Martino feel ill to the stomach.

'It was because of me,' Martino said guiltily. 'But I was the dumb one. Gian and I shouldn't have got on the train. We should have known better than to listen to Monte.'

'I'm glad I hit him. He deserved it,' Nardo muttered. 'He wanted you to be lost.'

'So why are you afraid of him now?' Taddeo asked.

Martino couldn't believe his ears. Was his tough brother afraid of Monte? It couldn't be true, but Nardo was squirming uncomfortably.

'Out with it,' Taddeo pressed.

'Nardo's afraid of no one,' Martino cried in his brother's defence.

'I'm not scared of Monte, but he doesn't play fair and he …' Nardo shook his head. 'Forget it. With some luck, Monte's father will get work in a different city to ours and I'll never have to see him again.'

At that moment, Elmo returned with a loud whoop. 'It's all on. Another three are coming so it will be a great match. Let's go.'

'I'm coming,' Nardo cried and ran to meet the other boys.

Martino looked at Taddeo. 'Why is Nardo afraid, do you think?'

Martino knew Monte was capable of anything. In Germany, at the refugee camp, he had drowned a litter of kittens just to get back at them.

Taddeo shook his head, his expression dark. 'Don't worry about it. There's nothing you can do anyway. You're just a little kid. Let's go play soccer.'

Chapter two

Dinner was a foul smelling, tough meat, served with gluggy rice. His mother told him it was mutton. Sheep. Of course it was!

Martino tried to eat it, but he just kept on chewing, unable to break it down enough for swallowing. What torture it was! As he thought of the sheep in the fields, he could feel his face tightening with disgust. He glanced at Nardo, sitting next to him. He had already pushed his plate away. Then he saw his little sister Isabella crying and clinging to Nonna, begging for something else.

'Isabella, just eat fruit,' Nonna whispered. All the children heard her and perked up. There was fruit! Martino looked around and spotted the basket of apples and oranges on a table beneath a window. That was for them? He sprinted with his brothers and the other boys to grab a piece, returning to the table in better spirits. The girls were slower, but also helped themselves to the basket.

As he bit into an apple, he saw his mother staring somewhat enviably at him. 'Want a bite?' he offered.

'Thank you, but no. You eat it,' she said. Looking back at her own dinner, she asked Nonna, 'Is this rice or glue?'

Martino was shocked. They wouldn't serve glue, would they?

'Tastes like glue,' Lisa replied. An old friend of her mother's, Lisa had lived most her life on farms and was used to eating gamey meat or slightly turned goat's milk, but even she was struggling to eat the meal in front of her. 'And this is one old sheep,' she commented. 'Believe me.'

After devouring two pieces of fruit, Martino was quietly listening to the adults talk at the table, when he started to close his eyes.

The next thing he knew, Nonna was pulling on his sleeve. 'Come on, Martino. Off to bed, my sweet one.'

In a daze, he leaned into Nonna and, with his family around him, staggered back to their shed. After changing into bed clothes, they all slumped into their respective stretchers, trying to get comfortable.

'Goodnight,' their mother said. She leant over Martino first to give him a kiss. 'You look sad. What's wrong?' she asked of him.

'I thought there'd be kangaroos in Australia. But there's only spiders and snakes and … sheep.'

'We are in Australia for a long time. You will have plenty of time to find a kangaroo.'

'At least we're in the Silver City.'

'We are?'

'Yes,' Marietta cut in. 'That's what they call this side of the camp. It's because the sheds here shine like silver. A man at the mess hall told us.'

Their father gave a snort. 'The Silver City … sounds nicer than what it is.'

'The other side is the Chocolate City …' Nardo piped up, wanting to show he had been listening to the man too.

'Because they have huts made of brown wood?' Isabella asked, taking a guess.

Martino and Nardo nodded.

'Chocolate. How I wish it was a real chocolate city,' Marietta moaned, hungry after only a dinner of fruit.

'Imagine, a whole city made of chocolate!' Martino exclaimed.

'You'd all get sick,' Nonna said, making them all laugh.

'No. It'd melt before we could eat it,' Marietta shot back.

'All right. Off to sleep now,' their mother said, chuckling

lightly. She closed the door against the insects. There were so many little things on wings fluttering about outside, things Martino had never seen before. He hoped they didn't bite or sting. The room darkened, and he became afraid. He started to wonder if there were snakes or spiders beneath their stretcher.

'Goodnight, everyone,' his mother whispered.

Everyone responded, then there was silence. Martino closed his eyes and decided to think of kangaroos instead of things that creep and crawl, and within minutes he had hopped off to sleep with them.

When he awoke, it was still dark. Morning felt a long way off and his family were sound asleep. Nardo was leaning against him heavily, making him hot. He nudged at him, but he didn't shift. Restlessly, he glanced down at his brother and saw that a stream of moonlight from the window had found his face. How handsome he looked in that pale light. As he gazed, he remembered what Taddeo had said about Nardo being afraid of Monte and he wondered what that meant. Had Monte threatened him? If only there was something he could do. Taddeo didn't seem to think he could help, but the problem was his fault.

Unable to drift back to sleep, he extracted himself from his brother and put his feet to the floor. Quietly, he crept to the door only three steps away, and opened it a fraction. He looked out. It was late; the moon hung high above the silent camp, creating shadows that leapt around on breezes. A buzzing sound blared in his ear, making him duck. The sound faded, then stopped. Frightened, he was about to turn back, when he saw a small, red glow not far away. Was it the eye of a beast? He stared, stunned frozen, then his nose picked up the scent of tobacco and he calmed enough to reason that it must be just the glow of a cigarette. He wondered who it could be, smoking alone outside their barracks. Intrigued, he stepped outside, and after closing the door softly, lightly stepped across the dirt path to stand behind a tree. Now closer, he could see the smoker more clearly. It was Cappi Coletta.

Cappi belonged to the family who had given his family a place to stay after their house in Fiume had been bombed. They were good friends, good people. His parents could not do enough for them. They would always be close and help each other … this thought had Martino thinking.

'Cappi,' he called softly, so as not to startle the lone, wiry Italian, whose hair was longish and as black as his eyes.

'Who is it?' the young man asked.

'Martino.' He came out from behind the tree and stood in the moonlight, showing himself.

'Martino! You're up late. Shouldn't you be in bed?'

'Can't sleep.'

Cappi nodded. 'Me neither. Not easy leaving your home country, is it? And then they bring us here, to the middle of nowhere!' He drew on his cigarette and exhaled. 'Can't smell the sea out here. It is strange not to have salt in my lungs. Might as well fill them with smoke instead.'

Martino smiled. 'We won't be here long,' he said. 'At least, I hope not.'

Cappi put the cigarette to lips now curving into a smile. 'No. Let's hope not. So, what is it then? Why can't you sleep?'

'I'm worried about my brother.'

'Which one?'

'Nardo.'

'Go on.'

'He's made a bad enemy …'

'Never a good thing,' Cappi said, his tone light. 'We all have enemies, but a bad one is a problem.'

'He's really bad,' Martino said. 'I think he might try and kill him.'

Cappi breathed out slowly, sending the stench of smoke in

Martino's direction. Sounding more serious, he queried, 'Who might kill him? Monte?'

Martino was surprised that Cappi had guessed correctly.

'You think Monte will kill Nardo? Is there a reason?' Cappi pressed.

'I don't think Monte needs much of a reason, but Nardo did hit him once—because of me.'

'I see. What do you want me to do about it?'

Martino was glad he was asking. Encouraged, he put forward his bold suggestion.

'The Australians are going to give our fathers jobs. Could you somehow tell them that Monte's father would be better off working in another city to my father?'

Cappi's lips twitched. He looked amused. 'That would make for a neat solution. But aren't you forgetting that Monte's father is Edrico, a friend of your father. Wouldn't they want to stay together? What makes you think I can interfere with a friendship?'

'My father would rather have a son alive than a friend in the same city. Look ... I know you have a way of making things happen. You saved Nardo once. You carried him to hospital.'

'So, you think me some kind of hero?' Cappi's face saddened. 'I fought in a war, you know? Lost my father and brother at the end of it. Couldn't save them, could I?' His voice had turned ugly, his expression uglier. He crushed the cigarette in his hand and flicked the bud.

'Sorry,' Martino said quietly.

Cappi looked as though he was about to walk off. He took a step towards the dirt path, then halted. He was still and tense, his face grim, eyes pained. He seemed to be struggling with himself. 'Nardo's a good kid,' the young man blurted at last. 'And Monte, well ...'

Martino patiently and politely waited for him to finish.

'All right. I can't promise you anything. These processes are complicated, but I'll see what I can do. No guarantees.'

Martino felt a surge of hope followed by a wave of gratitude. 'Oh thank you, Cappi … just for listening to me. Thank you.'

'No promises.'

'No. But thank you.'

'Now go back to bed and get to sleep.'

'Yes.'

'And Martino?'

'Yes?'

'You're a good brother.'

Martino did not know if it was true. His older brothers didn't want him around most of the time. 'Tell Nardo that. He hardly knows I exist.'

'Brothers know. They don't always show it. But …' Cappi's voice had thinned. 'Brothers …' He stopped talking and strolled away.

Chapter three

September, 1950
Greta Migrant Camp, New South Wales

'Come outside! Now! Kangaroo!'

Martino opened his eyes and bolted up. Gian's face loomed large.

'Where?'

'Follow me.'

Martino, wearing a T-shirt and shorts, leapt out of bed and followed his friend. Behind them were the rest of his family, curiosity drawing them out.

Trudging through dew-drenched grass, Martino was led to the edge of bushland, a section not burnt, on the outskirts of the Silver City. There he saw a small grey kangaroo, sitting peacefully in the early morning sun. It was on a slight incline, munching on the moist grasses.

Gian's family was there: his mother Bianca, father Roberta, his nonna Gilda, and his sisters and brother. Martino also saw Cappi's mother Lisa and her tall and gracious daughter Lena. Lena was holding hands with her husband Rico, an engineer, and holding on to their legs were their daughters, five-year-old Vittoria and Elisa, aged two. It was quite the gathering!

'What a bizarre creature!' Nonna cried.

'It's so cute,' a sleepy Isabella said, wanting to get closer, but Nonna held her back.

'Don't frighten it away,' the older woman advised.

Martino stared, awestruck, then remarked, 'It's like a giant rat!'

Everyone laughed.

'I wonder how high it can jump?' Daniela mused, and Martino saw her turning to Taddeo for an answer. Her long blond hair was a mess of tangles down her back.

Taddeo smiled. 'Hopefully, we'll get a chance to see,' he told her, and Martino looked back at the kangaroo, waiting to see if it would hop.

'I'll show you,' a voice boomed across the grassy slope.

Martino felt someone push him aside to get closer to the native animal, and then saw Monte striding purposefully towards it. What was the sturdy twelve-year-old going to do? He watched on, feeling a sense of dread.

Monte wasted no time in charging at the kangaroo, trying to grab hold of its weighted tail. The roo turned on him and stood to its full height. It no longer appeared small and vulnerable but feisty and calculated. Could kangaroos bite? Monte laughed and shaped up to fight it, making fists and dancing around on his toes. The roo gave him a furtive glance then retreated, hopping away at a steady pace. While pleased to see it in action, Martino was sorry to see it disappear into the thick scrub.

Monte's mother Tazia charged through the gathering to confront her son. 'Why did you do that?' she asked, sighing hard. 'You've scared it away. I didn't get to see it!'

Monte's father joined her, whispering harshly on his approach, 'Why do you think he did it? He just likes trouble. I've told you ...'

'Sorry Mama and Papa. Everyone wanted to see it hop. I made it hop,' Monte replied with a gentle shrug. He flicked his long fringe away from his eyes.

'Oh well. Nothing more to see here. Let's go,' Nonna said in her commanding voice, and the gathering turned to start walking back to the barracks.

Martino did not turn. He had caught hold of Nardo's face. Fear. Yes, he was seeing what Taddeo had observed. Martino glanced about and saw Taddeo wandering off with Daniela and everyone else drifting back to camp. When he looked back to Nardo, he saw him staring at Monte. It was then that Monte flicked something out from his pocket. A knife. Monte was flashing a knife, directing the twist of its shiny blade in Nardo's direction, his eyes conveying it was intended for him. Threat delivered, the older boy thrust the weapon back in his pocket and ambled away.

Nardo peered sideways, noticing Martino's wide-eyed gaze. 'Go back to camp, Martino.'

'Not without you,' Martino replied protectively.

Nardo, pale and edgy, seemed annoyed, then conceded. 'All right. Let's go back.'

'Nardo …' Martino began, struggling to keep up with the fast pace his brother was setting.

'No. Leave me. Just go away.'

'But …'

'Drop it. Nothing happened.' Nardo then broke into a run and flew away from him. There was no point giving chase. Nardo was faster.

When Martino reached their room, Nardo was busy dressing and then hurried out again. He couldn't stop him and didn't even try. Inside, he hung about. His mother, Nonna and sisters plucked out their clothes and towels and headed to the communal women's showers. Taddeo hadn't returned, probably still talking with Daniela. Alone with his father, he saw that he was dressing in his best trousers and white shirt with collar.

Still agitated by what he had seen pass between Monte and Nardo, Martino desperately wanted to tell his father about it. He knew he should. Nardo was in real danger, and if something were to happen because he hadn't spoken out …

'Papa …' Martino launched. 'There's something I need to tell you.'

'Not now, Martino. I have a very important meeting at the employment office. I want to try and eat something before I go. I'll need my wits about me. Maybe they want to discuss my new job.'

'But Papa ...'

'No, Martino. I need to be focused. This will affect the next two years of our lives.'

Martino suddenly understood the seriousness of what his father was saying. Two years was a long time. 'Why two years, Papa?'

His father was examining his coat, so Martino's question went unanswered. It was the coat his father had been given yesterday on arrival at the camp. He'd also been given a hat, a pair of boots and a few shillings.

Not one to be ignored when he had a burning question, Martino posed louder, 'Papa, why two years?'

'Huh? Oh, well in exchange for our passage to Australia, we were told that we would have to work for the government for two years. After that, we can work where we want and live where we want.'

'What work will you do?'

'That's what I'm about to find out. Should I wear the coat?'

'If it is an office job—wear the coat. If it is an outside job—don't.'

His father looked at him for a long moment. 'You know, you're right. No coat.'

'Don't you want to work in an office?'

'I'm afraid we won't have much choice. We are here as labourers.'

'Didn't you used to be a mechanic before the war? Won't they let you work on cars?'

For a moment, his father's eyes filled with memories and his faraway gaze softened with a sad longing. 'One day I will work on cars again. For now, we take what we can get or we may end up sitting around this camp forever! As for you, Martino, the best thing you can do is learn English and learn it fast. Then you can be a big help to your Mama and Nonna, and to me!'

Martino nodded. He wanted his father to be proud of him. 'Okay Papa. I will try and learn English—fast!'

'Good, good. Now I best get going.'

'But Papa, I'm worried about Nardo and Monte. They ...'

'Oh, not now, Martino. I have no time to hear about kids' squabbles. Nardo is a strong boy, capable. He'll take care of himself. Goodbye.'

His father ducked out of the room, almost as quickly as Nardo had.

'Good luck,' Martino thought to call after him.

It wouldn't be until later in the day at dinner in the crowded mess hall that Martino would hear news of the interviews at the employment office. With his family and their friends all seated at the same table, he kept trying to catch Cappi's eye to see if he had had a meeting too, and if it had gone well. But Cappi kept his head bent over his plate and was slowly scooping little pieces of food into his mouth.

The food, if it could be called that, was mutton chops served with gravy, peas and sloppy potato.

'Can't we get spaghetti?' Isabella had cried when the plate was put before her. At the word 'spaghetti', Martino's stomach grumbled.

'Not tonight,' Nonna replied sadly.

'I don't like these ...' Nardo announced, pushing peas around with his fork.

'One quick mouthful,' Nonna urged, though it hadn't escaped Martino that her peas were still swirling around in the gravy in her metal dish.

Then he heard Monte's father Edrico say. 'It seems there's not much permanent work around. Lots of temporary jobs, but men are not being placed for a long time.'

A long time! Martino was alarmed to hear it. He wanted to get Nardo away from Monte as soon as possible.

'Why bring us here if there isn't the work?' Roberto shook his head.

'Job markets change. This is a country of growth, the work will come,' Martino's father assured them. He was looking hopeful, despite the glum looks on his friends' faces.

'I don't like the sound of some of the jobs,' said Roberto. 'It seems we get the jobs the Australians won't do—the grimiest, and the dirtiest.'

'It's true,' Edrico backed him up. 'I've talked to a few of the men around the camp. Many of the jobs are terrible. A lot of migrants have got work at a project in the Snowy Mountains. They're building dams, power stations and tunnels. The work's gruelling, underground, and I heard they have to stay there for months at a time while their wives and children remain here.'

Martino couldn't believe it. It had not occurred to him that just the fathers could be sent away to work. The thought of having to stay at camp with Monte horrified him! No. That couldn't happen.

Rico leaned in and, glancing around, addressed their table softly, 'I've not told them I'm an engineer.'

'You haven't?' Roberto was astounded. 'How have you managed to keep it secret?'

'I just did.'

'You should tell. You will get a much better job and you'll find one straight away,' Edrico pointed out.

'I can get an engineering job at the end of the two years. For now, I don't want to be sent too far away from Lena and my daughters. It's best if we all stay together and get jobs in the same town. Lena and Lisa don't want to be separated from you. I've requested that we should stay together—that is more likely if I'm put down for general labouring, same as you.'

Martino was starting to despair on hearing that Rico had made such a request, when Monte's father countered, 'I want to stay together too but … there are some jobs I'd do anything to avoid, even separate from my good friends. Selfish as it may seem, I confess, I don't want to go down in the mines, couldn't. It would be unbearable.'

Cappi then joined the conversation, which surprised the group, as he rarely spoke. 'I'm certain to be given farm work. They know I have farming skills. I don't expect you to follow me. I'll go alone. Staying together is nice but I wouldn't have you suffer with me.'

'I go where you go,' his mother Lisa said vehemently.

'Me too,' Lena added.

'Then that's me in,' said Rico.

'Farm work probably means sugarcane cutting up north,' Edrico said slowly. 'It's hot, sweaty work and I've heard it's brutal on the hands.'

'If you get any better offer, take it,' Cappi urged. 'I mean it. You too, Rico.'

'We'll see,' said Rico. 'I've already told them we want to stay together, so we'll see what comes of it. At the end of the day, there won't be much choice.'

'I've heard you can say no to work postings a couple of times before they'll take away our pensions. If I get assigned to the mines, I'll say no to it. I'm with Edrico, I can't work underground,' Roberto declared.

'Eventually, my friends, all our roads will lead back to the capital cities. Wherever we go, we will see each other again at the end of the two years,' Ettore pointed out.

'I thought your road leads you back to Italy,' Edrico challenged.

'We all want to go back to Italy when we can,' Ettore agreed. He looked down the table and saw Martino listening intently. 'Isn't that right, Martino? We can go back one day, yes?'

'Yes, Papa. I'd love that.'

Everyone at the table smiled, sharing his view. They then returned to their meals of fried meat and tinned peas, swirling in thin, salty gravy. In such a moment, it was hard not to think of Italy and miss it dreadfully.

Chapter four

A couple of weeks went by and there was no news of job placements.

Monte was spending most his time in the Chocolate City and, as far as Martino could tell, was leaving Nardo alone. Martino was starting to relax about it. It seemed that the threat to Nardo had passed. Maybe Monte had just wanted to scare him and had now put their conflict to rest.

Another improvement to life at the camp was the food. His mother had become concerned at how little he and his brothers and sisters were eating. Wanting to find out if she could prepare her own food, she went in search of women who had been at the camp longer to see if it was possible. Her quest had her come across a group of Polish women cooking soup outside their barracks in big metal pots. She asked other Italians how they were preparing the food and learned that a butcher visited the camp once a week on Saturdays. From him, she could purchase better meat cuts, such as veal, sausage and pork.

His mother had told her friends and they had commenced working together to buy the meats and, as soon as could be arranged, caught a bus into the town of Greta to buy an oil cooker, a large pot and some seasonings. Martino watched as they set up their own cooking area outside, something they weren't sure if they were allowed to do, but no one told them to stop. Then Nonna happily directed in the creation of fine smelling broths or stews. Martino loved sitting near the bubbling pot, inhaling the aromas and waiting for the nice, flavoursome meal to be served. How he wished the butcher could come more often!

When not watching the cooking, Martino was mostly running about, playing soccer. There were always children to play with and it didn't matter if they couldn't speak Italian. He played with children from the Ukraine, Estonia, Poland, Germany, Austria and Hungary.

At night, he sat around the light of a bonfire with his family and friends and other Italian families who they had met at camp. Wine put the adults in a cheery mood, and once this state was achieved, one of the Italians brought out his accordion and played jovial music. He liked to sit with Gian, pointing out the strange behaviours of the adults affected by the combination of wine and music, and they would laugh together.

One morning though, his love of soccer led to a match of far greater consequence than usual. It had all begun after breakfast when a small group of boys from the Chocolate City had walked up to him and his brothers.

'Saforo,' one of them called on approach, and the three brothers had turned on hearing their family name.

'How about a serious match? Silver City versus Chocolate City, adults and children allowed, up to fifteen a side. Today, at three o'clock.'

They were instantly excited and asked questions, determining the place, the referee and the makeup of their team, then ran off to sort their own team out.

They found their friends Elmo and Gian, who agreed to play then decided they would need adults to join them if they were to have any chance of winning. They found their fathers seated in the shade around a small table. They were playing cards with Edrico, Rico and Cappi.

'What are you up to?' Roberto raised a bushy brow as they approached.

The children, seeking a spokesperson, looked to the eldest, Taddeo, to explain. He started to tell the men about the pending match in enthusiastic detail, only to be interrupted by Nardo.

'We want you to play with us,' he put to them.

'Us?'

'Yes, all of you,' Martino confirmed.

His father was smiling. 'I haven't played in years and my head is heavy with last night's wine. When is this match?'

'This afternoon,' Nardo replied. 'Please, Papa! Play!'

'I'm no good,' said Roberto quickly, shaking his head with a deep chuckle. 'I'm unfit, terribly unfit.'

'Papa, please!' Elmo begged him, his face falling.

'You can't disappoint your boy,' Edrico said. 'Is my son Monte playing?'

'He's joined the opposition, the Chocolate City,' Taddeo said hesitantly. 'In goals, as keeper.'

'He has? That sounds like Monte,' Edrico mumbled somewhat darkly. 'Well, I won't play against him then.'

'Cappi? Rico?' The boys looked to the younger men aged in their early twenties. They would be valuable to secure. 'Come on. We have to win this. The other side is mostly Croatian,' Nardo said.

That seemed to pique the men's interest.

'Italians versus Croats, you say?' Rico peered at Cappi, who had straightened.

'Tempting,' Rico said, his blue eyes flashing. 'Count me in.'

Once Rico had put up his hand, the others caved in one by one, Roberto agreeing last, but not least as far as his sons were concerned.

'We'll have the best team now,' Martino said.

'It doesn't make fifteen. You better go and see who else will join. We're going to need a full quota if we're to have any chance,' his father told them.

Martino ran off to help assemble a full team. Soon they had put together a side consisting of all Italians except for two Hungarians, a father and son.

When mid-afternoon arrived, they met on what would be the field, just a flat section of crisp grass, partly shaded by tall gum trees. The players were allocated positions. Martino was happy to be put on the right wing, where he could do a lot of running.

Then the spectators started to arrive. Hundreds of people began to take their places around their field; some dragging chairs from the nearest mess hall, some willing to sit on the ground and risk the ants. The soccer match seemed to have whipped up great interest amongst the migrants. A camp officer of British heritage turned up with a whistle to conduct the tough task of refereeing.

Martino stood on the field, his mouth gaping. He had never played before such a crowd.

'Hey, Martino. Turn your top inside out,' Nardo told him.

He did so, knowing it would help to tell the teams apart.

Then, at seemingly no time in particular, the whistle blew and the match began.

Martino should have known that having Nardo as striker and Monte as opposition goalie was inviting trouble. Nardo loved to score goals. It was what he did. And Monte hated to lose. It was a bad combination.

The adult players ran in short bursts and walked to catch their breath. Martino and the other children had the advantage of being young, and tapped into energy generated by nerves and excitement.

About fifteen minutes after kick-off, Martino saw Cappi kick the ball to Nardo, who was in full flight, sprinting towards the goals. The ball found his brother's feet at the right moment and he easily slotted it past Monte, who didn't have the speed to stop it.

The huge crowd to the left clapped and cheered as Nardo's team members slapped him on the back.

'That was fantastic,' Martino told his brother, in awe of his ability. But then he turned and beheld Monte. A chill ran through his body. Monte was clearly infuriated, an abusive tirade spitting from his lips. The rant went on so long that the referee was forced to approach him and, putting a finger to his lips, indicated that the keeper should quieten down or else. Reprimanded, Monte scowled and swept his longish hair back from his face. Although he had ceased his spiel, as soon as the referee turned his back, he spat on the ground in disgust.

Martino returned his gaze to Nardo and saw he had lost his victorious smile, his mouth now a grim, straight line.

'Don't worry about him,' Martino threw at him, although his words sounded thin.

'Sure,' Nardo said though it was clear he was rattled. Neither of them had ever seen Monte that irate.

The whistle sounded. It was time to recommence play.

Sadly for Martino and his team, their sense of triumph was to be short-lived. The opposition retaliated quickly, with an impressively swift Croatian sidestepping Roberto, and then evading Elmo in goals, to kick the ball through the goal markers.

The riotous applause from the spectators on the right of the field was deafening. Laughing, Monte did a couple of cartwheels across the face of the goals. When the celebration quietened, the players reassembled and faced each other squarely. Martino could feel the tension. He saw a desire to win gleaming in the eyes of the players around him. There was much flexing of legs, being pulled back in needy stretches, much raking of sweat-drenched hair, and many chests rising and falling.

Martino, too, was breathing hard. He wanted to do his part to help his team. Staying focused, he did what he always tried to do on field: he passed the ball to Nardo, putting it before him right in front of goals, twice. Both times Nardo took the shot, but both went wide, causing a loud collective sigh from their supporters.

Martino observed his brother's pained face and understood. The pressure was too much, the price of winning too high. Nardo did not want to upset Monte again. Scoring would be like slapping a hunting lion.

The half-time whistle sounded. The score was still drawn at one each.

Martino trotted over to join his team, huddled in a corner. Most had flopped to the grass in exhaustion, some even laid down flat. Italian women handed them metal cups of water. Martino guzzled his thirstily.

When his heart settled to a lighter beat, its thumping fading like a bass drum being marched into the distance, he found his voice. 'Hard game,' he panted to Gian.

'Tell me we don't have to go back out there,' Roberto gasped. He looked unwell.

'I won't tell you, though I think you know there are two halves to a soccer game,' Ettore responded.

Before long, the other team started taking to the field. They walked slowly, but their heads were up, and they looked calm and in control.

'Come on team,' Taddeo called. 'Let's go.'

Martino strolled back on.

The whistle blew and the ball was rolling.

Within minutes a Croatian player scored, creating such a cacophony of noise from one side of the crowd that Martino put his hands over his ears.

Searching for his brothers, Martino saw they appeared close to tears. They did not want to lose. Whipped up by the emotion around him, as soon as the whistle shrieked, Martino was running, kicking, tackling and pushing until his heart felt like bursting. At last, the ball was kicked from a corner and Cappi leapt to head it. The ball soared over Monte's shoulder and a goal was claimed. They had equalised. Martino was relieved. A draw would be a good result, he thought. No winner, no loser, and hopefully a calmer Monte.

There was only five minutes of play left. As they gathered for kick-off, Martino sidled up to Nardo. 'A draw is good, Nardo,' he pleaded. 'It's better this way.'

Nardo winced. 'You don't understand. I hate this. I want to score, but ...'

Suddenly, Cappi was beside them. 'If you want to score, do it. Forget the keeper. I've got your back—on and off the field. I've got your back. You win this, for yourself, for us, for Italy. No fear! Okay?'

Nardo stared at him. 'You don't know ...'

'I know more than you think. Just win it.'

Martino was uncertain. Why was Cappi egging him on? It wasn't safe. He was worried. 'You don't have to ...' he squeaked, but somehow his fear fed Nardo's courage. His brother picked up his feet, picked up his pace and ran to the field's centre.

Play resumed.

Nardo pushed up towards the front and Cappi shot him the ball from midfield. Nardo's feet brought the ball down and he danced it forward. He glanced up.

Monte was ready and lethal in his balanced stance.

Nardo's foot caressed the ball, pushing it one way, flicking it the other. Monte became confused and shifted to the right, and then the left. Thump. He kicked it straight—straight through Monte's legs, making him look a fool.

Although worry was churning in his stomach, Martino couldn't help but smile. The joy of winning was contagious. Everyone—his players, their supporters, and even the referee— had joyous laughter on their lips and in their eyes.

Cheers erupted—the loudest all game.

While Nardo was being surrounded by his players, Martino braved a glance back at Monte. The goalkeeper was frighteningly still and silent. No abusive tirade this time! His hands were clenched tightly by his sides.

Martino shuddered. Monte was obviously crushed. He looked around for Cappi and saw him walking alongside Nardo.

Cappi better protect Nardo, he thought. What had he promised … he had Nardo's back?

They returned to the field and the ball was back in play for just over three minutes.

When the whistle finally blew again to announce full time, they were declared the victors. Martino saw Nardo being carried on shoulders. He saw his mother blowing kisses at him. Nonna was shouting at the top of her voice, 'That's my grandson, that's my Nardo.'

But all Martino could think of were Monte's eyes, two slits of pure malice, fixed on Nardo's back. What had he done? As much as he loved to win, loved to see the joy that was now filling the field and surrounding them, he dreaded what would follow. Monte would not let this rest, he was sure of it. He vowed not to let his brother out of his sight.

That night, the Italians had more reason than usual to enjoy their wine around the bonfire, and the accordion came out early. The Silver City was noisy, the Chocolate City quiet. The music played and the Italians danced.

Away from the bonfire, under moonlight on a hill overlooking the camp, Martino was with a large group of children, his brothers among them. After several cups of red cordial, organised for them by the referee, they were high on sugar and playing chase. Running and shouting at night added an exciting quality to the game. Martino was pleased that Monte was nowhere in sight and so was happily screeching with pleasure as he ran to avoid being tagged.

Suddenly, he noticed Nardo galloping down the hill towards the toilet block. Keeping to his pledge, he started to follow, then saw what he had been dreading. Monte. Emerging from trees to the side of the toilet block. Not wasting a second, he pushed his legs to a sprint, pumping them hard, heading downhill but now towards the glow of the bonfire. He had to get help. He had to find Cappi. But he didn't have to go far. Cappi was at the bottom of the hill, seemingly waiting.

'Where are they?' he shouted before Martino could reach him.

'At the toilets.'

Martino was beside himself. He didn't know what Monte was going to do, but his mind was picturing the knife. Oh please, let Nardo be safe, he thought. He was angry at himself for not telling his parents. He should have said something, though he wondered if that would have helped. Monte had a habit of lying his way out of things.

Martino reached the toilet block and halted, madly searching for Nardo or Monte. Where were they? He heard a shuffle and looked towards the sound in time to see Monte flinging himself off a large, metre-wide cement pipe, landing on Nardo, crashing him to the ground. To his horror, Martino spied moonlight reflecting off a knife's blade.

'He's got a knife!' Martino alerted Cappi, who was a little way in front of him.

The two boys, locked in combat, were rolling across the grass, each gaining the upper position for mere seconds before being rolled again, until Monte had Nardo pinned. Martino could see Cappi running towards them. Hurry, Cappi, he thought and then he let out a squeal. The knife was hovering over his brother's chest. He was close enough to see Nardo bracing, terror stamped across his face.

And then miraculously, Monte was rolling across the ground, clutching at his own chest. Cappi had kicked him.

Martino raced over, hoping his brother was all right.

'It's mine. Don't,' he heard Monte pleading.

But Cappi ignored him and reached down and took the knife from the boy's hand. He shoved the knife's handle inside the waistband of his trousers. He then rested his boot on Monte's bruised ribs.

'Boys shouldn't be running around with knives,' Cappi told him.

'I wouldn't have used it.'

'Didn't look that way to me. You seem to have it in for Nardo. Whatever it is, it's over. You've had your fun. You've scared him. It's enough.'

Monte did not reply. Cappi put more weight on his foot, wresting a cry from the boy's hardened lips.

'Don't,' Monte urged between gritted teeth. 'Or I'll tell my father.'

Cappi looked amused. 'What will you tell him? That I hurt you after taking your knife away?'

'What knife?'

Cappi's expression hardened. 'Stay away from Nardo and his family. Got it? I don't care who your father is or what lies you tell. I don't care about much at all. So if I have to come looking for you again, I won't be holding back.'

There was an edge of hysteria in Cappi's tone and Monte seemed to register it.

'All right. Got it,' the boy spat.

'Now go, before I … just go!'

Monte sprang up and darted away towards the barracks.

Cappi took a moment to calm himself and then turned his attention to Nardo.

'Told you I had your back.'

'I was beginning to wonder.' He slapped on a brave grin.

'How did you know where I was?' Nardo asked.

'Martino told me.'

'Martino?' Nardo was surprised. He glanced behind him and saw his younger brother standing worriedly nearby.

'He's the one who has your back,' Cappi said.

'Thanks Martino. Were you really looking out for me?'

Martino felt strangely embarrassed. 'Yes.'

Nardo nodded. 'Thanks.'

Martino shrugged it off, but it felt nice to have his brother seeing him, really seeing him.

'You're lucky to have each other,' Cappi said. 'I'll get back now. I need a wine and a smoke.'

Martino watched Cappi make his way back towards the laughter, light and music and knew that he was lucky, very lucky. He reached in his pocket. His penny was still there. He carried it with him everywhere, every day. He wondered if it had helped Nardo that night.

'Who would have thought ...' Nardo was saying. 'My little brother, Martino, has my back!' He got up and walked over to him. 'Come on, let's go.'

'Can you wait for me? I need to go to the toilet,' Martino asked.

'You know what? Me too. Didn't quite get there!'

Chapter five

October 1950
Greta Migrant Camp

'Well, I asked,' Martino's mother told her family as she entered their room.

'Will they make it?' Isabella asked.

'They seemed understanding, so I think they will. It might not be the spaghetti you're used to but it will be better than more mutton. Now go out and play.'

But before they could, their father burst in. 'We've been notified,' he said in a rush.

'About the job?' Nonna asked.

'Yes, yes. We're going to North Queensland, at the top east of Australia. Roberto, Rico and Cappi have been placed with us too, but not Edrico. How strange! He's not going with us. He's going to work in Newcastle. There's a job for him at the BHP steelworks.'

'North Queensland! So far! Why isn't Edrico coming with us?' His mother appeared baffled.

Colour was draining from Martino's face. Nobody noticed him slowly sitting down on his stretcher bed. He was responsible. The weight of it was heavy. Cappi had somehow made it happen, but instead of feeling happy and relieved, he felt guilty. He was separating his father from his friend. He knew the two men had shared much together and now they were being torn apart in this big, strange country. His father looked sad.

While it meant they would travel far away from Monte, and for that he was grateful, he wondered if it was still necessary. Monte had not come near them since that night.

'I don't know how it happened. We all requested to stay together. Perhaps they don't think he'll be able to handle the tough conditions up north,' his father was saying, trying to figure it out.

'Tough conditions? What job is it?' His mother sounded concerned.

He hesitated to respond but with all eyes on him, he breathed out, 'Cappi and Rico will be cutting cane. Roberto and I will be building roads in the tablelands.'

'Oh Ettore ...'

'What's wrong with that?' Isabella asked.

'Nothing, nothing. It is a good job. I'm very happy.'

'Won't it be hard, building roads?' Taddeo asked.

'It won't be for long.' He shrugged. 'I can do it. I'm strong, yes?'

'The strongest,' Martino readily agreed, but everyone looked at him, for his words had been flung out on a sob of tears.

'Come now, Martino. What's wrong? It's not so bad.'

'But it is, Papa. And it's my fault.' Before he could stop himself, he was blurting, 'I didn't want Monte to be with us and so I had his father sent away. It was me. My doing. And now you will lose your good friend and are going north and not to a nice factory. Now you will build roads, a hard job, all because of me!'

He was sounding hysterical, he knew it, and his brothers and sisters were staring at him with confused expressions, but his father seemed to understand his blubbering and knelt in front of him.

'Calm down, Martino. It is all right. Rico asked for us to stay together and Cappi was always going to be sent north to the cane fields. The only change you have perhaps brought about is that Edrico gets to go to the factory, and believe me, for that he will thank you. He will cry and kiss your hands in gratitude. Edrico is today the happiest Italian in Australia. If it was you who did this, you have done him a great favour.'

'I have?'

His father nodded. 'And if I am a true friend, I will be glad to see him happy, even if it means we are apart for a couple of years. Two years is not so long.'

'You're not mad at me?'

'I'm a little surprised that you could arrange such a thing, and I won't ask how, but I'm not mad. We will all be together. Your mother has her friends: Lisa, Bianca and Lena. And you can attend the local school with your friends: Gian and Elmo, Francesca and Daniela … all of them! But not Monte. You see, you get your wish, and we're all happy.'

Martino tried to smile. Put like that, it didn't seem so bad. His father did look happy, or at least he was being successful in making them think he was.

'I have to take this paperwork to the reception for mailing,' his father said, coming to his feet. 'Once this is sent to Canberra, it's all locked in. We could go as early as next week.'

His mother wiped her hands on the folds of her long skirt. 'Okay. Let's not hold up the process. Send it off.'

* * *

That night in the mess hall, Martino was astounded to be served spaghetti with pieces of meat in a tomato-based sauce. It seemed the camp's cooks had listened to his mother.

Martino's stomach ached in anticipation. He picked up his fork and placed it in the pasta, spinning his fork to wrap the strings around it. But the pasta strands were slippery and slid off his utensil. He stabbed at them and shovelled them into his mouth.

Sugary tomato sauce lit up his tastebuds. He was ecstatic. Swallowing quickly, he took a gulp—then felt something sharp jam in his throat. It was lodged there. It hurt. He tried to breathe in, but couldn't. A gagging sound filled his ears. Was he making that noise? Air, where was it? Panic set in. He stood up.

As he came to his feet, so did every adult at his table, but his father reached him first. His lips were parted and he felt his father's fingers plunging into his mouth … his head was fuzzy, he was seeing coloured lights … a second later and cool air was passing over the searing pain in his throat. His lungs sucked it in and expanded. Martino was dumbfounded. What had happened? As his vision swam back, he looked at his father's fingers and saw they were clenching a sharp bone.

He looked at his father's face and saw fury rising fast. As his mother came to his side, his father stomped to the back of the mess hall towards the kitchen.

Everyone in the hall heard his shouting, though only those who could speak Italian would have understood. Martino heard him venting his outrage.

'Who in their right minds would cook spaghetti with mutton chops? You put bones in there. Bones! Who would hide such small, sharp things in a meal and serve it to children? You could have killed my son with your stupidity. All we get is mutton— even in the spaghetti. It is too hard to believe!'

His father stomped out of the hall, too angry to return to his half-eaten dinner.

Martino, his throat sore, looked to his Nonna for comfort.

'Don't worry, child. I should have taken charge weeks ago, but now I see I must do something. I'll visit the kitchen tomorrow and teach the Australians how to cook.'

'Will they let you, Mama?' Martino's mother asked, worried about interfering in Australian ways.

'It is worth a try, I think. Tomorrow. I promise.'

The following day, Nonna invited Martino to come with her to one of the kitchens at the Greta camp, saying it would be good for him to see the making of the spaghetti so he would not be afraid to eat it for fear of more bones.

They wandered in, uninvited, frightening the five Australian cooks with their sudden appearance. The aproned women, with their tied-back hair and bright lipsticks, stopped short, their eyes wide.

'Don't be afraid. We are here about the spaghetti,' Nonna said.

At the word 'spaghetti' the women started to nod, showing a glimmer of comprehension. Then, trying to be friendly, one of the cooks grabbed a big metal pot and plunked it on the stove. She snatched at a can with the word 'Heinz' plastered across it and, using a can opener, yanked back its tin lid. Martino watched as sloppy white tube spaghetti in a bright red sauce was splashed into the pot. Another of the women then hurried over with a pan of cooked lamb chops and began to scrape a couple in on top of the tinned spaghetti. Nonna rolled her eyes but kept her calm. She held up a hand, indicating for the woman to halt, then waved at her to stand back.

'I need flour, salt, eggs, oil ...' She cast her eyes about and saw the ingredients she needed on a nearby shelf. 'Martino, fetch me that tin, that container, that bottle and the eggs.'

Martino quickly did her bidding.

She cleared some space on the wooden table, then began to sift the flour and salt into a soft, white mound. With her fingers, she deftly made a hole in the centre of it and cracked in the eggs.

'You see what I'm doing? Flour, salt, make a hole, insert cracked eggs, whip the eggs with a fork. Now add a dash of oil.'

Nonna then put aside the fork and started to massage, bit by bit, the salted flour into the whipped eggs, her fingers moving quickly, expertly around the well she had created. Martino figured he was just as impressed as the Australians to see a golden dough emerge.

Carving the dough into four sections, Nonna pointed at two women and Martino. 'Come, you knead. Work the dough. Add flour if it's too sticky. Add a drop of water if it's too dry. Like this ... okay?'

Martino did as Nonna told him, surprised to be helping with the cooking. The women stepped up to the table and did the same, all copying Nonna. The kitchen was usually strictly the women's domain and Martino was never allowed near it. But here he was cooking next to Nonna, all in the aid of teaching the Australians about spaghetti. He was feeling quite special.

'Bravo, bravo,' Nonna said to them and the women smiled in return. Once thoroughly kneaded, she asked them to stop. 'Let the dough rest while we see about the sauce.'

With the cooks watching on, Nonna diced the lamb, removing the bones. Without tomatoes to hand, she drained the Heinz spaghetti, extracting the red liquid from the pot. Now she had a sweet meaty sauce. Returning to the dough, she helped the women roll the pasta and cut it into thin ribbons, unravelling long strands. The pasta was boiled up and Nonna assembled the meal on to four plates.

'Eat, eat,' Nonna said to the women.

Martino leapt at the dish put before him, shovelling the light pasta, dripping with red sauce, into his mouth.

'Oh Nonna,' he said. 'You've brought Heaven to Australia. Thank you, thank you, thank you.'

'You like?' Nonna asked the cooks in Italian, her tone helping them understand. They nodded, their faces beaming wide smiles, their eyes shining appreciatively.

'It is delicious,' one of the women said.

'Delicious,' the other two echoed.

And just like that Martino had learned another English word. He was sure he would always remember that one.

* * *

Over the following nights, Martino realised it was not just the Italians who were pleased to be served the new dish at the camp.

Every nationality, fortunate enough to dine at that mess hall, welcomed the change, savouring the finely cut lamb with the pasta and red sauce. Nonna continued to help in the kitchen, bringing with her Gilda and three other women, who were keen to volunteer their services. Such talented assistants ensured the pasta turned out fine and light each time. Nonna found tinned tomatoes in the camp's stores, along with a few spices, and a richer sauce was created. No one missed the gravy and peas.

At last they had eaten their final meal of spaghetti at the Greta Migrant Camp. The next day, Martino and his family and friends were taken by trucks to the town's train station. When it was time for the Cairns-bound migrants to board the train, they did so, waving as they went to those who had come to see them off. Martino waited while his mother and father kissed and hugged Edrico and Tazia, saying goodbye and good luck repeatedly. Monte stood away from his parents, not saying a word.

'Time to go,' Nonna called out.

Martino was keen to be on a train again, though he was hoping this time he would see more than sheep. Once in the carriage, the younger passengers huddled around one window, while their parents clustered around another. At this point, there was much waving and shouting.

Sandwiched between Nardo and Gian, Martino peered out and was a little unsettled to see Monte standing directly in front of their carriage window. He was staring at them from the platform, a smug look on his face.

'Hey, Martino,' he shouted.

Martino's eyes narrowed. What did he want?

'Have fun in Cairns,' Monte said, his lips curving into a sly smile. Then he held it up, a coin wedged between his thumb and pointer finger. With playful delight, he casually tossed the brown penny up and down.

Oh no, Martino thought. It couldn't be! Wanting to race out

and snatch the coin to see if it was his, he looked to the train door. It was shut. The window in front of him was open but too small to climb through. Trying not to panic, he slid a shaky hand into his pocket. He had put his penny there that morning. His fingers clawed desperately at the pocket's seams, finding nothing. It couldn't be true. How had Monte managed to steal it? He bit down on his lip.

'Martino, is that yours?' Nardo asked.

'Oh, Martino, no!' Gian cried. 'Not your kangaroo coin!'

Martino couldn't look at them. His silence confirmed what they feared.

'I'll get it back. It may take time, but I will get it,' Nardo told him.

'No,' Martino said. 'This has to stop. I don't want you hurt because of a dumb coin.' His chin wobbled.

'Monte can't hurt me. I'll get it back.'

'No. I don't want it. Let it go, Nardo.'

Martino hung his head. It wasn't true. He wanted the coin, but a part of him felt that perhaps he owed the boy something. He had sent his family away from them. If it had cost him a coin, then so be it. He looked back up, meeting Monte's eyes.

'Have it,' he shouted to him. 'I don't care.'

The train was moving away from the station. Passengers were waving at the Greta camp residents who had come to see them off. There was much shouting of advice and final words of farewell.

Monte put the coin into his pocket and smirked.

Martino held his gaze, defiant.

The train screeched away from the station and Martino took his seat. His mind was fixed on that lasting image of Monte's victorious grin. Why did he enjoy hurting people so much? he wondered.

'What's all the glum faces about?' he heard his Nonna ask. He glanced up and saw her standing in the aisle, on her way to her seat behind them.

'I want to go back to Italy,' Martino said.

Nonna looked at him squarely and nodded. 'I do too. But we aren't going to Italy. We're going north to the tropics, more than two thousand, three hundred kilometres away. I daresay your love of trains will end with this journey.' She looked sad. 'Here. Something for the trip.' Nonna handed each of the children a piece of chocolate.

Martino stared at his piece, gripped between his finger and thumb. The size of a coin, he thought, and the tears began to roll.

Chapter six

Late October 1950
Cairns, Queensland

The rocking motion was constant. The musical chugging was always in his ears, though it was occasionally punctuated by shrill whistles and the explosive pant of air brakes.

Martino longed to feel solid ground beneath his feet. They had stopped in Queensland's capital city of Brisbane to change trains and then had a break in travel at another township, but apart from those short chances to walk around and stretch the limbs, he, along with the other passengers, had sat for four days, their eyes fixed on windows, their expressions listless as they took in a rural landscape that stretched endlessly north.

Farms, grasslands and bushland went on and on and on. Scrappy bushland covered hills, mountains and plains. The farms went from sheep to dairy, back to sheep, then came the crops of wheat and, once they entered northern Queensland, they started to see the true and staggering extent of the sugar industry. On and on they chugged, past field after field of tall, lush sugar cane. Sometimes the cane was burning under hungry, high flames that swirled and danced bright yellow against billowing black smoke. Martino hated to think of Rico and Cappi out in those fields under that hot, cruel sun.

To help pass the time, he joined the other children in sharing scary and funny stories, making up silly songs and playing word games. But those activities didn't last long and he soon found his eyes once again glued to the passing scenery, willing the tedious rail journey to end.

Finally, the steam train pulled into Cairns station and came to a merciful stop after a melodramatic chorus of screeching and wheezing. Martino thought the poor, old train sounded exhausted.

He followed his father, who alighted from the train and walked with the other migrants through the large, red brick station. Eventually they came out and stood in the shade of a tin awning on a cement footpath. It was hot. That was his first and lasting impression of Cairns. He had thought Greta had been hot, but he now considered it cool in comparison. Buses were waiting for them and so they did not extend their legs for long.

Even though all the bus windows were open, the heat on the bus, especially coming up through the thin floor, was intense. The seats were hot to the touch, and within minutes of boarding Martino was red in the face, sweat meandering down in beads from his hairline. Nardo and Taddeo tugged on wet shirts, while Marietta and Isabella fanned each other with an old comic book, groaning when it failed to provide relief. The bus was cutting through air cooked by heat radiating off bitumen roads, which were close to melting point. The breezes were frustratingly hot.

Travelling up a shopping strip, Martino stared at the shoppers, obviously dressed for the heat in light, loose clothing. The men were wearing broad brimmed hats. The women were in skirts and dresses with colourful prints. Soon they were no longer passing shops, but ugly industrial sheds and workshops. What was more, he gathered there must have been a storm the night before, because the wide, flat roads were mud-slicked and covered with leaves and sticks and other debris. He even spotted a dead snake lying by the roadside. The scent in the air was sharp from torn leaves, snapped branches and stripped bark.

When the bus pulled up and parked, he rubbed at tired eyes, struggling with his disappointment. They were out front of another camp, consisting of two, long barrack-style buildings, one in front of the other. They were white walled and topped with tin rooves. Running along the front of the first building was a dirt drive, now muddied from the previous night's downpour, promising a slimy entry. The combination of heat and leftover storm sludge created such steamy conditions that to Martino the sheds may as well have been long, tin ovens.

'This can't be it!' Nonna cried, her voice carrying from the back of the bus to the front. 'Look where they've brought us. To the end of the world!'

Heads turned. Martino, too, looked behind him and saw his Nonna waving her hand with emotion.

'I'm not getting off this bus.'

'Mama, please,' Martino's mother hissed. 'Don't make a drama.'

'But Contessa! Look where we are. Where's my beautiful Italy?' she wailed, and several other women began to cry. They howled loudly, encouraging more women to join their lament.

Martino looked worryingly to his mother. What was going to happen?

'Don't worry, children. Just get off the bus. All of you,' his mother said. 'We're here now.' Her voice cracked on the words, but she stood and bustled about, prodding them to hop off.

Slowly the passengers disembarked, quiet and desolate, except for Nonna and Gilda and a small group around the same age, some much more elderly.

The passengers leaping down from the bus were met and welcomed to Cairns by a city official and two camp officers. Hands shaken, they were guided into the nearest building. Martino's mother, on seeing Isabella nearly take a slide in the mud, picked her up and carried her inside. His father went in, hauling their suitcase, and his older sister and brothers followed.

Martino chose not to go in. Concerned about Nonna, he wanted to wait for her. He watched intently as the camp officers, dressed in shorts, light shirts and hats, approached the bus driver.

'They won't get off,' the ginger-haired driver explained. Amusement was sparkling in his eyes. 'I've never seen anything like it.'

Baffled, the camp officers tried to entice the passengers to alight. 'Come on, we have cold drinks waiting for you,' one of them said. He mimed holding a cup and taking a swig of drink.

Martino looked on as Nonna and the others shook their heads.

'Gawd, now what?' one of the officers whispered to the other. 'We can't force 'em off. They'll come when they have to.'

'What about the driver? He can't be expected to wait round.'

'Who me?' the bus driver spoke up. 'I'm all right. I don't have to be anywhere else. This was my last pick up for the day. Let 'em take their time.'

'Righteo! How about comin' in for a cold one yourself then?'

'Good-o. Could do with a beer, if you've got it?' the bus driver put to them, smacking his lips.

The officers smiled. 'We'll fix you up.'

Standing abruptly, the driver grabbed his bag from beneath his seat. He turned to his disgruntled passengers. 'Don't think much of the place, hey?' he said. 'Can't say I blame ya! Days like this, hot and humid, saps the life out of ya. You'll get used to it.'

Martino was sorry to see the driver go inside with the three men. He leapt from grass tuft to tuft through the mud to get back to the bus and climbed on board. 'Nonna,' he called to her. 'You have to come inside. It is cooler off the bus.'

'I don't care. I want to go back to Italy.'

'But we're not going back, you said so yourself. We're here, in the north, and we need you. I need you. To teach the Australians to make spaghetti. Please, Nonna. You have to or I'll starve to death.'

'Martino … my dear boy, look at the place. I know you cannot understand, but I was raised in a city of beauty, of classical Hungarian architecture. Before the war, I went to galleries, museums, concerts … But here! Here? We are in the middle of nowhere.'

'Nowhere needs you.'

Nonna sighed. She glanced at Gilda and the other older Italians, their faces as gloomy as her own. They were looking to her for direction. 'All right, Martino. You are right. We should go in.'

Martino helped Nonna hobble off the bus, the others following. He held her clammy hand as she stepped carefully along the muddied path. On her request, he helped her find the toilets, and then they made their way to the mess hall.

After a cup of cordial, they were served stewed mutton sitting in watery gravy upon which peas and carrots floated. They picked up spoons and ate in abject silence. It was deathly quiet; such was the sound of misery.

Martino sloshed the food around in the army-style square metal pans that featured a strange handle. How was he going to eat that? After being spoiled at Greta with lashings of spaghetti, it was going to be a hard task. He put the gravy to his lips and sipped, trying not to gag.

The very next day, his father had to leave, along with the rest of the men destined to spend weeks working in the Atherton Tablelands.

His family followed him outside to a parking area where the trucks were waiting. Martino saw his mother was close to tears. She was wearing a sky blue dress that pinched at her waist. His father, sensing her distress, turned to her and drew her into his arms. He smoothed her hair back from her face and kissed her on the lips.

'Take care,' he said huskily. 'I'm sorry about leaving you here. I'm sorry, about everything.' He lowered his eyes and pressed his forehead to hers.

'Don't be sorry. This is not your fault. The war was not your fault.'

'No. We will get through this. Goodbye.' Then he turned and picked up Isabella to give her a last cuddle. 'Take good care of your mother and Nonna, hear me?' he said, addressing his sons.

'Yes, Papa,' Martino and his brothers replied promptly.

'Try hard at school. Try to learn English, yes?'

'Yes, Papa.'

'I best go. Goodbye.' He put Isabella down and walked briskly towards the trucks loading up the workers.

'Goodbye,' they shouted after him.

They watched the trucks depart, waving wildly. When he was gone, they stared at the empty street, not knowing what to do or say. Nonna broke the awkward silence.

'He will be back before we know it,' she said, sounding overly bright. 'Let's go see what they have concocted for breakfast!'

His family strolled to the mess hall. Martino didn't follow. Unable to face food, he ducked away, running back to one of their rooms.

The rooms were so small that his family had been given two, side by side. They didn't have ceilings and were divided by high partitions, rather than walls. This meant sound travelled easily from room to room throughout the barracks. Martino could even hear conversations taking place three or four rooms away. Inside each were narrow beds, a cement floor, and a board with nails upon which to hang clothes. He lay down upon his bed and felt tears trickle down to the firm, thin mattress.

'Martino, here you are. Don't you want breakfast?' It was his mother, coming to check on him.

He shook his head.

'Bacon and eggs.'

'I don't like hot breakfast.'

'I could find some bread.'

He shook his head again.

'All right. Stay and rest. I'll send Gian to come and get you when it's time to play.'

Sure enough, after a short while Gian turned up.

'Come on sleepy head. Let's explore.'

Martino lifted his tear-streaked face and, on seeing the cheeky smile of his friend, nodded. 'All right. I'm coming.'

Gian had seen his tears but didn't ask. He, too, was feeling sad that his father had gone.

First they went in search of trees to climb. The terrain was flat and uninteresting, though on the outskirts they found trees; most were gums with trunks too smooth and branches too high to climb. They leaned against the trunks, watching the noisy, colourful birds above. Martino had seen them at Greta, but here there seemed to be more of them. He liked their songs, or strange squawks, but there was one bird he loved most of all: the one that sounded like a human laughing—its explosive humour was contagious. The mosquitoes were a different story. There were too many of them! They hummed about his ears, pricking his arms and legs with vicious intent. Martino and Gian took to counting how many they could swat.

While their mothers and nonnas were occupied with chores and their older siblings could wander off into town, for Martino and Gian life in those early days of the camp was boring and hot. Certainly too hot for soccer until the sun went down, and then it was too dark and the cane toads came out, croaking in the grasses.

* * *

On the fourth day, Martino was relieved to notice something different. Cars started pulling up at the front of the centre, and out of them skipped Australian women, dressed in bright skirts or checked and spotted dresses.

Having finally found a climbable tree, Martino and Gian and their brothers sat on branches to observe the strange procession of women making their way to the mess hall. They carried plates hidden beneath tea towels, trays of cups and saucers, and cake boxes. A couple of other women heaved large cardboard boxes. At around noon, they observed a group of migrant women being led to the hall.

'I see Mama and Nonna,' Martino pointed out. 'I wonder what's going on.'

'Some kind of party?' Elmo suggested.

'Do you think we're invited?' Martino asked.

'Nah. Surely, it's just a girl thing,' Nardo replied, sounding resentful.

'We should go see.' Gian jumped from the branch.

The boys did not need a lot of convincing. Leaping after him, they crept to the hall and peered through the windows.

To Martino's amusement, he saw that the well-dressed ladies were arranging the Italian women and other migrants in a circle and trying to teach them a dance. He laughed out loud on seeing Nonna refuse to copy the silly steps. Her protests only drew the attention of a large, busty Australian woman, who grabbed hold of Nonna's hips and gave them a mighty shake to encourage her to wiggle them!

Music was being pounded out of an old piano by a woman in a yellow dress. Next to her was a woman singing a funny, melodic song. The girls—Marietta, Isabella, Daniela and Francesca—were laughing as they 'put their left foot in and their left foot out' and 'shook it all about'. They then tucked their hands beneath their chins and turned around, swinging their hips with gusto. Nonna thought it was belittling, but on seeing the younger women and girls laughing, tried to make more of an effort to participate.

As the dance came to an end and they were being shown steps for the next dance, Nardo's eyes lit up on a table across the far side of the hall. 'What's over there?'

'Let's go see,' Martino whispered and the boys took off around the building for a closer look.

Standing slowly, the mischievous bunch gazed through

open windows to take in the table below. Laid out on the white tablecloth were plates of assorted sandwiches cut into little triangles. In Italy, lunch was mostly crusty thick rolls and chunky slices of cheeses and meats. Martino was intrigued and wondered what was inside them. Also, laid out were pink-iced cupcakes and triangles of sliced white bread with the crusts cut off. These were covered in butter and multi-coloured sprinkles. The food was the prettiest and daintiest he had seen.

'Looks nice,' Gian said in awe.

Their mouths were watering. They looked at each other, thinking the same thing. Their time in camps, especially during the food shortage experienced in the German winter, had taught them how to be light of finger. With the women dancing, the boys saw the perfect opportunity to pilfer the enticing fare.

'Let's just take one thing each,' Nardo said and the others nodded enthusiastically.

Their eager hands reached over the sill to snatch at cupcakes and fairy bread. They then crouched and stuffed the stolen treats into their mouths. So delicious … and there was so much more to be taken. As Martino stood up and looked back inside, he saw that all the children, boys and girls, were lining up and being offered the trays of food. They were being allowed to take as much as they wanted. He was astounded. The food was for them. Fancy that! He had wrongly assumed it would only be for the mothers and girls.

'Look! They're giving it away. We're missing out,' Martino told his fellow thieves.

They stood and stared, then the race was on as they bolted around to the door and, laughing hysterically, joined the end of the queue.

'Whose birthday is it?' Martino asked his mother as he polished off his third piece of fairy bread.

'It is not a birthday party. It is a welcome to Australia party,' she told him. 'These women belong to the Country Women's Association. They have brought us food and clothing.'

'They are nice ladies,' Martino said.

'Yes, they are.'

Martino was confused to hear sadness in his mother's tone. He glanced up to see her eyes holding tears.

'Are you okay, Mama?'

'Oh yes. Just tears of happiness. I feel so grateful to these women. They have gone to a lot of trouble. I didn't expect it.'

'Oh, sure,' he said, not really understanding it. He never cried when he was happy. Not giving it much more thought, he trotted off. Maybe he could eat one more of those ridiculously thin sandwiches, he thought.

Martino didn't know it, but his mother had continued to observe him as he bounded over to the table and stood there, opening a sandwich to examine its contents. He looked so small and scrawny. His legs were mere stalks, seemingly too thin to hold his weight. She loved to watch him eat.

It had not been easy on him or the other children, she thought. So much to learn … a new language, culture, foods … it had all been so strange. But this kindness shown by these women—that she understood and it warmed her heart. For the first time since their arrival, she was feeling a sense of community in Australia and she hoped that one day she and her children might become a part of it. It was a hope that was sparked that day and with each breath, each daily prayer, she tried to keep that desire alive.

Chapter seven

Late October 1950
Cairns Immigration Holding Centre

Monday arrived. The Monday. The Monday they were to start school in Australia.

Not long off the school bus, Martino found himself standing awkwardly at the front of an assembly. Rows and rows of school children were facing him and the other migrant children starting school that day. He gazed back. He noticed some were curious, some looked confused, and some appeared openly hostile.

A plump nun, aged in her middle years, shuffled in her black dress from the office building and, breathing hard, made her way over to a flagpole. A round-faced boy started to beat on a drum and another tall, lanky boy stepped forward to raise the flag. The school children lurched into song.

Martino knew it was the Australian anthem. It had been played for them on the ship, but he did not know the words so he just stood and watched as the other children drawled through the lyrics of 'God Save the King'. Their lacklustre performance could have been a result of singing the song too many times, or due to the heat circling their bodies, rendering them light-headed and lethargic.

Flag raised and anthem done, the Catholic nun, no doubt the head Sister, turned and beckoned them to step forward.

Martino did so.

The nun addressed the school, pointing every so often to the migrants huddled nervously behind her. What was she saying? Martino wondered. A fly was pestering his nose and he wiped at it every few seconds. At last, she finished and small palms created a spattering of nonplussed applause. Those small palms then stayed locked together as heads bowed and the nun took them through a short collective prayer. Mutterings of 'Amen' were heard before all the pupils were dismissed. There was a scurrying of legs and ponytails as they raced to escape the punishing sun and get to class.

The Sister then approached the new children, took out a sheet of paper and started to read down a list.

'Martin?' Martino put up his hand, knowing the Australians preferred to drop the 'o' in his name. 'Stand over there.'

Eventually, Martino saw that they were standing in age groups. He stuck close to Gian, hoping to stay together and get in the same class. It worked. The nun grabbed hold of them and pushed them forward, pointing to a building. 'Go in.'

The other children, including Nardo, Marietta, Francesca and Elmo, were being poked in the shoulders in the direction of the next wing of classrooms. Being older, Taddeo had already made his way to the college, located at the back of their school.

'Good luck,' Nardo called to Martino.

Martino was surprised. Nardo was good for wrestling and liked to beat him in competitive games. It was unusual for him to show kindness. 'Good luck to you too!' he returned.

Glad he had Gian by his side, Martino walked to the building and tentatively went inside. He crept to the first classroom door that presented and stood there, too afraid to knock. Gian came up and hid behind him. A stern-faced nun ceased her teaching and called out to them.

'Come in, come in.' Her tone was impatient.

The room had large open windows and a high ceiling. Nine pupils—three girls and six boys—were sitting straight-backed at wooden desks. Two boys were staring in undisguised horror at them, while most of the girls smiled.

'Hello,' the nun said. 'I'll be your teacher for the year.'

'Hello,' Martino and Gian mumbled back, having been taught a range of simple English words on the ship out from Italy.

'I'm Sister Parker,' she pointed at herself. 'What are your names?'

'Martino.'

'Gian.'

Giggles erupted, but when the teacher spun to see who had found the names amusing, the class fell silent.

'Right, now we've got your names worked out, sit over there.' She pointed at two wooden desks along the room's left side. 'Go, sit,' she said loudly.

Martino did so quickly. He was happy to be no longer standing out front.

'Here you go,' said Sister Parker in a singsong voice and she gave them each a fountain pen and a notebook. An inkwell sat in a hole in the desk.

'Now, where were we? Oh yes … we're looking at the letter P and writing down as many P nouns as possible on the board.' Sister Parker looked at the Italian boys and phonetically pronounced the letter 'P' by pushing so much air past her lips that she could have extinguished many candles.

The class found her exaggerated 'P' amusing and laughed. Martino glanced behind him at Gian, who shrugged.

'Anyone else think of another noun starting with the letter P?'

Martino couldn't comprehend what she was saying and watched helplessly as the children around him shot up their hands. He was usually clever in class. In Italy, he had often answered the questions promptly and correctly. Adopting an expression of understanding, he tried desperately to catch English words he knew. But to his frustration, the Sister was talking impossibly fast. This was not going to be easy.

At each response, the teacher turned to the board and wrote a word with thin, squeaky chalk. At times, she would call to

Martino and Gian and point at the board then at their paper, indicating that they must write the word in their notebook. Martino copied the words as best he could with neat, little strokes of ink. Afterwards, he looked at his page, and although he could not understand a single word he'd written, he did gather they all started with the same letter. If only he could call out some Italian words, starting with P.

Maths, sport and art were a welcome relief, as Martino could add up and subtract, recognising the sums on the board. And he could catch a ball and draw a picture without needing to know the language, but for most of the day he was left to sit like a fool, listening to the continuous stream of foreign words and writing some down. After a long while, he became tired of listening without comprehension and grew bored. He gazed out the window to examine the tall trees and odd birds flying between them, only to have the teacher shout at him for daydreaming. He apologised in Italian—making the class laugh. It was awful.

Lunchtime was worse. The only good part was that each child was handed a small bottle of milk to drink on their way out of the room. After that, it was a struggle.

The other children would not let him play with them. He approached a group of boys playing a game with a bat and small ball. A chubby boy glared at him.

'Get lost, wog,' he sneered. The other children laughed.

'Yeah, nick off, dago,' another kid said, giving him a shove.

'Come on, Martino,' Gian called him away.

'Why won't they let us join in?' Martino asked his friend.

'I don't know, but it's not like we can ask for a reason.'

The day eventually came to an end. The school bus picked them up from the front gate and they were dropped off outside the camp. On their return, Martino saw his mother, Nonna and Isabella waiting for them, standing in the same spot where they had waved them off.

'How was it?' Martino's mother sang out as they strode up the dirt path.

'It was all right,' muttered Taddeo.

'Terrible,' Nardo snapped.

'Martino, Marietta?'

Marietta burst into tears and flung herself into her mother's arms.

'They pulled Francesca's ribbons out of her hair and wouldn't give them back,' she cried.

'Who did?' their mother said, alarmed.

'Some girl and her friends.'

'Did you tell the teacher?'

'No. I ... I tried to snatch them back, but she held them too high for me to reach.'

Their mother looked over at Francesca, who was with her mother and saw she still had ribbons in her hair. 'She seems to have them back now.'

'Yes, I pulled the girl's hair until she gave them back.'

'Marietta! That's not like you.' Marietta erupted into tears again. 'Well, maybe next time just tell the teacher,' her mother said more gently.

'But the teacher doesn't understand a word I say!' Marietta cried, starting to sob. Nonna handed her a handkerchief.

'And how was it for you, Martino?' his mother asked.

'They speak English too fast.'

'Learning a new language takes time,' she replied in a sympathetic tone, stroking Marietta's curly hair until her sobs quietened.

'They should just give them English speaking lessons for the first couple of months,' Nonna said, scowling.

'What were the other boys like?' his mother ventured.

'They speak English,' Nardo moaned.

'I see. Well, there's cold cordial waiting for you in the mess hall.'

Martino nodded. His clothes were damp with sweat. His feet were sliding in his sandals. Something cold would be nice, he thought.

* * *

Day three and Sister Parker was still talking in a fast stream of words that meant nothing to Martino. The other children were writing furiously, while he and Gian sat idle. He glanced around and saw some children sniggering. They thought him stupid! He looked at his blank page and cringed.

There was a light tap of fingernails on his desk. He peered sideways. A kind-faced girl with fair hair and milky white skin was trying to gain his attention. Covertly, she pointed to a book and whispered: 'Book.'

'Book?'

She nodded then quickly returned her eyes to the board before she drew the attention of the teacher for talking out of turn.

Martino smiled. Book. He had learned another new word for the day.

'Grazie,' he whispered back. 'Thank you,' he corrected.

She smiled.

'Martino, is there something you want to tell the entire class?'

'No, Sister.'

'Good. Then be quiet. I trust you understand that!'

The class laughed.

At lunchtime, feeling vulnerable, Martino and Gian sought out their older brothers. Martino felt that by staying in a group they were less likely to be targeted by bullies, and there did appear to be a lot of them. Fights were always breaking out. With numerous migrants from various countries in the school, many clashed, even with each other, and without common languages to resolve issues, fists often went flying. Nardo stood up to some of the toughest, winning fights with his fists, until his reputation went before him and he and his group started to be left alone.

One afternoon, when they all met up at the gate to wait for the bus, Taddeo joined them, hobbling down the street from his college with an obvious limp.

'What happened to your leg? You okay?' Nardo asked him.

'Nothing. It's fine.'

'Why the limp?'

Taddeo ignored him.

At the end of that week, Cappi and Rico returned from their first stint of cane cutting. They were covered in soot, their skins black as coal. From a distance, Lisa didn't recognise her son or son-in-law, and it was only when they drew nearer that she realised they had come back.

'My goodness,' she gasped, unable to embrace them for the filth. 'Go shower and give me those clothes.'

After they cleaned up, Lisa and Lena were shocked to notice that the men's hands were covered in blisters, stings, cuts and boils. Lena ran for Nonna, who came with ointment. Her ministrations were met with complaints and the embarrassed men repeatedly told her that they were too old for her creams and attention.

'Shush now. This will help,' Nonna silenced them, and so they sat reluctantly and allowed themselves to be treated. It did seem to cool their burning skins.

Afterwards, Rico and Cappi attended the evening meal.

'What happened to your hands?' Martino asked Cappi. He couldn't stop ogling the cuts and lumps. The other children were equally as shocked by the sight of their injuries.

Cappi grunted, indicating it was nothing.

Rico leaned in.

'Cutting cane is not easy. We use a curved blade with a wooden handle,' Rico explained. 'In the morning, the dew makes the cane wet and slippery and it is easy to slip up and cut yourself. The cane also releases syrup, which attracts bees. See I got stung there and there.'

The children's eyes widened. Lena held on to her husband's elbow, shaking her head with dismay.

'I never want to cut cane,' Martino burst out.

'Then keep learning English,' Cappi suddenly spoke up, pointing his fork at him.

'I am, I am,' he said, answering in English, making everyone at the table smile.

'Your fathers will be back next weekend,' Nonna told the children.

'Will they be covered in cuts and sores?' Martino asked.

'I hope not!' his mother cried. 'Now eat up.'

True to his Nonna's word, a week later the workers returned from the Tablelands, full of tales of hard labour, discomfort and misery. Their sun-baked skins were covered in mosquito bites, sores, blisters and cuts. They described a rainforest the likes of which they had never seen, with trees as old as time and tall as giants.

The children were thrilled to see them. On seeing his father saunter into camp, Martino ran up to greet him, asking, 'What do you have there?' His father was holding a bag in one hand and two chickens in the other.

'Wait and see!'

They reached their room where his father kissed his mother, then he indicated the bag, holding it high. 'In here are chocolates! I will give them to your mother for safekeeping and she can hand them out to you when you are good. Have you been good while I've been away?'

'Yes, Papa,' Martino answered with his brothers and sisters. They were all smiling.

'Good.' He handed them each a chocolate, then swayed on tired feet. 'Now I will go and have a shower!'

Martino didn't see his father again until dinnertime, as once cleaned up, he had sought his bed for a nap. While he rested, Martino was put to work by Nonna and told to stand guard outside an old horse stable. There, his mother, Nonna and other Italian women cooked the chickens that many of the workers had brought back with them. In each empty stall, they had dug a hole and set up an oil cooker. In secrecy, they cooked the poultry and laboured over a homemade tomato sauce, northern Italian style.

Martino was only too willing to aid in the production of the fine meal. The smells coming from that stable made him giddy with hunger. He had barely been eating the dreadful camp food. The meal served that night was incredible. He had not known food could taste like that. He would recall it long afterwards. He would also recall sitting next to his father, as close he could get, watching him devour the chicken in appreciative silence. It was one of the happiest moments Martino had had in a long time.

'Was the work hard?' he asked, seeing his father's blistered hands.

'It was. I won't lie. It's hot work. I can't believe we've only been at it two weeks. But you know what the hardest part is?'

Martino shook his head.

'Not seeing you and your brothers and sisters and your mother—even Nonna!'

The family laughed.

'It gets lonely out there,' he went on. 'But there are stars, so bright, so many of them. I swear the Tablelands bring you closer to them.'

'I wish I could see those stars,' Martino said.

'So, how's school?' his father put to his children.

'We can't understand the teacher,' Nardo answered. 'Some of the Australian children don't like us.'

'Then you must learn the language and fast,' he instructed. 'Remember, Martino. I told you the language is the key.'

'Yes, Papa. I remember and I have been learning it.'

'Good, good,' he said. 'Keep it up.'

'I'm finding it hard,' Taddeo confessed.

'You are older. It will be more difficult for you. At my age, I'm finding it almost impossible!'

Taddeo smiled at his father's admission.

'But what about soccer?' Nardo cut in. 'They don't have teams at this school. How can I become a great soccer play if I can't even play it?'

Martino gazed at his father, awaiting his answer. He too was upset that soccer wasn't as popular in Australia as it had been in Italy.

Their father looked disappointed. 'No teams? Well, don't stop playing. Do it at lunchtime and invite the Australian kids to play with you.'

'They don't want to play,' Martino said simply. 'They play rugby and cricket.'

'Don't worry. Keep trying, keep asking,' he said, urging them to persist. 'How could anyone not like soccer, hey?'

Martino started to smile at that. It did seem impossible to dislike the game, and it was true that the other migrants were keen to play it at lunchtime and some Australian boys had asked to join, sometimes.

'All right, Papa. We'll keep playing when we can.'

'Good. Let me know how it goes.'

* * *

The next morning, their parents came into their room just as they finished dressing for the day. His father waited to get their attention.

'What is it, Papa? Are you going again?' Martino asked.

'No, not yet,' he said. And then he gave him a wink. 'Martino, I won't be here for your birthday next week. I've made you a present. It's outside.'

The children exchanged looks of surprise. A present! They flew out the door and scanned the grounds, but couldn't see anything.

'Come with me,' their father said.

They followed him until they came in sight of the tree they liked to climb, and there, hanging on a rope, was a tyre.

'When I bought the chickens, I saw this tyre in their field,' their father said. 'I asked the farmer if I could have it and if he had any rope. He was glad to be rid of it. And there you are! A swing!'

'But, Papa—the centre's officers …' Marietta queried.

'It's all right,' their mother assured them. 'Your father asked the head officer here about it and he agreed, as long as Martino shares it with all the other kids at the camp.'

'Yes, I will,' Martino said, willing to agree to anything in order to keep it.

'Off you go then. Give it a try.' They were about to run off when something caught their father's eye. 'Wait a moment.'

They halted.

'Taddeo, you're wearing long pants … why? It is the tropics. You can wear shorts,' he said, staring at his ankle.

'True, it is a bit hot. I'll change later,' Taddeo replied, his eyes downcast.

'Want to tell me what happened?' His father bent down and lifted the trouser hem. A long purplish welt was revealed, alongside several others, suggesting a harsh beating—perhaps a couple of weeks ago, given many of the welts had faded into a pale blue. 'Nardo do that?'

'Of course I didn't,' Nardo protested.

'That looks sore,' Isabella said, looking up at her brother with sorrowful eyes.

'Why didn't you say something about it?' his mother cried.

Martino sucked in his breath. The beating must have been severe to leave such deep markings.

'It's nothing,' Taddeo murmured, hanging his head evasively.

'What happened? The truth—now,' his father demanded.

'My teacher,' he said softly.

They were all stunned.

'Your teacher! Why? You've always been an excellent student, too kind for your own good. Tell me, Taddeo. This I must understand.'

Taddeo hesitated before saying, 'My teacher wrote two English words on the blackboard and asked me to say the English words. I couldn't pronounce them. I didn't know these words and they were long and difficult.'

'So he hit you? Hit you for not knowing English?' His father was practically spitting with fury.

'Yes,' Taddeo whispered.

'What is his name?'

'Mr Adams.'

'All right. Off you go, play on the new swing.'

'What are you going to do?' Taddeo asked.

'Don't you worry about it. Go play.'

The following day, when the sky was softening after a spectacular dawn of pink and apricot streaked clouds, Martino was awoken by his father and asked to dress. He did so sleepily, wondering what his father was wanting of him.

'Come with me.'

He went outside and they walked to the front gate, where a bicycle was leaning against the wire fence.

'I need you to show me the way to Taddeo's school. Hop on. I can ride us both there.'

Perplexed, Martino sat on the front of the bicycle seat and

found his balance while his father slipped in behind. Martino was observant and knew which way the bus went. He was easily able to guide his father, who pedalled quickly up the wide, flat roads.

'Taddeo goes in there,' he said, pointing to the building, located around the corner from his primary school.

They hopped off the bicycle and leaned it against the fence.

'Martino, go and ask that boy over there where we can find the classroom of Mr Adams.'

Martino now had enough English to ask for directions and the boy, on seeing his imposing father standing behind him, answered helpfully.

They soon found the teacher, a man in his early thirties, who was dressed in a white shirt and brown trousers. He was writing on the blackboard, chalk crumbling beneath his heavy strokes.

His father called from the doorway. 'Mr Adams?'

'Yes. Can I assist you, sir?' The man turned and straightened to an average height. As his eyes settled on his visitor, he was surprised to see a rugged, dark-haired man, dressed casually for labouring. His olive skin looked darkened by the sun and his hands were rough and blistered; combined with his Italian features—the strong nose, the dark eyes, the course hair— these were tell-tale signs of a new migrant. Within seconds of his appraisal, he braced himself for a barrier in language and perhaps even in intelligence.

'Can I help you?' the pert-nosed teacher rephrased the question, making it louder and slower.

Standing outside, Martino saw through the window that his father did not respond but marched over to the board, snatched the chalk from the man's hand and wrote two Italian words on the board—'Insegnante idiota'.

'Say them,' the outraged father said in Italian and knocked his knuckles upon the words. He pointed at the teacher and again knocked on the words. 'Go.'

The teacher shook his head, a little confused at first, then realisation dawned. He recalled his treatment of the migrant boy, Taddeo, and his right cheek started to twitch nervously. The father had to be at least a head taller and his solid, muscular arms were twice as thick as his own. He looked at the words and hesitated. How to pronounce them? He wasn't quite sure …

Martino observed his father glaring at Mr Adams, a teacher that Taddeo had described to him only the night before as being very strict and cruel with a fondness for whipping students with a stinging cane, and he started to grow concerned. He had an urge to shout 'Watch out!' to his unsuspecting father. But Martino was failing to comprehend how capable and hardened his father had become after living through a long and terrible war, one in which he had been forced to work for the Germans and was later shot and thrown in prison for it. His father had seen death, executions, bombings, disease and extreme poverty and, in recent weeks, had known backbreaking labour in extreme heat. As such, Mr Adams in his neatly ironed shirt with his soft and flabby arms did not intimidate him in the least.

'Can't say it?' his father inquired, now speaking Italian louder and slower. And to Martino's astonishment, his father calmly reached out and grabbed the stammering man by the back of the neck and very deliberately whacked the teacher's forehead against the blackboard.

'Say the words,' he said.

The man shook his head helplessly.

'See? It is not easy to speak another language. Don't ask the impossible,' he fired in rapid Italian, and with greater force thumped the teacher's head against the board before striding off.

As he reached the door, he saw Martino gaping.

'Come,' he said gruffly. 'The trucks will be leaving soon. I can't be late back.'

Martino was shocked. He had never seen his father use

violence against anyone before. Although he did have a quick temper, he wasn't one to strike out. He couldn't believe he had harmed a teacher, someone they had always been told to respect! All in support of Taddeo. Martino felt a surge of love for his father. As he sat in front of him on the bicycle on the way back to camp, he felt something, a sense of being that had been eluding him since he arrived in Australia. He felt safe.

When Martino told Taddeo what he had seen, his brother was mortified. He feared the teacher would certainly get back at him. And yet, weeks went by without any recrimination. It seemed his father had made a lasting impression. Taddeo told them that he was surprised by it. He hadn't thought anyone or anything could ward off Mr Adams and his cane whipping. But it seemed his father had.

Chapter eight

December 1950
Cairns Immigration Holding Centre

'Now take this to the store room,' his mother told him, piling several bed sheets into his arms. 'I'll follow.'

Martino couldn't see where he was going for the load in front of him. He tried to peer around it, his arms aching as he went. The camp officers issued fresh linen on Fridays and it was usually Marietta's job to help their mother hand in their used sheets when she got back from school. On that terribly hot afternoon, Marietta was complaining of a headache and had taken to her bed. Martino had tried to scamper off with Gian, heading for the swing, but his mother had grabbed him by the sleeve.

'Oh, no you don't. I need your help,' she had said.

Martino walked in front of his mother, going slow as he was afraid of tripping.

'Come on, Martino. Nonna is waiting. She will need help carrying back the fresh ones.'

'I'm going as fast as I can,' he said, his voice muffled by the sheets.

He pushed open the half-closed door with his big toe and threw his load on to the floor. It landed in a pile just near Nonna's outstretched hand. For a split second, he couldn't understand why Nonna was lying on the cement floor. He knew the heat was making everyone tired, but surely she'd go back to bed for a nap? Then, almost as quickly, he knew that something was wrong. He saw a bruise on Nonna's arm and forehead.

'Mama! Mama!' he began shouting.

An ambulance was called. His mother went with Nonna to the hospital. He was left at the camp, Taddeo put in charge.

Martino had been beside himself. Was Nonna going to be okay? What was wrong with her? He knew that old people got old enough to die, but Nonna was not that old. She wasn't even sixty!

His mother returned later that night, tired and downcast. She explained that Nonna had fainted from the heat. She was not coping with it. She should be allowed to come home for Christmas, which was on Monday, but didn't know who would pick her up from the hospital. It was a holiday and many of the camp officers would be home with their families or working to serve the migrants a Christmas lunch.

Martino was sad to hear it. No Nonna on Christmas Day! It would be the worst Christmas ever, he thought. Nonna always made it fun.

Somehow their situation was brought to the attention of the Country Women's Association and to their surprised delight, on Christmas morning, a car pulled up at the camp and a woman with brown, curly hair, dressed in a dark green skirt and white blouse, hopped out and opened the passenger door.

Out stepped Nonna.

Word of her arrival spread quickly and her family hurried outside to greet her. When Martino reached the side of the building, he saw a woman holding Nonna by the hand, leading her up the dirt path. He thought her the kindest person on the planet.

Cheers rang out as Nonna gave them a weak smile. Even the other migrants were pleased to see her returned in time for the festivities. She was sat by the window in the mess hall. A small portable fan was set up for her, though it simply served to whirl hot air.

To Martino's dismay, she spoke and ate little.

'Nonna, try some Christmas cake,' he said, bringing her a small piece in a bowl. She was always bringing him food; now it was his turn.

'Thank you. You are a sweet boy, but I'm sorry, I don't feel like it. It will make me sick in the stomach,' she explained.

'Can I get you some cold jelly?' he offered, trying to think what else was on their Christmas table.

'No, no. Nothing.' She closed her eyes and drew in a ragged breath. She was so still for the next few moments that Martino grew scared. He felt compelled to reach out and rest a hand on her papery elbow.

'Nonna,' he whispered fearfully.

Nonna breathed out and Martino exhaled with her, feeling terribly relieved.

The cooler months did come and Nonna's energy returned. Martino was pleased to see her back, bustling about and lending a helping hand in the camp kitchen. Migrants were being employed to cook and serve at the camp, and the food had certainly improved. Spaghetti was once again a regular dish on the menu.

However, warmer days started to revisit them in the spring of 1951, and almost at the first hint of high humidity, Nonna's health took a turn for the worse. The family watched in alarm as she grew thin, frail and despondent. She was frequently pining for the past, talking about Italy. As the heat increased, her health worsened and she had another fainting spell.

'Mama, what's going to happen? The heat is making Nonna sick and it is not even summer,' Martino asked. He had just delivered a glass of water to her in her room where she was lying down.

'I know you are worried. I am too,' his mother said. 'When your father comes back this weekend, I will speak to him. We have to do something.'

* * *

Contessa waited for the right moment to speak to her husband. She asked him to walk with her outside after the children had gone to bed. The air was warm and the moonlight bright. Toads croaked in the taller grasses and the mosquitoes bit at her ankles. Arm in arm, they ambled across brittle grass, not venturing too far from the camp but far enough not to be overheard. Inside, Contessa had found it impossible to have a private conversation.

Then, she broke down.

'I can't live here another year,' she said, tears spilling. 'The heat! The air is so thick it is hard to breathe. Mama hardly eats— she's too thin! I can't stop worrying. The summer will kill her! And the boys keep coming home from school with bruises from fights, especially Nardo. They try to hide them from me, but I see them. Taddeo is struggling to learn the language. Marietta cries herself to sleep and I can't figure out why. Now that I'm doing shift work at the cannery I hardly see the kids, and Nonna is not well enough to look after them. I can't do it anymore!'

Ettore took her into his arms and felt her body convulse with shuddering sobs. He had never seen her so upset. She had given up. Worry had set in, and over the past long, insufferable year it had worn her down.

'I miss home,' she said, so softly he could hardly hear her. 'I miss Fiume and Trieste and the port. I miss Italy.'

He listened to her crying, understanding her sorrow all too well. He longed to be back in the seaport town, living the life that they had enjoyed before the war. In fact, he wanted it so much that he found he could no longer look back. Reflection submerged him in a depression too deep for resurfacing, and so he had adopted a mindset of only looking forward. With a painfully precious past and an unbearable present of constant hard labour in debilitating heat, the future was all he had.

'I will see what can be done,' he said, kissing his wife lightly on the lips.

'Can something be done?' She had so little hope left.

'I'll see. I'll go to the migrant employment office and explain about Nonna's health. Maybe I can spend my second year of contract in a cooler place to the south of the state. It couldn't hurt to ask.'

'Oh, Ettore. Thank you. Please try. We have to do something.'

* * *

About a month later, Martino was with his family in one of their rooms, getting ready to go the picture theatre in town to see the animation movie, *Alice in Wonderland*, when there came a knock on the door. Expecting it to be one of their friends, Taddeo opened it and was surprised to see a camp officer standing there.

'I have a letter for your father,' the officer said.

Hurrying to the door, their father reached out for it. 'It came yesterday, but you didn't get back from the Tablelands until late,' the officer said in English. Martino understood and translated for his father.

'Grazie. Thank you,' their father said. He closed the door and, without a word, sat down on the nearest bed, his fingers tearing at the seal and struggling to pull out the single sheet. As he read, they all stared.

When he finished, he bowed his head and Martino thought he was upset.

'Bad news, Papa?'

His father's head snapped up and his smiling eyes were glistening. 'We can move to Brisbane. There is a job at the Ford factory. A higher paying job!'

'Are you sure?' his mother asked in a shrill voice. 'They say you can have it?'

'I'm to visit the office to sign a contract and then we can leave in two weeks.'

'Two weeks,' she cried. 'Brisbane is south. It must be cooler.'

'Not as humid,' their father put in.

'Oh, wait until I tell Nonna!'

Their door swung open. 'I heard every word!' Nonna had been in the adjoining room, separated only by the partition.

'Brisbane. We're going to Brisbane,' his mother said, hugging Nonna.

Her excitement was contagious and Martino found himself jumping up and down with his brothers and sisters.

'Yeah! Ford? Does that mean you can work with cars again! It will be better, yes, Papa?'

'Yes, Martino, much better.'

'Oh no. Now we have to tell the others,' his mother despaired suddenly. She pressed her lips together, a worried look pinned to her face. 'Bianca and Lisa ...'

Martino was instantly thinking of Gian.

'Can't they come too? Couldn't their father ask for a move?' Taddeo proposed and Martino knew he was thinking of Daniela. They were close and had become closer during their stay in Cairns.

'I don't think so. Roberto has been struggling with the heat. He often gets put on duties back at the tents, but I don't think they will see it as reason enough for a transfer. Nonna's case is stronger.'

'How do we leave them?' his mother asked. 'We have been with them since we left Fiume. They are like family.'

'They will be so upset,' Nonna agreed, concerned for their friends.

'It will only be for one year ...' his father said. 'Then they can come to Brisbane.'

'Yes.' His mother nodded. 'Just one year apart and then we'll be together again.'

* * *

Two weeks was not long enough to get used to the idea of moving and separating from their Italian friends. News of their departure sent shockwaves through the camp, their friends quick to express sorrow at what promised to be a difficult parting. But they understood. They had been worrying about Nonna's deterioration too and were relieved that she would be escaping the fast looming summer.

Still, it didn't make it any easier. The parting took place on a sunny Tuesday. Like the day of their arrival, there had been a furious storm the night before, and the air was heavy with the scents of damp earth and torn foliage. Martino awoke early to make sure he could have one last play with his friend Gian before they went.

The boys ran to their tree and climbed the branch, from which their tyre was strung.

'I can't imagine school without you,' Gian said. His eyes held fear. 'I wish you weren't going.'

'You still have your brother Elmo,' Martino pointed out.

'Yes, but he's not as fun as you.'

Martino smiled. 'No. He's too serious. Want to swing?'

They both stood on the tyre, clinging to the rope. They swung back and forth over the dusty ground.

'What is Brisbane like?' Gian asked.

'Don't know,' Martino shrugged. 'Maybe that's where all the big red kangaroos are'

Gian laughed. 'Sure they are!'

'Think this swing will stay here?' Martino wanted to know.

'Of course, it will. It will stay here forever.'

They were quiet for a while. 'Let's climb back up.'

They both pulled themselves up and sat in the elbows of branches. They could see over the roof of the barracks to the rear yard, where a woman was hanging out some washing. They laughed at the size of her underwear. A beep made them look to the front. An old farmer's truck had pulled up.

'That's our ride,' Martino said. He felt a stab of panic. 'You will come to Brisbane next year, won't you?' he asked.

Gian nodded. 'I hope so. My father hates the work here. He wants to get a job as a painter in Brisbane.'

'Oh, good.'

The boys watched as Martino's family came out of the barracks, his father waving to the driver. Nardo and Taddeo were carrying heavy bags, while the girls brought out boxes of food and toiletries. Nonna was wearing the best of her three blouses and his mother was in her blue dress.

A small crowd started to gather around them, preparing to wave them off.

Roberto, Cappi and Rico weren't there. They were away working. They had already said their painful goodbyes.

Lisa, Lena, Bianca and Gilda were standing in a circle around Martino's mother, who appeared to be talking non-stop. Martino knew his mother talked a lot when she was nervous or excited.

Taddeo and Daniela were leaning in towards each other. Not touching, not kissing, not talking, but just being close.

'Do you think they'll marry one day?' Gian asked, following Martino's line of sight.

'No. She's too pretty for him.' Martino smiled.

'Taddeo's too nice for her,' Gian countered with a laugh.

The truck's front cabin door was opened and Nonna was being helped inside. Once she was seated, Martino's father started lifting his brothers and sisters into the back of the open truck.

Martino's mother was hugging each of the women around her, clinging to them. They appeared to be wiping at tears.

And then his father was shouting: 'Martino!'

'Looks like you're going now,' Gian said to his friend.

'I better go. Don't have too much fun without me. See you in Brisbane,' Martino sang out, sliding down the tree and running until he reached his father.

He was hastily thrown into the back of the truck, where they had wooden crates to sit upon in amongst the bags and boxes. His father climbed back in, reaching for his mother and holding her tight. She was putting on a brave face, though her eyes were red from crying. He glanced at Taddeo, who was looking down at his feet, his mood sullen. Nardo looked serious, and Marietta and Isabella were holding hands.

With a roar of the engine and a puff of exhaust, the beat-up truck pulled away from the kerb. As it spluttered up the road, Martino looked behind to see Elmo, Daniela and Francesca running after them, shouting enthusiastic goodbyes.

Martino and his siblings waved back, finding their smiles.

From his bumpy seat, Martino lifted his eyes to see his friend still sitting in the tree. They waved at each other.

'Don't fall out,' Martino shouted to the kid he had known as long as he could remember.

'Don't fall off the truck,' he yelled back.

The truck took the corner and the tiny figure upon the branch was cast from view.

Chapter nine

October 1951
Enoggera Barracks, Brisbane, Queensland

'At least it is not so humid here,' was all Nonna managed to say as she surveyed the large, canvas army tent before her.

The Saforo family had been delivered to yet another migrant holding centre, this one based at the Enoggera Army Barracks, located six kilometres northwest from the heart of Brisbane. However, the barrack buildings were full and they had to reside in a tent pitched on the grounds. For Nonna, it was hard to take in. She wiped away beads of sweat lounging on her upper lip. While less humid, it was still steaming hot. The tent was squatting in a field dotted by towering gum trees. Insects, including dragonflies, were hovering over the brown, straw-like grasses and the sun was hitting the tent's canvas, cooking the air within.

'Don't worry, children,' Martino heard his mother saying, taking steady breaths. 'Now that your father has work at the Ford Motor Company his pay will go up. I will get work too. We will soon save for a deposit on a house.'

'Mercy be. Imagine—a house again,' Nonna murmured dreamily.

'We will have our own kitchen and a garden with vegetables and you can go to the same school … not all this change all the time.'

Martino clung to her words, hoping they would soon come true. But he knew it would be months before they would have a deposit big enough to buy a house. He knew he would just have to get used to sleeping in the crowded tent, walking the long distance to the basic showers and toilets and, no doubt, eating more tough lamb. He could feel fear building as another first day of school was scheduled and, worst of all, he would have to go there without Gian.

'Please let us save money quickly,' he said in his nightly prayers. 'Please make this year go fast.'

Despite the usual challenges of camp living, Martino saw that some things were taking a turn for the better. His father had come home from his first day on the job at Ford, covered in grease-slicked skin and reeking of oil, but smiling and nodding agreeably. He was enjoying working indoors, out of the reach of the beating sun, and the best part of all was that he could come home to his family each night.

Taddeo was happier too. He had been allowed to leave school and get a job. Struggling with the language, his results were poor and unlikely to improve. He had argued that he would be of more use to the family bringing in a third wage than sitting in class. It was a convincing argument. Decision made, he went with his mother to a nearby textile factory and they both applied there for work.

They had returned ecstatic. Apparently, there was plenty of work and they had both been employed on the spot. Martino laughed as his mother teased Taddeo about all the factory girls, who had stolen fanciful looks at him while he signed his employment papers. It seemed most of the factory workers were female. But Martino noticed that Taddeo didn't respond to her taunts. Probably because he was still thinking of Daniela, he thought. She was going to be hard to replace in his heart.

While Taddeo was proud to become a wage earner, Nardo couldn't help but feel a little jealous.

'Thinks he's a man just because he has a job,' he whined, stripping a piece of bark outside the tent one afternoon.

'Well, he does earn money now,' Martino pointed out. He was trying to do his maths homework, his book laid out on a large cardboard box beneath a nearby gum tree. Taddeo and their parents were still at work. Only Nonna was there to mind them, and she was occupied giving Marietta a haircut on the other side of the tent in a patch of shade. Isabella was sitting nearby, playing with her doll.

'Anyone can earn money,' Nardo scoffed.

'Well, go on then,' Martino challenged. 'You do it.'

There was a long silence as Nardo considered his options.

'I know what sells! Right, you and Isabella, come with me. Get those spades and old sacks from the army shed.'

'I'm still doing my homework.'

'Well, hurry up and finish it. We have work to do!'

'What will we need spades for?' Isabella wanted to know, putting down her doll. She looked pleased that Nardo was including her.

'You'll see.'

And they did. Half an hour later, Isabella and Martino were in a nearby cow paddock, shovelling manure into old potato sacks.

'Why don't you shovel?' Isabella complained, looking at Nardo sitting on the fence.

'Because it was my idea and I have to do the hard work—the selling! Now come on you two, go faster. We need lots of it!'

Martino wished he had a peg for his nose. The manure piles, some sloppy, some dried, stank in the hot sun, making for the most disgusting of tasks, but Nardo was right. They had to do something to contribute to the family's savings and he wanted to help. For an hour, they filled a dozen sacks, placing them into a small wooden cart.

Over the next two afternoons, Nardo dragged the cart around the neighbourhood and managed to sell all their stinking produce. It was a good time of year for planting and the fresh manure was in much demand. Martino would never forget the look on his father's face when they handed over six shillings.

'How have you done this? Not stolen?'

'No, Papa. Martino, Isabella and I have set up our own business.'

'And it smells bad!' Isabella complained loudly.

Martino laughed, but Nardo gave them a scathing look and snapped, 'It's worth it!'

Their father praised them repeatedly and gave them a chocolate for their earnings, and Martino would have been happy for that to be the end of it. However, Nardo was spurred on by their success and wanted the manure business to keep going. So it did, all through spring. Martino added the shovelling of manure to the long list of things he regularly dreaded.

Over the following months, Brisbane life settled into a routine. His parents and Taddeo laboured hard, too hard, complaining of tired feet every night and going to bed not long after the sun. Nardo, Martino, Marietta and Isabella attended the local Catholic school, which was just a short walk from their camp and, if they weren't shovelling or selling fertiliser, they were helping Nonna with her chores.

Martino liked the little school. The nuns were kind and the children didn't bully him. He was the only Italian in his class, and while he was starting to pick up more English, it was still a struggle. He very much felt the odd one out and missed Gian terribly.

Then, just like that, everything changed.

Early one Sunday morning, in the autumn of 1952, Martino walked with his family to Enoggera tram station. He was told they were going to church. They wore their best clothes and shoes and set out beneath a blue sky marked by a few scudding white clouds. They boarded the tram and sat near the rear door.

'Isn't this the stop?' Martino asked when the tram door opened to let a few people off but his parents made no move.

'Yes, but we are trying a different church today,' his father said. Martino didn't think to question it. They were always doing something new.

The tram travelled past dairy farms and wooden houses set on large blocks. It was a quiet, peaceful area and Martino, interested in where they were going, craned his neck, looking for a church. At last, his father stood up and signalled to his family that they would get off at the next stop.

Hopping off, Martino saw a strip of shops including a baker, butcher, shoe repairer and newsagent. No church though. His father crossed the road and they all followed. They walked a couple of blocks, passing wooden houses on stumps surrounded by large yards. There were farmlands on the other side of the road.

'Where are we?' Marietta asked.

'Stafford,' their father replied.

'Where's the church?' Martino added, casting his eyes about. It wasn't the kind of street for a church.

When his father did not respond, he became suspicious.

'Where are we going?' Nardo started to nag.

'Keep walking,' their father commanded, and Martino and Nardo exchanged a puzzled glance. What was going on?

They turned down a quiet street, then another. Midway down that one, their father announced, 'Ah, here.'

Martino looked at the house their father was facing. It was a simple, box-like Queenslander: a wooden house set on high stumps, with a single-gabled tin roof and stairs leading up to a covered front veranda.

'Are we visiting someone?' Nardo asked.

'Someone from your work?' Taddeo said.

'No.' His father turned to them. He looked nervous. His lips had gone dry and his tongue flicked over them.

'This everyone … this house … take a good look at it. Go on,

Isabella turn around. See this house? This … is your new home. It's our house. Ours!' he declared proudly. 'No more sleeping on the floor of a tent!'

Bewildered, Martino pushed past his shocked brothers and sisters to claim an uninterrupted view of what would be his first home. For as long as he could remember, he'd only lived in camps. He had always taken dinner in mess halls, queued for food that had been cooked in bulk and taken turns to enter showers, which often ran without warm water. He could not believe what he was seeing! It was better than what he had struggled to imagine. This was all theirs. The notion of privacy was strange to him. He stared at the house in awe. His eyes hungrily took it in. The large, white structure was set on a flat dirt patch. Along the front, enclosing the yard, only an arm's length away, was a fence of iron railings with V-shaped bars and a little gate. The sides of the yard had wooden palings running down its length.

Nardo opened the gate and entered the property, peering back at his father for permission.

'Go on, all of you. Explore. I have the key,' he said.

Eager to see the backyard, Martino and his brothers took off at a sprint down the side of the house, coming to a massive area of overgrown grass. At the rear of their property's boundary, they found a water-filled hollow. Wow! What adventures it promised. It was not exactly pretty, but Martino thought it perfect. A yard! Plenty of space for them to play—enough to kick a ball. And they wouldn't have to share it. What a thought!

The back door at the top of a flight of stairs was flung open.

'Come and see inside,' Nonna called to them with childlike excitement.

The boys couldn't run up the stairs fast enough. Once inside, they ran from empty room to empty room, their feet stomping noisily along the floorboards in the hall and kitchen, while their footfalls were muffled on the carpet in the living room and bedrooms. Martino found his way back to the front door and saw that it sat in the middle of the veranda. From there, a hallway ran to the main living room, passing two bedrooms on either side of it. But what excited him most was not the size of the bedrooms, but the fact the house included a bathroom.

'Look, look,' he screamed. 'Mama, Papa—come quick!'

The entire family hurried to see what he was making a fuss about to find him standing in a bathtub.

'We have a bath,' he shouted with a wide grin. For the first time in his life, Martino could not wait to wash himself.

'It is a fine thing.' His mother smiled back at him.

When they all calmed down, their father allocated the bedrooms. The boys were led to a room adjoining the main living area. 'You boys will sleep in here,' he said.

'Wow! Our own room. Look at the size of it.' Martino was impressed.

Then the girls were led to the room to the right off the hall.

'In this room, will be Nonna, Marietta and Isabella.'

'We have windows!' Isabella cried, running to peer out. She saw it overlooked the veranda and the front of the street. She could see the houses opposite. Her cheeks were flushed and her ponytail was bouncing around with her.

'And we will be in the room across from you,' their mother said, indicating the room to the left off the hall.

'We have a window too,' Nardo felt compelled to tell his six-year-old sister.

'So, what does everyone think of it?' their father had to ask.

'It's the most beautiful, best thing ever!' Martino beamed. 'You were right, Nardo. It was worth bagging all that stinking manure. When do we move in?'

They all looked to their father.

'How about today? Let's go and pack up the tent.'

There were cheers all round.

'But we don't have beds yet,' Marietta cut across the din.

'We'll sleep on the floor!' Nardo shouted.

'We don't have to,' their mother posed with a mysterious tone to her voice. 'The factory that Taddeo and I work at makes mattresses. My boss heard that we were moving to a house and let me buy mattresses at wholesale prices. They are being delivered this afternoon.'

'Brand new?' Nonna couldn't believe her ears. For the past eight years, they had slept on all kinds of bedding—from flimsy stretchers to hard bunks to scratchy, old, lice-ridden mattresses on the floor.

'Yes. They will take out some money from Taddeo's and my pay over the next three months.'

'Bless you! And they arrive today?' Nonna was clearly amazed.

'Yes, this afternoon.'

Nonna nodded, then wiped at tears and Marietta burst out a long-held sob.

'Now, now,' their mother said gently, pulling Marietta to her. 'It's all right now.'

'I never believed …' Marietta went on.

'Neither did I,' admitted Taddeo.

'Never believed we'd do it? Buy our own house?' their father asked.

'I believed it,' Martino said. 'Now we have a house … can we have a pet?'

His father roared with laughter and his large hand reached down and cupped his shoulder.

'First, we need furniture,' he said. 'We need to fill these rooms, fix up the yard, grow a garden … the list goes on. I'm sorry but I don't think a pet is high on the list.'

Martino was sad to hear it, but understood. 'I'll help earn money for furniture,' he said seriously.

'Me too,' said Nardo.

'Good, because we don't own this house. The bank does. And we have to keep working to pay it off.'

'Yes, Papa,' the children responded together.

'All right. Now, your mother packed some biscuits. Let's eat them on the back steps, and then go and pack up our tent.'

Martino sat on the highest step, nibbling at his biscuit to make it last. It was his first snack in their new home, and his happiness was overflowing, spilling beyond his senses so that he could not feel the full extent of it. That moment, sitting in the shade on wooden stairs, overlooking an overgrown yard, was the first real day of living in Australia—really living, not just staying. Now he had a place, a place with a house and a yard, a place to call their own. No more moving for a while, surely!

Chapter ten

March, 1952
Stafford, Brisbane

'Now hurry up and eat. You will need energy for your first day at your new schools,' Nonna said. 'Taddeo, you best eat fastest. Your mother will leave very soon.'

Martino didn't need Nonna to tell him to hurry. He was enjoying a freshly baked pastry dripping in butter and it was demolished within seconds.

He was perched on a red padded chair at a shiny table that had silver trim and legs. His father had spent weeks saving for it.

Other, smaller items, such as things for the kitchen, sheets, towels and clothes, had been donated to them by local parishioners only too keen to welcome newly arrived Roman Catholics into their fold. It turned out there was a strong Catholic community in Stafford. Martino was impressed by their generosity. Of course, he kept hoping that someone would donate to them a dog or a horse, but it was not to be. No matter. He was loving his new home.

That morning, he ate happily, dressed in the comfort of his bedroom and then brushed his teeth in silence and without interruption, having the bathroom all to himself for a full three minutes.

Taddeo and his mother flew out the door to catch the tram to work, and Nonna left with Marietta and Isabella, walking them to the nearby Catholic school.

That left Martino to trek to the local public school with Nardo. They had finished the term at the Enoggera Catholic school near the barracks, but now that they were settled in Stafford, it was time for them to attend the area's new government-run school. Being walking distance away, it made more sense.

Martino and Nardo crossed the main road to the shops and then walked several blocks until they came to a large and impressive three-storey, red brick building. That was it. It had to be. The sign said so. Martino felt small and insignificant standing before such a severe building. Rows of windows stared at him, making him shrink beneath their glare. Buttery pastry started to churn in his stomach and he swallowed hard. This school was enormous—much bigger than the ones they had attended in Italy, Cairns and Enoggera.

'Where do we go?' Martino whispered to Nardo.

The grounds were empty. The students were already in class and teaching for the day had begun. They were late and lost.

'There.' Nardo pointed at a sign that read 'Office'. 'That way.'

They made their way in and two ladies behind a high desk smiled at them. Using the little English they had acquired, they managed to make themselves understood. At first the ladies, dressed in white blouses and grey skirts, were confused and there was a flurry of activity as they searched through files and paperwork. Finally, they seemed to locate the necessary documentation and there were smiles of comprehension.

'Are your parents with you?'

The boys shook their heads.

The thinner lady pursed her lips, obviously disapproving. Then, with a sympathetic smiled, she addressed them. 'All right. That's all right,' she muttered, pressing her lips together. 'We can have these signed another time. All right. I can show you to your classes. Follow me.'

She delivered Nardo to his class first, leading him into a room of about twenty children and a stern-looking male teacher. She then took Martino to the ground level and he was handed over to a female teacher. She appeared to be a few years younger than his mother, with light brown hair and soft, dark eyes. It was strange not to be facing a nun.

He was seated at a desk at the front of the classroom.

'Please everyone, clap your hands to welcome your new class member—Martino Saforo,' she said.

The children clapped politely. At least this time no one had laughed at his name and she had pronounced it in full.

'Martino, where are you from?'

Martino reluctantly answered, using a blend of English and Italian to explain that he had come from north Italy and had spent a year in Cairns before moving to Brisbane. He heard a few giggles at his low level of English and was glad when his response came to an end.

But the teacher was curious.

'Martino, please come out the front and tell the pupils a story in Italian,' she beckoned.

'Me tell story … in Italian?'

'Yes. Please do.'

The request had taken him off guard, but he got to his feet obligingly and walked slowly to the front. When he turned, he saw faces that were amused but also, strangely, interested.

With a deep breath to steady his nerves, he launched into the story of *Little Red Riding Hood*. As he rattled off the familiar tale, the children laughed and smiled. It seemed they found the different language intriguing. He warmed to the performance, loving being the centre of attention, and added some hand gestures until one of the children cried out in triumph, 'It's *Little Red Riding Hood!*'

'Yes,' Martino said in English, smiling gleefully. 'It is.'

While he was off to a good start, once class got underway he found he became lost in the teacher's rapid speech. He desperately looked around him to see what the other children were writing, searching for words that would allow him to understand, and was happy if he could figure out even a small part of it.

When the lunch bell sounded, Martino was surprised at how nervous he was. He had learned in Cairns that the schoolyard was a different world to the classroom and he didn't know what to expect. A bigger school was likely to have more bullies, he thought, an assumption that had him creeping out to the lunch area, searching desperately for his brother.

But Nardo, who had turned eleven, was in the senior area and he wasn't allowed in that section. As a junior, he was expected to eat in a separate courtyard. He sat down, away from the other children gathered in groups, and took out his lunch: a large, crusty, submarine-style bread roll that his Nonna had made, filled with ham and thickly sliced cheese and tomato. He peered about. The other children had triangle cut sandwiches with Vegemite or jam or honey. How he wished he had their neat, little lunches. Opening his mouth wide to bite into his massive bread roll would draw attention to himself. So instead, he picked at it with his fingers, trying to break pieces off and pop them into his mouth. Then, to his absolute dread, a mocking voice addressed him.

'What on earth is that?'

Martino glanced up to see a boy at least two years older pointing at his lunch. A couple of kids nearby laughed as they sighted the bread roll.

Feeling vulnerable, Martino slid the roll back into his lunchbox. 'My mother give me,' he tried to explain, distancing himself from the strange choice of lunch.

'Oh, a mama's boy—mama's spaghetti boy,' the boy teased, and others gathering to watch the encounter giggled.

Martino remained quiet. The boy was much larger, stronger, meaner … he didn't want to engage him. Timidly, he looked down at his feet, which felt hot and sweaty in his second-hand black shoes. He was hoping the boy would just go away.

'Look at me, wog boy,' the bully commanded, turning serious. He nodded to a friend, who suddenly grabbed hold of Martino, bringing him to his feet. Martino tried to twist free, but his arms were held firm and his wiggling only served to cause him pain.

Then, to his horror, a cigarette was taken from the boy's pocket and lit.

His eyes widened in disbelief. What was happening? What had he done to deserve this? He turned to the onlookers, appealing to them to intervene, but many were smirking, some cheering, egging the bully on.

'Want a smoke?' the bully asked, bringing the lighted stick menacingly close to Martino's terrified face. 'Whoops, sorry,' he said, and he brought the red glow down on Martino's wriggling arm, holding it there for too long a time.

Martino screamed as his skin burned and blistered. He bucked in pain, causing the cigarette to be knocked to the ground.

'Don't waste my smokes, wog,' the tough boy shouted through gritted teeth, and he punched a still-bound Martino in the stomach. He was instantly winded and gasped for air. He felt the sickening blow of another punch. Surely a teacher would come soon, he thought, as he struggled to take in breath.

The young spectators were no longer smiling, no longer cheering. The attack was more sinister than they had anticipated and even they knew a line had been crossed. Not so the bully. He continued to punch his young victim over and over, in the face and stomach, but Martino did not, would not, cry.

'Break—you—dumb—dago,' the bully ground out the words, sweat streaming down his plump cheeks.

But Martino did not want to give in to this fat-lipped, flat-nosed bully. He didn't want to give him the pleasure of seeing him cry. He gritted his teeth against the pain and closed his eyes.

The boy, frustrated and irate, took a few breaths, tensed his arm and swung it back to give it as much momentum as he could. Just before he was about to let it plunge into Martino's face, he felt his arm lock.

The boy turned in time to see another wog-looking kid holding his arm, but this foreigner was bigger.

'Don't touch me, wog,' the boy seethed, not realising to whom he was talking. The kids in Cairns had learnt the hard way. Nardo was not one to be messed with, and you certainly could not beat up his younger brother and expect to get away with it.

Nardo had hold of the bully's arm, which had been stretched out taut. In one swift motion, he brought up his knee. Crack. The bully's arm was snapped over it—a clean break. Nardo let go, allowing the arm to dangle on a disturbing angle. The yelps and screams the boy emitted were sickening to hear, and all the children, who were sorry to witness the act, fled in shock.

'You all right?' Nardo asked his brother.

Martino shook his head. His nose and bottom lip were gushing blood. His stomach and ribs ached from bruises and it was painful to breathe. The cigarette burn was an ugly irregular blister upon his arm.

'We best get you home. Nonna will fix you up,' he said.

Martino couldn't even nod; his face was so sore. He let his brother lead him out of the school grounds and together, quietly and slowly, they walked home. He was aware that Nardo was carrying both their bags, something he was incapable of doing in his state.

Nonna opened the door to insistent, loud knocking and gasped in horror.

'Mercy be, what has happened here?' she cried, ushering the two boys inside.

'They didn't know us,' Nardo said. 'Now they do. It won't happen again.'

When their parents came home, they were alarmed at the

extent of Martino's injuries and wanted to go up to the school to complain. Even Nonna was keen to march up to the office. But Martino and Nardo shook their heads and argued vehemently against it.

'It is all right now, Mama and Papa. I took care of it,' Nardo assured them.

'Martino, is it true? Will you be safe now?' his mother wanted to know, clearly distressed.

'Yes,' he said softly through swollen lips. 'Nardo took care of it.'

'How did he do this?' his father asked, becoming concerned. He looked to his serious-faced son. 'What did you do?'

'I fought back, and won,' he replied, but did not elaborate.

His parents exchanged a worried look, then their father said, 'All right. If you say so. But if one of you come home like this again, there will be hell to pay up at the school. Got it?'

Martino recalled how his father had confronted Mr Adams and shivered. He did not want his father going up to the big school. For a start, his teacher and the principal wouldn't be able to understand him and, furthermore, it wouldn't change anything when it came to the schoolyard bullying. His father's temper wouldn't solve a thing.

'All right, Papa. We will be okay in future,' Martino mumbled.

The next day at school, the boys made a beeline for the office. They knew that Nardo would be in trouble for breaking the boy's arm and they had left the school without permission in the middle of the day. They thought it best just to face it head on.

When the grey-haired, grey-bearded headmaster called them into his office, he regarded Martino's beaten face and burned arm with some alarm.

'What happened to you?' he asked the small, skinny boy.

Martino held his steady gaze. Surely it was obvious, he thought. He didn't want to have to say it.

'Looks like you got in a fight,' the principal prompted.

'Yes.'

'And from what I've heard, I'm guessing your brother stopped the fight.'

'Yes.'

The headmaster turned to Nardo. 'You broke a boy's arm. That was an excessive use of force. The boy's right arm will be months in plaster. I've had his parents up here complaining. You can't just break bones in my school! If you have a problem, and I can see by your brother's face that perhaps you did, you come and tell me about it. Got it?'

'Yes, sir,' Nardo and Martino responded together.

'And you don't just go home when you feel like it. You come and see me. Got it?'

'Yes, sir.'

'Now, I want to speak to your parents. They need to know about this.'

Martino and Nardo exchanged a worried look, then Nardo spoke. 'Our parents don't speak any English and both work during the day. They don't get home until late, after six o'clock.'

'Then who looks after you when you get home from school?'

'Our grandmother. She doesn't speak English either.'

'I see. Well, I'm going to send home a note with you. You can translate it to your parents. It's informing them of my decision to give you, Nardo, twelve cuts of the cane—six for excessive violence on one hand and six for truancy on the other.'

The headmaster then looked at Martino. 'As for you …' He cringed at the sight of the black and blue face and blistered arm. 'You go to class, but stay out of trouble. Next time you're in my office, there'll be cuts for you too. Understand?'

'Yes, sir,' Martino said meekly.

'You can go now.'

But Martino didn't want to leave. He wished Nardo didn't

have to be punished for coming to his aid. He opened his mouth, wanting to say something in his brother's defence.

'Go on,' Nardo whispered to his brother. 'I'm all right.'

Martino bit his lip and reluctantly took his leave. As he walked out of the office, he heard the whooshing of the cane and the slap of it on skin, over and over and over.

Chapter eleven

March, 1952
Stafford, Brisbane

Nardo ripped up the note to his parents on their way home.

When they got there, Nonna opened the door for them. 'No more fights?' she asked them at once.

'No more fights,' Nardo said tiredly.

'No one came near me. Not to fight or play,' Martino said flatly, walking down the hall, his shoulders slumped. 'I hate school,' he added, before rushing into his room to flop down on the bed. He struggled not to cry.

'Now, now,' Nonna clucked in the doorway to the bedroom. 'Don't give up so soon. It has only been two days. Give it a bit longer. You said you liked the teacher.'

'She feels sorry for me,' he moaned, remembering the pitiful looks she had thrown him. His lips throbbed, his jaw ached and his left eye was so puffy that he could hardly see out of it.

'Anyone with a decent heart would feel sorry for you after that beating.'

'I don't want pity. I want a friend. I want Gian to be here.'

'I know. We all miss our friends. Give it time. Learn the language.'

'I am. I've got nothing else to do.'

'Wait.'

Nonna disappeared for a few minutes, and when she returned she slipped something into his hand. Martino lifted his head long enough to look down at it. In his hand was a piece of chocolate in a shiny wrapper.

'Chocolate?'

She nodded, smiling. 'Don't show the others. Enjoy it, then go downstairs and kick the soccer ball around—that always cheers you up.'

Martino found himself following her advice. He devoured the sweet and then went outside in search of a ball. With no one to pass it to, he kicked it against the side of the house: left foot, right foot, left foot, right foot.

Learn the language, he thought, as he kicked the ball. Better yourself. Be smarter, and don't get caught out by the bullies.

After half an hour, Nardo had finished his homework and joined him.

'Pass it,' he said.

Martino did as instructed and for the next half hour, the brothers kicked the ball back and forth between them.

'Your kick is strong,' Nardo remarked after a while. 'And you've always been accurate. Want to ask Papa if you and I and Taddeo can join a club? They'll have teams and competition soccer, like in Italy. Now we've settled here, we should see what clubs are around.'

Martino had not thought of joining a football club, but the idea held strong appeal. A club would mean training under a coach and making soccer friends.

'That sounds great. I'd love to play for a club,' he answered, his spirits rising. 'You ask. You're older than me. You're better at asking.'

Nardo grinned. 'All right. I will tonight.'

It was at the end of a beautiful meal of soft and plump gnocchi in a cream sauce that had been lovingly prepared by Nonna when Nardo posed the idea of club soccer to his parents. Martino was scraping his plate clean with some bread, but stopped mopping up the sauce as Nardo spoke. Taddeo, too, stilled with interest, his eyes shining with hope.

There was a long minute of deliberation, then their father

responded, his tone apologetic. 'I wish I could sign you up. I just can't afford three pairs of boots for it. Let's wait for next season. I will save for it.'

'We can ask the club if we can buy second-hand boots,' Nardo suggested.

'Nardo, I have no money. After we pay the bank each week for the house and we have been buying furniture and I am trying to start up our vegetable garden and I pay for electricity ... money is going out everywhere. I can't even afford second-hand boots, and I don't want to ask for more charity—not for all three of you! What about your sisters? You don't think they want to take a class? You don't think I would like to go to the tavernetta of a Friday night with the other Italians at the factory? And ...' He glanced at their mother. 'You tell them. It is your news to tell.'

All eyes turned to her. She scanned their faces and took a ragged breath. 'I'm three months' pregnant. I'm going to have a baby.'

No one spoke. Martino tried to absorb the news. A baby? He did not know his mother wanted another one.

'The baby will come in the spring,' she went on. 'What do you think?'

'Boy or girl?' Martino thought to ask.

'I don't know yet.' She smiled. 'Whatever it is, it will be our first Australian in the family!'

Martino's mouth dropped open. Yes, of course. It would not be Italian if it was born in Australia. How strange, he thought. Lucky baby will grow up learning English.

'It is wonderful news, Mama. I will help you with it,' Marietta said.

There were lots of smiles breaking out.

'So, you see, boys, with a baby on the way, we will need to save every penny. Next season, we will see about soccer,' their father said. 'I promise.'

Martino looked to Nardo, who slowly gave a tilt of his head in agreement. Taddeo nodded too, his face glum. They would just have to wait.

Resigned to living without soccer, Martino was prepared to be patient, like his brothers, and yet, for him at least, it would only be a short wait. A few weeks later, the game with the round ball came into his life. It came suddenly, unexpectedly, but not first without a fight.

It happened during morning break at school. As usual, Martino was sitting by himself, finishing off a crunchy bread stick, when a ginger-haired boy swaggered over to him. Martino looked up to see pale skin marked by a sprinkling of freckles.

'Heard you can take a beating,' the boy said in a strange accent. He sounded more curious than hostile.

Martino shrugged and, not sure what the boy wanted of him, slowly returned the bread stick to his lunch box, freeing up his hands. Don't get caught out, he thought, sizing up the boy. They were of the same age and year level. They seemed evenly matched. Martino didn't want to fight him, but he had learnt one thing since they had come to Australia, and that was it paid to stand up to bullies. Cappi had warded off Monte with a kick to the chest; his father had put Mr Adams in his place with a couple of thumps; and Nardo had dealt harshly but effectively with the state school bully by breaking his arm. Nardo's brutality had served to keep others away. But now this boy was fishing, perhaps for a fight, and Martino knew it wouldn't serve him to back down, to show weakness.

'Got some old bruises on your face. Must've taken a few hits. Come on, show us what you've got,' the boy beckoned, almost playfully.

'No.'

The ginger-haired kid smiled.

Before long, Martino found himself throwing and dodging

punches. He was panting hard with exertion, trying to protect his face, trying to hit back. It was tough work! Eventually, a teacher on playground duty came over and pulled them apart.

'Off to the office,' she shouted. 'Now!'

Martino and the boy sat quietly next to each other in the principal's office. When the headmaster turned up and heard that they had been caught fighting, they were promptly issued six cuts of the cane each. Side by side they received the cuts, both refusing to cry out during the painful punishment. Martino didn't try to blame the other boy for starting the fight. The principal hadn't asked anyway.

Walking away from the office and down the steps of the administration block, Martino glanced sideways at the boy, who gave him a wink.

'Ouch,' the boy confided with a huge grin. 'That headmaster really knows how to whack a stick!'

'He's been practising on my brother,' Martino said, offering a weak smile and shaking his sore hand.

The boy began to chuckle. 'I like you, Saforo. You're all right,' he said suddenly. 'I'm Tommy. See you at lunchtime.'

Sure enough, later that same day, during the longer lunch break, Martino was tracked down by the boy who found him hiding behind one of the classroom blocks, eating a salami and cheese roll. Martino thought for sure he wanted to pick another fight, and was waiting for some snide remark to be made about his lunch.

But then the freckly-faced boy said straight out, 'Coming to play soccer?'

'What? With you? Now?' Martino asked, his surprise obvious.

'Sure. After you finish eating. I'm Scottish. We know how to play soccer. I'm guessing you do too, seeing as you're Italian.'

Martino nodded. 'I can play.'

'Great. Can't wait to see how good you are. There's a few of us who play on the oval at lunch. I need someone stronger on my team. Hope you're up for it!'

Martino couldn't believe what was happening. He was making a friend, a soccer friend. He couldn't wait to show Tommy how he could play. 'I can eat this on the way home from school. Let's go,' he said.

He ran with Tommy to the oval and a few other boys jogged over to them. Tommy introduced Martino as Marty and the boys shouted out a quick hello in greeting. Then they were divided into small teams and were off, chasing a ball. Martino ran as hard as he could, joy pumping into his heart. He wanted to impress so he could be invited back to play, so he did his best and, with concentration and effort, pulled off a cracking goal.

Tommy ran up to him then, a broad smile on his face. 'I knew you'd be good, Saforo. Welcome to my team. Meet me here at lunch every day, okay?'

'Sure, Tommy. I'll be here.'

* * *

'How did you go today?' Nonna asked when he got home, a sympathetic smile at the ready.

'Great. Excellent,' Martino announced and quickly told her all about Tommy and the soccer game, though omitted their fight and the consequent caning.

'That's wonderful to hear,' Nonna said. 'Now I can relax. You have a friend and all will be well.'

Feeling on top of the world, Martino ducked into the kitchen, grabbed some bread and dipped it into a pot of simmering tomato sauce.

'Hey, what are you doing in my kitchen?' Nonna shouted. She came rushing in to swipe at him, but as usual he was too fast for her. He laughed as he ran down the rear steps into the backyard.

'And stay out,' she called after him, shaking her head, though she was smiling. Her monkey-faced Martino was back to normal, and so was she!

Chapter twelve

As expected, the baby came in spring, two and half weeks before its due date.

Martino visited his mother in hospital along with his family, eager to meet his new sister. They went up in a lift and down a long hall before coming into a large, cheerless room consisting of many other beds occupied by women. The beds were curtained off and Martino was pleased when one of the dark curtains was pulled back to reveal his mother.

While she seemed happy to see them and told them so, her face was pale and her eyes were tired and sad. She was holding the baby, wrapped in a blanket, close to her chest.

'What is it, Mama?' Marietta asked once they had all quietened. She didn't speak.

Nonna then spoke, her expression grave. 'Today you will meet your beautiful, little sister Maria, named after your aunty in Bergamo, Italy. But you need to know, she has a problem with the right side of her body. Her right hand does not work and she will walk with a limp.'

Martino was confused. What did she mean the baby's hand wasn't working? Weren't all babies born strong and healthy?

'Why is she broken?' Martino wanted to know. He immediately regretted his question as it made his mother turn away from them, bury her face against the baby's blanket and start to cry. His father moved to comfort her.

'There was an accident at work,' Taddeo told them. 'I was

there. Mama was hit by a trolley. Remember, she spent a night in hospital a few weeks ago, then had to stay home from work?'

Martino remembered. Nonna had told him that his mother was in hospital so the doctors could check on the baby in her stomach. They said the doctors had told her it was time to stop work so the baby could keep growing well. They hadn't mentioned an accident.

On seeing baffled expressions, Taddeo explained, 'We didn't tell any of you. We didn't want you worrying.'

'The accident hurt the baby?' Isabella inquired, her voice just above a whisper.

'The baby is not in any pain. She is lovely, with the sweetest face. And we will love her and care for her. She is the luckiest girl in the world,' Nonna replied. 'Come and meet her and you'll see.'

Martino thought Nonna was right. The baby's face was perfectly shaped and she had dark, wispy hair. She looked so small! One by one, they took turns holding her and kissing her.

Martino was in awe of the baby as she was placed in his arms. He was worried he would drop her. He could see her right arm was hanging strangely. A work accident had done that, he thought. Mama was working so she could help pay for their house. The thought made him feel uncomfortable. He wished it hadn't happened. He wished his mother didn't have to work and have accidents. Poor baby. It didn't seem fair. For a moment, he was glad such a thing hadn't happened to him when he was a baby, then felt guilty for thinking that way.

He peered into sleepy, half-open eyes and felt his heart soften. She was special, he decided. Look at that face, that nose, that tiny mouth! He loved her straight away. Don't worry little one, he thought. I will look after you.

* * *

His mother was not allowed to leave the hospital. They wanted her to stay while more tests were carried out to examine Maria's paralysed right side. They were told it could be at least two weeks before his mother and Maria could be discharged. To Martino, two weeks sounded like a long time. He wanted the baby to come home with them straight away.

'Hurry home,' he shouted as they left.

Home wasn't the same without his mother in it. Even though Nonna was there, and life went on as it always did, he missed her, especially at night when she wasn't there to kiss him goodnight.

He continued to go to school and found that he was at last enjoying it. He and Tommy had become fast and thick friends. They played soccer every lunchtime, and as he walked and talked with Tommy to and from the oval, he started picking up more English.

He thought he was fitting in. He thought things were improving and all would be well, particularly as his mother and Maria were due home the next day, something he was really looking forward to. But that wasn't to be the case.

He and Nardo were walking home from school; their bags were heavy and the sun was strong on their backs. They rounded the corner and wandered into their street, then stopped. There, on the opposite footpath in the shade of a tree, was a group of boys. Martino saw among them the bully who had given him the beating on his first day of school. The boy's arm was no longer in plaster. He and the other boys were holding various weapons. He saw cricket bats, pipes and sticks. Before they knew it, the boys were crossing the street towards them.

'Run!' Nardo cried, breaking into a sprint.

Martino did. Fear made his legs feel lighter but less controlled. He pushed on them, trying to find his balance. Despite the heavy bag, he hurled himself down the road, the sound of others chasing coming from not far behind. Nardo reached the front door first and snatched at a note pinned to it. He opened the door and pushed Martino inside ahead of him, then threw himself into the hall and slammed the door, locking it tight.

Heaving for breath, Nardo read the note out loud: *Gone to the shops. Back soon. Nonna.*

Martino was partly relieved that Nonna wasn't there. He wouldn't want her to get involved. But a part of him wished she was home. Nonna would know what to do.

Curious to see if the boys were still outside, Martino and Nardo hurried into their sisters' room and peered out the window to the street. They saw the boys hanging about their front fence. Instantly, they crouched back down.

'They're out there,' Nardo croaked.

'What if Nonna comes home? Do you think they'll hurt her?' Martino was worried, imagining Nonna trying to get through the front gate, now blocked by the boys.

Nardo's expression became pained. 'They better not!'

'Come out, wog boys! You like to fight? We'll give you a hiding,' the bully shouted. The sound of bats and sticks whacking and scraping against their steel fence was frightening.

'What are we going to do?' Martino breathed. They were vastly outnumbered. There had to be at least eight of them.

'What's going on?'

The boys looked up to see Marietta and Isabella in the bedroom doorway.

'When did you get home?' Nardo asked.

'Five minutes ago,' Marietta replied. 'We're having cordial. Want some? Nonna must've left us a jug. She's at the shops. What are you doing in our room and what is that noise outside?'

'Don't go to the window,' Nardo warned sharply.

'Why not?' Marietta asked, trying to see out.

'Get down! I mean it,' Nardo shouted.

The girls bobbed down uncertainly.

'There are boys outside. Boys who want to kill us,' Martino told them.

The girls fell quiet and heard the voices outside shouting abuse.

Nardo's eyes searched the room, seeking potential weapons in case the group advanced on them, but he only saw a collection of plastic dolls sitting on the bed.

'I'm scared,' Isabella piped up. The first grader was still wearing her wide-brimmed hat from school and was now trying to fold it down over her ears to block out the noise. 'What if they try to come in?'

'They better not,' Nardo seethed.

'The front door is locked,' Martino pointed out.

'What about the back door?' Nardo asked, looking to his sisters. They shrugged.

The yelling and nasty slurs grew louder, the names uglier.

'I wish they'd go away,' Marietta cried. She did not know why the boys were calling them such horrible things. Tears welled.

'What is going on?' demanded a voice behind them.

The children turned to see Taddeo, his brows knitting together.

'How come you're home?' Martino asked. Relief and confusion were making a mess of his thoughts.

'I finished early today because I worked late yesterday. How come there's a bunch of kids hanging over our gate? I had to come in through next door and jump our back fence. Want to explain?'

'The boy who beat up Martino is out there, and he brought friends,' Nardo responded.

Taddeo took that in and listened to the abuse and the scraping of bats and sticks outside. Suddenly, there was a loud thud as something hit the side of the house. It was followed by a few more knocks. What were they doing? Throwing rocks? Martino figured they must be. That was what it sounded like.

'They could break a window!' Marietta cried.

'How many are there?' Taddeo asked.

'Too many,' Nardo snapped.

'Eight,' Martino offered.

'Where's Nonna?' Taddeo demanded.

'At the shops,' they all answered.

Taddeo looked at his cowering sisters. Marietta had her arm around Isabella. 'Go and hide,' he told them. They nodded and scampered off to find a hiding place.

'What are we going to do? Hide too?' Nardo asked. Knowing his brother detested confrontation, he half expected him to advise it.

'No. We're going out there,' Taddeo said calmly.

Nardo and Martino simply stared at him in disbelief.

The older boy took a deep breath. 'We can't let them damage our house, or worse—Nonna will be on her way home soon. We don't want her caught up in this. We have to get rid of them.'

The brothers exchanged concerned glances and nodded in silent agreement. For Nonna, they would do whatever it took.

'What's your plan?' Nardo asked Taddeo.

'Follow my lead.'

Taddeo walked to the front door and his brothers joined him there. He unlocked it and rested his hand over the handle.

'Remember, they think we're crazy Italians, so let's give them crazy. Be loud and wild. Do what I do!'

The boys, horrified by the thought of going out there, nodded.

'Let's do it,' Nardo bravely agreed. 'Let's be crazy.' It was a crazy idea after all. Three against eight!

Taddeo took a deep breath. 'Now,' he commanded. He flung open the door and charged outside, shrieking like a maniac. Nardo and Martino followed, yelling their lungs out.

Running straight to the side fence and using fear-fuelled strength, Taddeo tore off three wooden palings and handed one each to his brothers, so they were all armed with a plank. Then

Taddeo bolted directly towards the group with savage abandon, his brothers doing the same, scaring the lifeblood out of the primary school toughs, who immediately turned tails and ran. The Saforo brothers did not stop giving chase until their feet were sore and their hearts were almost bursting from exertion.

They walked back, their chests heaving. Despite being victorious, they did not talk. They did not want to discuss what had happened or, more importantly, why it had occurred. It was too ugly a topic. Martino hung his head. He may have made a couple of friends, but it seemed there were always going to be a few who didn't accept him. Being Italian in Australia meant being different. It wasn't easy.

They replaced the palings, Taddeo fetching a hammer to knock them back into place, and they returned to their anxious sisters and perplexed Nonna.

'Thanks Taddeo,' Martino said over a cup of cordial.

'No problem.'

But it didn't end there. Later in the early evening there was a knock at their door and their father went to answer it.

'Boys, come here and tell me what the police want with us?' he called down the hall.

Martino and his brothers were shocked. The police! They walked to the door, and Martino felt small and afraid as he was put in front of two stocky and stern looking men in blue uniforms, hats in hands.

'So, sons, tell your father what you were up to this afternoon then,' an officer with a large rounded belly requested of them.

Nardo spoke up, his Italian words coming out in an urgent rush. 'We had to defend ourselves, Papa. We didn't hurt anyone. There were eight of them, only three of us. They came here. They asked for it. They came to our house, started throwing rocks, they picked the fight.'

Their father held his hand up, requesting silence. Martino

couldn't be sure, but he thought he could see a flash of relief in his eyes. What had he thought the police wanted?

'We will talk about this when the police have gone. Right now, say sorry and tell the officers it will never happen again.'

The boys apologised—they were used to saying sorry in English by now.

The uniformed cops, satisfied the strict Italian parent would see to the matter, left the family, but not without a parting word.

'Keep out of trouble,' the old, chubby policeman told the boys. 'Next time, you come with us,' he pointed at the oldest boy. The front door was closed.

Martino was upset at the thought of the police taking away Taddeo. What would they do to him? Lock him up in jail? Nervously, he turned to face his father. They were in the hall, where the light was dim.

'You chased these boys off … didn't hurt any of them?' their father began.

'That's right,' Taddeo replied softly.

'Those boys came here, looking for a fight, calling you out?'

'Yes.'

'Your sisters were here. They heard these boys?'

'Yes, they were scared, Papa,' Taddeo explained. 'I told them to go hide.'

'Nonna was on her way home. We were worried about her,' Martino added.

His father's eyes widened and his hands closed into fists. He took in a deep breath. 'You did good,' he said, sounding proud. 'You defended your home, your sisters. You had no choice and no one was hurt. Well done, all three of you. Now, go and see Nonna about dessert. You've earned it.'

Taddeo and Nardo raced down the hall, eager for a sweet, but Martino didn't move. He looked to his father, wanting to ask him something.

'Yes, Martino? What is it?'

'When you saw the police ... what did you think they wanted?'

His father ran a hand through his hair and exhaled heavily. 'You don't miss much, do you?'

Martino waited for him to reply.

'I admit I was worried. I was worried about our immigration status. I was worried we had done something wrong, not filled out the paperwork correctly or something. And it reminded me of another time. The last time officials came knocking on a door, it was in Italy. My name was on a list for arrest. Bad memories, Martino. The police standing there brought back bad memories.'

'I'm sorry, Papa.'

'It's not your fault. It's just the way it is. Now, hurry ... before your brothers and sisters eat all the biscuits.'

Chapter thirteen

October, 1952
Stafford

Martino wanted to be happy that his mother was finally home and there was a baby in the house. Yet he couldn't believe what she was saying to him.

'But why?' he gasped. 'Why do I have to change schools? I like the Stafford school. I have made a friend. A good friend. His name is Tommy. He lets me play soccer and teaches me English. Ask Nonna! It is true.'

'No, Martino. The boys there are too rough. I talked with your father about what happened yesterday. About you getting into trouble with some boys and the police turning up. I can't have you getting hurt again.'

'But I wasn't hurt.'

'Your brothers can't always be there for you, Martino. They are strong and can take care of themselves. You are a slight boy, all skin and bones. I can't sleep for worry about you, and with a baby to take care of, believe me, I need my sleep when I can get it. I can't afford to have you getting into fights. I want you to go to the Catholic school. You'll be safer there.'

'No, Mama. I want to stay where I am!'

'You'll make friends just as quickly at the Catholic school. Trust me, Martino. You'll be safer and happier with nuns watching over you.'

Martino didn't believe her. He didn't want to believe her. He argued with her, he cried, he begged, but his mother would not change her mind.

And so, he started a new school again, and again, he was the new kid, the wog, the foreign one with strange sounding English and an odd packed lunch. Strange faces surrounded him—again.

Change. Always change. He was tired of it. Different countries, camps, cities, schools. Back to no friends.

By the end of the first week, he could see that the nuns were not as his mother had promised. They rarely smiled and were strict and mean. He was afraid of them.

He came home on the Friday, sullen and miserable.

Nonna found him at the side of the house, kicking the ball against the wall: left foot, right foot, left foot.

'Here,' she said, slipping a chocolate into his hand. 'Not liking your new school?'

'It's horrible,' he said, putting his foot on the ball to bring it to a rest. He looked at the chocolate. It wasn't enough to bring a smile to his face.

'School is not forever. You learn what you can, take from it what you can and then, one day, you will be free to run your own life.'

'Can't wait to grow up then,' Martino sighed.

'It will happen sooner than you think. Don't let those pesky nuns bother you.'

His lips at least twitched at that. He found it amusing to hear Nonna say such a thing about the nuns.

'They pick on me,' he confided.

'Let them pick. They can't change who you are, and you are becoming stronger and smarter every day. The harder it is, the better person you become.'

'I'm going to be perfect after all this,' he commented, making his Nonna smile.

'You already are perfect. Perfectly adorable,' she told him, planting a kiss on his cheek.

Martino grinned, knowing that was just his Nonna talking. She was always nice to him.

'Now, cheer up and eat your chocolate.'

He did. He shoved the block into his mouth, loving its creamy texture.

While Nonna meant well and her words had soothed him, the next week at school was unbearable. He was constantly getting into trouble with the nuns and, despite trying, he couldn't make friends. Soccer was not played on the oval at lunchtime. There was no boy like Tommy inviting him to play. Being three-quarters of the way through the school year, the boys already had their set friends and they weren't prepared to let a stranger, a foreigner at that, break into their groups. Struggling to fit in, he decided there was only one thing to do.

Not go.

No one knew. He had to walk to school by himself. It was easy to set off in the direction of the school, then, once out of sight, turn away from it. He didn't do it every day. Just every now and then to give himself a break. On his return to school he told the nuns he had been sick, and as they knew he had parents who didn't speak English they just had to believe him.

For the next couple of months, on his chosen days off from school, he explored much of his local area. He found he liked swimming in the creek, despite the stink of the nearby tannery. He taught himself to ride horses that he came across in surrounding paddocks. It wasn't so much stealing them, but borrowing them for a while. He preferred being outside—running, climbing, kicking balls, going fast. No one at home knew he was frequently skipping school. It was his secret. It was freedom.

It was the only way for him to cope.

And then came his ninth birthday and a gift that would help take him further afield on his days of roaming free. He got a bicycle! It was second-hand but his father had cleaned it up and it looked new to him.

Now his 'days off' from school saw him riding up and down

streets, passing hobby farms of dairy cows, horses, strawberry patches or pineapples. He pinched fruit simply because of his habit acquired in the European migrant camps and it was easy to do. They were long and happy days. He wished Gian was with him to enjoy them, and sometimes he found himself chatting to his friend in his mind, telling him things, showing him things. Gian was with him in spirit, even though he didn't know it.

One afternoon, after a relaxing day of riding, climbing trees and eating mulberries, he heard a bell clanging in a nearby school and knew it was time to head home. He was at least two suburbs away and thought he better hurry. Even if he went his fastest, he was going to get home later than his expected arrival. He hopped on his bike and took off at a hard pace.

When he was turning into his street at the T-junction, he saw a newspaper deliveryman driving toward him. The old driver was known to swerve his car from one side of the street to the other, throwing papers out his side windows into people's yards, and Martino knew to be cautious of him. But he was in a hurry, and rather than stopping and waiting for him to pass, he tried to keep clear and chose to ride as fast as he could to reach the safety of the footpath. Somehow he misjudged the speed of the car, and before he could react, it clipped him.

He sensed his leg being smashed against the car's headlight, the broken glass easily slicing through his lower leg. The impact sent him flying high through the air, and on landing the wind was knocked from his lungs.

He heard a chilling scream … it sounded like his sister Isabella. Her voice rang out across the neighbourhood, 'Come quick! Martino's been hit. Martino's been hit by a car.'

Then she was standing over him, her skipping rope in hand. Nonna, Marietta and Nardo arrived shortly after, crowding around him.

'My God in Heaven,' Nonna wailed on reaching him.

Martino tried to speak but his mouth was dry. He turned and saw his bicycle was a mangled mess beside him. No! Not his new bike!

He heard his sisters whimpering.

Why were they upset? It wasn't their bicycle. Seeing them overreacting, he decided to play along and give them something to worry about. He began to flutter his eyes and close them, staying very still.

'No, no, Martino, stay awake, don't go to sleep,' Nonna pleaded.

Martino made his arm go limp.

'Oh, sweet Jesus,' he heard Nonna exclaim. He was clearly doing a good job of his acting.

'Martino!' Nardo called urgently. 'We need a doctor! Doctor, doctor,' he yelled in English.

'Help him,' Marietta screamed.

'Help!' Isabella echoed.

'It's all right! I'm not dead,' Martino piped up, opening his eyes. He thought they would laugh. Surely they would see it was funny. They were all panicking for nothing.

'We thought …' Nonna began, her hand clutching at her chest.

'You were just pretending? How could you?' Nardo scolded his brother.

Martino had enjoyed playing the trick, but he could not know why his family members had so readily believed it. He had not seen his injured leg and shock was shielding him from the worst of the pain.

Nonna pulled herself together then spoke, trying to stay calm, 'You gave us a scare,' she said. 'Can you feel any pain? No, don't look at your leg.'

'I can't feel it,' he said.

'Lie still. The ambulance will come soon. The driver has gone into a house to call it.'

'Ambulance? I don't need an ambulance.'

'Don't move. The ambulance will be fun,' Nonna told him.

* * *

A few days later, Martino was still in hospital, his leg giving off a foul stench. It seemed it was infected. Everyone was speaking in whispers around him. He did not know what was going on and just wanted to go home. But his Mama kept saying he had to stay. His leg needed to get better.

One early evening, when his father was visiting the hospital after work, Martino overheard him talking to a doctor with the assistance of a translator. They were out in the hall, their voices low and hushed, and yet he was still able to take in every disturbing word.

'Listen here. That leg does not come off. I won't have a cripple for a son. We didn't come all this way just for this. My son will die before I let you cut off his leg. Understand? No, no, no.'

The doctor, sounding alarmed, spoke rapidly to the translator.

'Your son will die if we don't amputate,' his father was advised. 'Do you understand that? You have no choice!'

There was a long, considered silence, then his father spoke slowly and measured.

'Do your best for him, but let me make it clear: the leg stays on.'

The translator conveyed the message to the doctor.

'No. It is a shock. You need more time to think about it.'

'No. I have thought about it.'

There was the sound of his father's heavy footsteps striding away and the lighter tap of his mother's heels as she hurried away after him.

Sometime later, his mother appeared at his bedside. She sat, her hands fidgeting. She wiped at his brow, pulled up his sheet, rubbed his arm.

'Am I going to be okay, Mama?' he asked, and heard that his voice was wavering.

She did not smile, but planted a gentle kiss on his cheek. 'Of course, you are,' she said. 'Doctors are very clever these days.'

'My leg ...'

'Will get better.'

'But I heard Papa talking to the doctor ...'

Alarm widened her eyes, then she spoke quickly. 'You heard but one conversation. There have been many conversations and the doctors know what to do now. Your leg will be just fine.'

'How do you know?'

'I know. My heart tells me.'

'Does your heart know things, know things for sure?'

'In this case, yes. You will walk out of here,' she said fervently.

But he found he didn't believe her. She had said the nuns would be kind and protective, but they weren't. She had said Australia was a place where dreams could come true ... but there he was, in hospital.

After he had arrived by ambulance, when the first doctor had come to examine his leg, he had seen it. He had seen the deep tear, the skin flapping back, exposing bone and muscle. It had been a horrific sight. Then, he had been sick.

As his mother continued to assure him he was going to be fine, he turned his head away. He didn't know who or what to believe. He wondered if God was punishing him for skipping school. If he had been at school, he would not have been riding into his street when the newspapers were being delivered. He would have been there sooner and the accident wouldn't have happened. Thinking like that wasn't helping him though. There was no going back and doing it differently. What was done, was done.

His gangrened leg stayed on.

His mother told him that the doctors were going to apply skin grafts to his shin area and that she and his family, the nuns at school and the entire parish of Stafford would be praying for his recovery. He hoped God was on their side, if not on his.

The operation went ahead. Martino woke up to a lot of pain. He was given medicine and told to go back to sleep. When he woke up, Nonna was there, giving him comic books and sweets and talking about home, trying to cheer him. For days, he lay in the big hospital bed, taking medicine, having his dressings changed and his temperature taken. His mother and Nonna took turns staying by his side, while the others went to work or school. He hated the mushy hospital food and kept telling Nonna how much he missed her cooking. She started smuggling in portions of dinner to him: cold pasta, salads, crusty breads, cheeses. Still, he missed the house and the yard and kicking his soccer ball, and there was nothing that Nonna could do about that.

A week before Christmas, Martino started to believe that his father had made the right decision.

He had to walk out. He wanted to. He needed to.

And he did.

Though on his departure, the doctor issued a warning to his parents, telling them that their son might never regain full use of his leg, that too much muscle had been damaged. With Christmas looming and Martino thrilled to be going home, his parents didn't have the heart to tell him.

Contessa turned to Ettore in the hospital hall and whispered, 'How do we tell such a thing to a boy with a dream of being a great soccer player?'

'We don't. Not yet. Not yet.'

Chapter fourteen

January, 1953
Stafford, Brisbane

Any kind of activity was painful and difficult. Martino found his leg was weak and would not take his full weight. He wondered if his muscle was asleep and would, in time, wake up.

Despite the pain and discomfort, Martino kept to his chores, joining Taddeo and Nardo to clean out the chook pen, water the vegetable garden and do the weeding. He hobbled everywhere, going slow, whereas before he had sped about. No longer could he take the steps at the back of the house two at a time. Instead, he had to lean on the rail and drag himself up, his leg throbbing at the end of the effort. He had to be careful, he told himself. It was just going to take time.

Over two years had passed since they had arrived in Australia. The government contracts holding their friends in Cairns had come to an end. News from them was exciting. Roberto had found work in a biscuit factory, Rico was to take up a good job as an engineer on a building project, and Cappi had been appointed to the role of groundsman at a school. All the jobs were based in Brisbane. They would soon all be together again. Only Edrico, who had been given a job in Newcastle, was not planning a move to Brisbane straight away. His wife, Tazia, had written that Edrico was very happy in his BHP job and they were saving a deposit for a house before applying for jobs in Brisbane. They were planning to join them in about six months.

Martino was pleased to hear it. Gian was coming. Monte was not—well, not yet.

Martino thought his mother and Nonna had never looked happier.

'I can't wait to show them the shops in the Valley,' he heard his mother saying as she nursed Maria, who was suckling on a teat attached to a glass bottle of warmed milk.

'I know. We must take them to the café we found. Wait until they see it has an espresso machine!' Nonna returned.

'As soon as Roberto gets here, I'm taking him to the tavenetta,' his father chimed in. 'It will be good to see him. I miss speaking to people of our dialect. The Italians at my work are hard to understand.'

'It won't be long now,' his mother pointed out. 'We can have fun again.'

It was true, Martino thought. There had not been much time for fun. With his mother back at work, Nonna caring for the baby and taking care of the house, and his father working hard and trying to establish a vegetable garden, there had been little time left for enjoying themselves. Martino was heartened by their chatter and began to share their anticipation. He, too, had plans for when Gian would come to Brisbane. He wanted to show him the horses in the local paddocks and the nearby creek and the little farms. Hurry up, leg, he thought. Get stronger! There would be so much to do when Gian arrived.

Finally, the day came when the families from Cairns were to visit. Their father left to meet them in the city. He was to guide them to the tram and walk them to their house. There could be no talking to his mother or Nonna, whose focus had become fixed on preparing the house and lunch for their guests. Marietta was put in charge of watching over Maria, and Isabella was recruited to help in the kitchen, while Martino and his brothers raked and tidied up the back yard.

The day was hot. Martino was wearing a singlet and shorts. After his chores, he hovered in the front yard, waiting for their guests to arrive, but eventually the heat drove him inside.

When the knock came at their door, Martino was beside himself. 'They're here,' he cried.

His mother, carrying Maria, went to answer it. He kept close on her heels.

The door opened and there were cries of delight. The baby! Everyone wanted to touch her and kiss her.

Martino, leaning heavily on his good leg, craned his neck, trying to see Gian. Suddenly, his friend's face appeared, the first of their guests to weave around his mother and step it into the hall.

'How long has it been?' Gian asked.

'Too long,' Martino said.

The hall was soon filled with noise and bright laughter as greetings took on the form of kissing on both cheeks and embracing. Taddeo was greeting Daniela, Nardo was laughing with Elmo, and Marietta grabbed Francesca by the hand. Lena's daughters, Vittoria and Elisa, were now aged eight and five, and were shyly hiding behind their mother. Isabella was trying to coax them away.

Then an introduction was made. They had learned by letter that Cappi had married an Italian girl, Amelia, the daughter of a farmer in Cairns. She arrived hanging on his arm, her smile deep, her eyes kind. She had long, dark hair down to her waist. Many kisses were foisted upon her in what Martino thought was a warm but overwhelming welcome. She looked overawed and pressed her body closer to Cappi, her cheeks flushed.

Martino watched on as his mother talked fast, wresting Amelia away from Cappi so she could join the other women in sitting in the living room, where platters of sliced meats, cheeses and olives were laid out. Bianca, Lisa, Gilda and Lena were loudly praising the house and the furniture. Nonna was instantly uncorking a bottle of red wine. His father took the men through the garlic-scented kitchen to the backdoor where he showed them the backyard and pointed out his tomatoes sprouting on vines. Then they returned to the living room, dragging chairs from the kitchen on their way so they could all sit as a group and eat, drink and catch up on stories.

Martino and Gian were still in the hall, smiling at each other. Martino couldn't believe he was there. He hadn't changed, though he was a little taller and his hair looked different: shorter and lighter.

'You're in Brisbane then? For good now?' Martino wanted to make sure.

'Yeah, we are. We're at New Farm. I'll go to the local school.'

Martino was disappointed. He had hoped Gian could go to the same school as him.

'Your mother wrote to us, saying you got hit by a car.' Gian stared at his leg.

Martino's face fell. He didn't like being reminded. Ruefully, he too looked down at his bandaged leg. 'Yes. It's still sore. It's been weeks. I had a big operation. The skin is very thin on my shin now. I have to be careful.'

'Lucky you weren't killed! When will it get better?'

Martino shrugged. 'Soon, I hope.'

'By the time the soccer season starts? Now that we're in Brisbane, I'm signing up to play at a club. Papa says I can go to the same football club as you.'

'We can train and play together? That's the best news ever. The season starts in March—I'm sure to be better by then. I can't wait! Papa promised we could play at a club this year.'

'I can't wait either. So, want to show me around?'

'Sure.'

Martino led his friend to the backdoor, all the while feeling embarrassed to be limping badly. 'Here's our backyard,' he said.

'Wow! Look at the size of it.'

Martino smiled, delighted at his friend's reaction. Suddenly,

Nardo and Elmo were behind them, pushing past and racing down the stairs.

'Come on, Gian. Let's have a kick.'

Despite the heat, the three boys began to play soccer, running up and down the yard, shouting and passing. Martino had no choice but to sit on the back step and watch. As they tackled each other, at times collapsing into a wrestle, Martino lowered his eyes. They were having too much fun without him. He stared at his outstretched leg and hated it. Why was it taking so long to heal?

The visit did not go as Martino had planned. He could do so little with his injured leg. For the most part, he was an onlooker, missing out on the boisterous activities, which went on and on. Only during lunch did he feel he was back in the group and had Gian's attention, yet even that was over all too soon. After the midday meal, the games swiftly shifted outside again, where the boys and girls started playing chase and then were granted permission to turn on the hose and play water games.

It was hard for Martino not to sulk. He was given a turn of holding the hose, but what he really wanted to do was run through the water stream and splash his feet in the fresh mud puddles. He was starting to understand what it meant not to have use of his leg and he did not like it.

Their friends took their leave just on sunset. By then, Martino was glad to see them off. He was tired of watching everyone else enjoying themselves. His father walked them up the street, seeing them to the tram stop, while he and his brothers and sisters waved from the front steps. Once their friends were out of sight, Martino chose not to go back inside with the others, but rather sank heavily to sit on the front steps. There, he watched pink clouds floating in a light blue sky. His leg was pounding so hard it was as though it had its own pulse. He thought he hadn't done much, but maybe he had.

He was still sitting there when his father returned. There was no more pink in the sky and the blue had darkened, allowing early evening stars to shine. His father slumped next to him and rested his large, calloused hand lightly on the knee above the bandages.

'How is it?' his father asked.

'Sore.'

They didn't speak for another minute or so. Martino had a question resting on his tongue, but he was too afraid to flick it to his lips. Once spoken, could he cope with the reply? His father wasn't looking at him, but he sensed that he too had something to say.

'Papa?'

'Yes, Martino?' Oh, his father sounded so tired.

'Will I be able to play soccer this season? With my leg … will it get better?' There, it was out. He had asked it.

It was then that Martino saw his father's eyes were glistening. Just from tiredness, or were there tears welling? He hoped they were not a reflection of sadness, but then his father said what he had been dreading to hear.

'No, Martino. You won't play this season and I don't know about the next. The skin on your leg is very thin and will tear easily if it is knocked or kicked. Soccer will be very dangerous for you. Besides, you can hardly walk. How do you expect to run?'

'The season is weeks away. I should be running by then, at least, won't I?'

His father was no longer looking at him. He heard him inhale air and slowly release it.

'Papa? How long do I have to wait before it is better?' Fear rose behind his frown. They had kept his leg on so that he could walk again, and if he could walk, he could run, he would run …

'We don't know. We see the doctor again in six months. We can ask him then.'

Martino felt as though his father had punched him in the stomach. He couldn't breathe. He sorted through the words, sifting the meaning so that he could absorb it. When he finally found his voice, it was a strangled whimper.

'Six months! You don't know! You don't know ...' Was he crying? His shoulders were heaving, his body shaking. Then he was on his father's lap, his leg jutting out in front of them, and strong arms were holding him against a hard chest.

'Martino, I didn't want this for you. I risked all for you to keep the leg. We have to believe it will come good. It has to! Don't give up on it. I'm not. I'm not giving up on it. Six months is not long to wait. Give it time. But don't give up. Fight.'

His father's words were ringing in his ears and would haunt him in the following weeks. Fight. Everything had been a fight, his entire young life had been a struggle, and so he should be battle-strong, right? He could fight for his leg to recover ... he had no other choice.

* * *

When the school year recommenced, it was deemed that Martino was well enough to attend. His heavily scarred leg, with its paper-thin covering, was concealed beneath a long sock that was part of the school uniform. Although hidden from view, Martino could not conceal his obvious limp. As he walked into school, he could feel his cheeks burning. Glances to his left and right revealed students gawking at him. News of his car accident had spread throughout the community and he was no longer just the odd foreigner; now he was the survivor of a car crash with a hideous leg and limp. Could it get any worse?

He recognised the children in his class; many were the same from the previous year. When he took his seat, some smiled at him. They never used to. They pity me, he thought sadly.

'Hey, how's the leg? Heard you got hit by a car,' the boy next to him asked.

'Yes. It was a bad hit. My leg will get better.'

'Did it hurt?'

'No. I couldn't feel it.'

'Lucky.'

'Yes.'

It seemed the children were curious. They had never met anyone who had been hit by a car before. He became a person of interest. Martino reluctantly answered their questions and finally accepted their pity, which he realised was coming from a place of kindness. It was nice they were talking to him at all.

On the third day of the term, most of the pupils were chatting to each other, the noise in the room rising to an unbearable level. Martino was finishing off his work and not talking to the child next to him, though he had been throughout the day. The ice broken, he had been talking to lots of pupils in and out of class. However, on that occasion, he was doing what he was told and was working hard.

When the nun called for quiet and was ignored, she stopped writing on the blackboard and, turning to face the class, her hands on hips, asked those who she considered to be troublemakers to stand up. Martino was, as usual, named among them.

After whacking three kids with a ruler across the palm of their hands and asking them to sit, she came to Martino: the last one standing.

'Put out your hand,' she commanded. She was a short, frumpy woman with a blockish face. Her gaze was angrier than warranted.

'But, Sister, I wasn't talking,' he told her honestly.

'Put out your hand,' she insisted.

'I wasn't …' he began again. *Whack!* The nun slapped the ruler across his scarred leg. He squealed, almost collapsing with the shooting, searing pain. He reached for his desk to steady himself. What was she doing? Perhaps she didn't know about his leg, he reasoned. It was hidden beneath the sock. Then she raised the ruler again and in panic he spluttered: 'Stop, Sister. That is my sore leg. I was hit by a car and … please hit my hand.'

He held out his palm, offering it.

Whether it was his tone or she just didn't like him, he did not know, but she slapped his hand away and started to hit his leg, over and over, again and again and again.

At some point, Martino snapped. His brain registered red for anger and white for pain until the red and white tumbled and converged in his mind, exploding into sparks. His brain and self-control switched off and all he knew was to hit back, to fight, to stand up for himself. This was just another battle to him. He swung out and punched the nun in the stomach, hard. The woman gasped and fell to her knees.

He froze, as did every other child in the class. What had he done? No child had ever struck back. It wasn't right to hit a nun. It was bad, very bad.

The nun righted herself. She stomped over to her desk, opened the top drawer and reached for a long pin. A couple of children gasped as they saw it. She only brought it out for severe punishment.

'Martin! Come here!'

There was no way he could trust the Sister with a pin. Given she had persisted to hit him on his sore leg with the ruler, chances were high that she would stab his leg with that terrifyingly sharp point. He didn't wait another second but started limping madly, as fast as he possibly could, towards the door. His leg was still sore from where the ruler had struck it and so his escape was clumsy and frustratingly laborious. He was breathing hard, throwing his leg forward and hobbling vigorously. Looking over his shoulder, he saw her thick fingers reaching for his shoulder. If only he could run!

Just then, the boy who he was sitting next to stood up and slipped in front of the nun, blocking her.

'Get out of my way,' she screeched, holding the pin in a menacing fashion.

'Sorry, Miss. We could hold him for you?'

'Yes, yes. Get him. Stop him. He's leaving the room.'

The boy took his time to reach the door, by which time Martino was struggling up the hall.

'Can't see him,' he reported back.

Furious, the nun came up behind him, but the boy continued to block her.

'Out of my way,' she shouted.

Slowly, he stepped aside. When she gazed down the hall, the infuriating Italian boy was no longer in sight.

'He went that way,' the boy pointed in the opposite direction to where he had seen Martino heading and she charged off in that direction. He smiled, glad to have done the Italian a favour. The poor boy had been hit by a car! He didn't deserve the nun's cruelty as well.

Martino pushed open the school gate and shuffled along the footpath, vowing to himself never to return. His vow was easily fulfilled with the backing of higher authorities, for the nun filed a report with the head Sister, and he was expelled, effective immediately.

When his parents received the letter, informing them of his expulsion, he confessed it was true, but when being asked to explain what had happened, he found himself lying. He couldn't admit to striking a nun. He told them a boy had hit him on his leg and he had hit back.

'We must find a school with even greater discipline,' his mother told him.

Martino shuddered. He could not imagine such a school and didn't want to.

Without having any say in the matter, he was sent to another Catholic school.

More strange faces stared at him as he dragged his damaged leg over to a desk and sat down. The nuns knew he had been expelled from his previous school and marked him as a mischief-maker. They expected him to be up to no good and shouted at him at every opportunity until he cowered in his seat, afraid to answer questions.

The teasing at lunchtime extended to some mild physical bullying. He was pushed and shoved and occasionally tripped. Once he would have regained his balance from a slight trip, but with his weak leg he went tumbling over, grazing his knees and elbows.

It wasn't long before he once again began to skip school, lying to the Sisters that he had to attend medical appointments for his leg.

He was free again. He left for school alone, hobbling in the direction of the tram, which he was meant to catch, then turned up the very first cross street to start his slow journey to a park or creek. He hobbled seemingly for miles, gritting his teeth against the pain and occasionally wiping at tears. Exhausting as it was, he pushed on, demanding that his leg work for him as it once had.

Over the next few weeks, he hardly went to school. On his return, the Sisters would send him to the office to explain his absence. He would pretend to go, then return to class, saying it was all okay. They had talked to his doctor. His lies had no end. He justified them to himself that it was part of his fight to get his leg back. Skipping school had become less about running away from the strict and unfair Sisters and more about his recovery. His focus and intention grew clearer. Without the use of his leg, there would be no soccer and without soccer, there was nothing, nothing to smile about. He had to exercise—it was the only way.

The days spent walking seemed to be helping. Perhaps he was

lying to himself that his leg appeared to be getting stronger. He wanted it to improve so much that he didn't know what to think. Was he limping less? Was he going faster? He hoped so!

With the soccer season about to commence, Taddeo, Nardo, Elmo and Gian bought second-hand boots and signed up at Thistles Football Club at The Grange. They started attending training two nights a week. When it was time for their first match, their fathers went to watch them play. Martino went too. It was hard to see them, sprinting across the field, engaging in fierce tackles that made him wince. His leg wouldn't cope with such clashes. Watching the speed and strength applied on the field sapped him of hope of ever joining them in a game and such thoughts were more than he could bear. He couldn't afford to think that way. He had to keep believing in his fight.

And so he continued to walk the streets, putting one foot in front of the other, limping, always limping.

On a day he actually went to school, during his first break, Martino was surprised to see a man dressed in overalls and a safari-style hat, the kind you'd wear in Africa, coming towards him. The face looked familiar, yet it was a moment before his brain could register who it was. He was the last person he expected to see at school. Cappi!

'Hello, Martino,' Cappi said, sitting down on the grass beside him. 'Finally, I have found you. You are difficult to come by.'

Martino hoped Cappi had not worked out how little he was attending the school and then felt a rush of embarrassment to be found eating alone, away from the other children.

'Hello, Cappi. What are you doing here?' he mumbled, trying not to turn red with shame.

'I work at this school. I'm the groundsman. Surely Nonna told you.'

'No, she didn't.'

'She asked me what school I was working at just so that she

could send you here. Wants me to keep an eye on you.'

Martino lowered his gaze, feeling even more ashamed. He didn't want his Nonna asking people to look after him. Since his accident, they were being too protective.

'Don't worry. I don't have time or interest in watching over children. I'm not going to bother you, though I could use a favour ...'

'What is it?'

Martino could see other children smirking at them as they were speaking Italian and it wasn't usual for a student to talk to the grounds staff.

'During lunch, I don't do much. I'm told to keep out of the way as there are too many children about. So I go into the storeroom and hang out there. Any chance of at lunchtime you could come and teach me some English? You see, I am thinking that one day I may have a child who will be born in Australia. My English needs to get better if I'm to talk to my own child, agree?'

'How is your English?'

'Bad. I picked up a little on the cane fields, but in Cairns there was a large Italian community, and I was lazy and just spoke to them. My wife, she speaks Italian too. But now, I want to speak more English and I'm thinking ... I'm here, you're here ... you could teach me.'

Martino wasn't sure. The other children would judge him badly, seeing him spending his lunch breaks in the storeroom with the Italian groundskeeper. He could almost imagine the teasing that would attract. Besides, he didn't think the nuns would allow it.

'Of course, I would have to repay you in some way ...' Cappi went on.

Martino glanced up. What did he mean?

'For instance, I know you are trying to rehabilitate your leg. You want it to be stronger?'

Martino nodded.

'I can help you train. After school, we can use the school oval. I'm allowed on it to mow it and water it and so on. While I'm doing my work, I will set you exercises.'

'Nonna wants me home straight after school. And the nuns ...'

'I have already talked to the head Sister about my plan. She thinks that by teaching me English, your English would improve and she was very happy to let you train on the oval, under my supervision, of course. I will talk to Nonna. Don't worry about that. Okay?'

Martino thought about it. Teaching English in exchange for an oval on which to train with a trainer. Why not? Maybe Cappi could help rebuild his leg. For some reason, he was feeling happier. Having someone to talk to during school time would be nice.

'Okay, Cappi. Sounds good. I'll meet you at lunchtime,' he said, and found that he was smiling.

Cappi smiled back. 'See you then, Martino.'

And so the teaching and training began. Nonna was fine for him to stay longer, knowing he was doing exercises with Cappi. She thought it a good arrangement. More importantly, it also meant he was no longer skipping school. He wondered if the nuns and Nonna had in fact put Cappi up to it, just to stop him from running wild around the neighbourhood. He suspected the nuns knew the truth, and Nonna, well, she had a way of always knowing everything. He was glad of it, for training on the oval gave his leg soft, flat ground on which to walk, allowing him to go further and gain more strength. Cappi knew good stretching exercises, which he would do before and after walking. He felt his leg now had a good chance of recovery.

At lunchtime, Cappi presented him with Italian sentences that he wanted translated. Martino would make the translations, then help him to pronounce the words correctly, and they would practise. Slowly, Cappi started to build a broad collection of common and useful phrases. Some of them were amusing, making Martino laugh.

'How do you say: *Can I buy you a beer?*' Cappi had put to him. 'Why are you laughing?'

'I don't think you will be saying this to your future child … not for many years,' Martino explained.

'But I may want to speak to other Australians and they like beer more than wine, so I think I will use this.'

'All right, Cappi. I will teach you it. But no saying it to the nuns!'

Months went by and Martino's limp started to diminish. Slowly, his walking grew smoother and faster. It happened so gradually that it took Nonna to point out his progress to him.

'Your leg is stronger. I see you are walking straight again.'

'I am, aren't I? The pain is hardly there.'

'That is good to hear. The doctor will be happy to hear it too.'

'I will be running before you know it,' he told her, making her smile.

'I don't doubt it. Whatever, you're doing, keep doing it.'

Not long after Nonna's comment, Cappi asked him to try jogging, keeping it light and slow. He did half a lap of the oval. There was some discomfort afterwards, but not as much as he had expected, so it was added to his exercise routine, and the distance covered was extended each week.

At then the day came when Cappi urged him to pick up the pace. 'Try to run,' he asked of him. 'I think you're ready.'

Martino pushed on his leg, trying to go beyond the small steps of a jog and to stretch his calf out to take longer strides. To his surprise and relief, the muscle was there. It had awoken and it was time to use it. He wasn't going fast and he felt his leg was weak and only half doing his bidding, but he was running.

It was at that time he was due to see the doctor for his

six-month check-up. The following day he arrived at school to find Cappi waiting for him at the front gate.

'Well? What did the doctors say?'

'They were very impressed,' Martino said, but he was not smiling and could hardly face Cappi. He wanted to hide his disappointment from him.

'Impressed?' Cappi could see Martino was upset and then understood. 'But not enough to let you play soccer?'

'No. Not yet. My leg is getting better and will get stronger. The skin covering my shin is still thin and not tough enough to take a knock. No soccer. What's the point of it all, Cappi, if I can't play?'

'Martino, you are lucky the car did not kill you. You are lucky to still have a leg. And now it will recover. Given you are so lucky, I think you will play soccer again. You are too lucky not to.'

Martino liked his logic, but he did wonder if his luck had run out. All he could do was hope it hadn't.

The soccer season of 1954 started without him. And the one after that in 1955. Even though he was training hard and running fast, the doctors only shook their heads. No soccer, too risky. The shin would tear, they asserted.

His parents had no choice but to refuse his pleas to sign up.

The news was devastating. Nardo was top goal scorer at Thistles. Taddeo was achieving high praise in defence. They had lots of friends at the soccer club, many of them other migrants. They brought home trophies from premiership and grand final wins and placed them on the shelf in his bedroom, where he could stare at them every day on waking. Anger was building, anger that made him run harder and faster.

Cappi listened and understood.

'You have come so far, Martino. Next year, you will be a teenager and will start high school at the new college. Your leg is stronger every year. Maybe next season you will be able to convince the doctors that it is strong enough to take a knock.'

'I don't know. Every year I get my hopes up. I don't want to be told "no" again.'

'When your leg is ready, you will play and what a player you will be! All this frustration will lead to great things for you. You will have something to prove and it will make you work harder. Have faith.'

'I want to have faith. It's just taking so long.'

'Then you need patience. Just wait. Give it time.'

'I have no choice, Cappi. All I can do is wait. I'm just so tired of it.'

'You don't think I get tired of learning English? My wife has just given birth to a boy. I want him to be raised with English in the house. Don't you think I worry that my English isn't good enough? That my son will struggle at school because he will be learning a blend of two languages at home?'

'Cappi, your English has come a long way.'

'Just like your leg,' Cappi put in. 'We are getting there. Yes?'

'Yes. You're right,' Martino agreed. 'We're getting there. You know enough.'

'And you will play soccer. You've done enough. Not long now.'

'I hope you're right.'

Chapter fifteen

January 1956
Stafford, Brisbane

Martino wanted to tell his father about his first day of high school, but found him lying on the sofa, his eyes closed. He had been sleeping there since he got home from work.

Every day now it was the same. Perhaps it was for the best. When his father was awake, he was tired and irritable, and he and his brothers and sisters could do no right.

That summer his father had started up his own panel beating business, going into partnership with a work colleague. It meant he was labouring seven days a week, occasionally coming home to spend a Sunday afternoon with them.

'Why do you have to work every day?' Martino once asked him.

'The time to make money is now,' he had replied. 'Running your own business is the only way. We can't be like these lazy Australians. They are always having days off and going to the races, the newspaper in their back pockets. They eat meat pies and grow fat around the middle. I can't be like them. I have to work now, make money and then, later, much later, I can relax.'

'But Papa, you work too hard. You look tired. The weather is too hot for your kind of work!'

'Yes. I know. It is hot. I am tired. What else can I do? I have a chance to make enough money to give us the things we want. I must take this chance and make the most of it.'

'All right, Papa. But please have fun with us sometimes?'

'I will. When I can,' he had said, but there had been no smile on his lips or in his eyes. His focus was not on fun, not that year.

Martino started high school at a newly opened Catholic college. He was twelve years old and fit. His English was fluent, there was no Italian accent, and he had some talent for mathematics. He now looked upon attending a new school as a fresh start and not something to be feared. Although he was going to miss his exercise sessions with Cappi, he was hoping he might make some new friends his own age.

In the first term, the school announced that a sports day would be held. Martino was excited about it and, feeling confident, put his name down for several of the track events. As it approached, he shared his enthusiasm with Nonna.

'I'm going to enter many races in the school sports day, Nonna. I think I can do well.'

'I hope you can. Is it on soon? Perhaps I can go to this sports day. I'll see if your mother can come too.'

'Really? You want to come? And you think Mama can take a day off work?'

'Why no? We are always watching your brothers play soccer. It's time we watched you do something. Your mother can call in sick. I don't think your father will be able to take a day off. His work is so busy.'

'I know. Papa is always working these days.'

'Yes. He works hard for us,' she said. 'I know you have your hopes up about the sports day. But remember this is a big college and there will be boys from all around the north side going there. Some will be very fast. So please don't worry if you don't win. You can run and that is victory enough.'

Nonna was gently running a brush through Maria's wavy locks. Maria was no longer a baby, but a pretty little girl of three. Martino could see the girl's right ankle was turned on an awkward angle. Speaking at that moment, Nonna's words could not have had more impact.

'Maria, want to come outside? I can push you on the swing,' he offered.

'Can I, Nonna?'

'Of course, you can. Martino will take you down. I'll join you in a minute. I'll see if I can find us some biscuits. Okay?'

'Okay. Can I go to sports day?'

'Yes, of course you can come,' Martino replied. 'I will run for you. If I win my race, if I come first, I get a ribbon. I will give you my ribbon. Deal?'

'Ribbon for my hair?' Maria asked.

'No. Just a ribbon to hold. Would you like that?'

She nodded, her eyes wide.

'That's if he gets a ribbon,' Nonna shouted after them. 'The races will be very fast.'

'I know, Nonna. You haven't seen me run. I'm fast.'

'You'll need to be,' she couldn't help pointing out.

On sports day, his mother and Nonna arrived at the respectable college, wearing new dresses with buttoned and collared tops and pleated skirts. His mother, carrying Maria on her hip, was in pale green; his Nonna in pink. They joined hundreds of other parents taking seats by the school oval.

Martino was on the field, waiting to be called for the first races. He saw them sit down, and as they turned and spotted him he gave them a long wave, smiling as they waved back.

Nerves were clenching the insides of his stomach. Use that energy, he thought and gave his scarred leg an extra stretch.

'I can do this,' he told himself. 'My leg may look bad, but it can run and run fast.' He couldn't wait to show everyone what he knew he could do. If only he could manage a good start.

They were summoning his age group to the start-up line for the one-hundred-yard dash. It was time.

He toed the line and glanced around. The boys seemed bigger than him, taller. They checked him out and seemed to become more confident as they peered at his leg, where the scar was peeping above his slack sock. He didn't bend to pull up the sock. Let them stare. Let them underestimate him.

'Take your marks ...'

His heart was pounding so hard it hurt.

Bang!

They were off and Martino was running, feeling the air pressing hard against him. How hard it pushed. He strained his legs, driving them through the resistance. He dared not look sideways, though he sensed he was in front. Yes! And in an instant—after his legs had been thrust to their limits, muscles pumped for all they were worth—it was over. He had crossed the line first! As he struggled to catch his breath, a Brother approached him and told him he had broken the school record for his age.

The boys in his race stared at him incomprehensibly. He had not attended the school-organised training or the practice races at the school. No one knew he was even a contender.

The second-placed runner came over to him. 'Good race, Saforo,' he huffed. 'You're a natural. Didn't you have a car accident?' He was staring at his leg, where the ugly scar and broad stretch of thin skin was now fully exposed.

'Yes, I did. My leg is okay now,' he breathed hard, his cheeks red from exertion.

'I'll say. Well done! Hey, why don't you train with us next week? There's a group of us who run on the oval at lunchtimes.'

'Sure. I'd like that. Thanks.'

Martino then turned to the spectators, searching for his mother. Instantly, he found her and saw she had a hand over her mouth in a sign of disbelief. She kissed her hand and threw the kiss at him. Nonna and Maria were on their feet clapping. He gave them a hearty wave and, as before, they waved back.

He was happy. It was a wonderful feeling and he wanted to savour it.

Still high from his win, he soon lined up for the mile run. Again he was tense with nerves. It was going to be a harder race. He hoped his leg would endure it. The starter gun sounded and off he pushed, his legs propelling him down the track. The race seemed to go on forever and, as he reached halfway, he found his lungs were burning, surely close to bursting? Somehow he took his focus away from the pain and kept up the hard pace he had set. When he crossed the line, gasping and spluttering, a blue ribbon was handed to him. Another school age record smashed.

It then became a theme. Every race he fronted ended with a blue ribbon—for Maria!

At the day's conclusion, his mother made her way down to the oval. Martino jogged over to her.

'You are so fast. How did you get that fast?' she asked. 'Your leg … the doctors said …'

He shrugged. What to tell her? That he had trained until he had cried? That he had done everything Cappi had asked of him because of fear his leg would never recover and because he wanted more than anything in the world to join his brothers and friends on the soccer field? There was so much he wanted to tell her, so much that had driven him to train, day after day, but in the end he shrugged and smiled and said simply: 'I like to run.'

She smiled, though she looked puzzled. 'I think you must like it very much. I'm so happy for you.'

As she kissed him on both cheeks, he looked around. The students and Brothers were gazing at him in a way that he wasn't used to—he was being looked upon with respect. They were seeing him, seeing him for what he could do. It was a good feeling. He hoped it marked the start of better days to come.

Later that evening, Martino waited patiently while his father put away some tools, had a shower and dressed for dinner. As he slumped on the sofa in the living room, Martino bailed him up.

'Papa, I have good news.'

'Yes? You had your sports day today. How did you go? Well?'

'Very well. I won all my races and broke the record for my age in each event.'

His father leaned forward, his surprise evident. 'Age champion? But how? Your leg …'

'I can run fast now.'

His father shook his head, finding it hard to believe.

'Looks like you made the right choice for me, hey Papa?'

Comprehension was in his father's eyes and he nodded slowly. 'Yes. We got lucky, Martino. You are lucky, never forget that. And, perhaps, you have Cappi to thank. I know he was training you.'

'Yes. I can't wait to tell Cappi. I'm lucky. I agree. Lucky, I have you.'

His father pinched his cheek. 'Go on. Maybe it was more than luck. You fought a good fight. Well done. So, with that kind of speed, let's hope we can get you on a soccer field, hey?'

'I'm always hoping for that.'

'Me too. Believe me. It is my wish for you, too.'

Chapter sixteen

September 1956
Stafford, Brisbane

Martino woke up and smiled. Picnic day!

Organised by an Italian association that had been formed in Brisbane, the picnics held at Sutton Beach on a peninsula north of Brisbane represented a long day of feasting and fun. Many Italians across Brisbane attended, most of them from Fiume.

He would get to see Gian outside of a soccer field.

Martino hurried to eat his breakfast and get dressed. Alberto would soon arrive with his pick-up truck to collect them for the ride to the beach. He picked up many families on his way north.

The horn honked outside, sending his Nonna into a flap. 'Come on everyone. He's here!'

Martino and Nardo helped carry the heavy picnic basket out to the truck. When they got there, they saw the back was already full of passengers, many just sitting on the floor where blankets had been laid out. His family piled in. Martino said hello to Cappi, who was with his wife, and squirmed his way over to be with Gian.

Their fathers sat on crates. Both wore knotted hankies on their heads for protection from the sun. Martino was pleased to see his father smiling and joking with Roberto. He didn't seem to laugh much anymore, not with all the stress of running his own business. At least he would get to relax that day.

About forty minutes later, the truck jostled over a long and bumpy bridge, giving them their first view of the sea, eliciting cheers from the jovial passengers. Soon after, they pulled up by a vast grassed area and, on leaping out, were embraced by cool and salty breezes, a welcome relief after being cramped against sweaty bodies for the trip's duration. A picnic spot selected, Martino and his brothers immediately went to work, helping their father and Roberto tie up huge tarps between trees to provide shade for the group. Martino's mother and Nonna worked with the other women to spread out the blankets and unpack the baskets.

As they prepared for their day, Martino noticed that other beachgoers were giving them a wide berth, choosing to walk further along the shorefront to steer clear of them. He understood. They were a large and rowdy group.

Tying off the last of the tarps, Martino was just starting to think it was going to be their best picnic yet when he saw a car pull up next to Alberto's truck. Moving for a closer look, he saw Edrico and Tazia sitting in the front of a light blue Chevrolet. In the back seat was Monte, who had grown into a fine-looking eighteen-year-old. He could have been an actor, Martino thought, such was Monte's resemblance to James Dean, with his thick, wind-tousled hair and slight curl of locks at the front, the dark sunglasses, the rolled-up sleeves and his confident lean, elbow out the window.

Fascinated as he was by Monte's appearance, Martino found himself groaning inwardly. He had not seen much of Monte in recent years. His parents were regulars at their social gatherings, but Monte had chosen to stay away, always with an excuse of being busy elsewhere. Why had he come today?

Martino had never forgiven him for his attack on Nardo at the Greta camp, or for taking his lucky penny. Even though that was years ago, he still didn't want to have anything to do with him.

His father and a few other interested Italians walked over to the car, drawn to inspect what was a new purchase. They gathered around it, compliments flying. Martino knew his father well, and knew he wouldn't be too pleased that his friend had achieved car ownership before him. He could already imagine his comments to his mother about it later that night.

'Coming for a swim?' Gian asked, running up to him. It was then that Gian saw Monte getting out of the car. 'What's he doing here? Is that their car?'

'Yes. Who cares? Race you to the water …'

They sprinted down to the calm sea and plunged in, swimming out to where their brothers were treading water. Without shirts, his brothers looked strong. Their arms were thick and muscular, their chests appeared hard and broad. Taddeo's blond hair shone fairer against the contrast of his summer tan. Martino felt small and scrawny next to them. They were swimming not far from the jetty, where the girls, including Marietta and Isabella, were gathered, chatting and laughing in their bright coloured swimsuits. Elmo eventually called out, asking the girls to join them in the water. They did so, walking around to the shore to wade in slowly.

Martino laughed as Nardo and Taddeo began splashing them unmercifully.

'Stop it,' the girls cried.

Martino was surprised to see Taddeo halt his splashing. His eyes were riveted on Daniela, now a playful nineteen-year-old, smiling coyly in a chic yellow strapless one-piece costume. His chivalry was rewarded with a harsh splash to his face as Daniela took the opportunity to retaliate.

'Right,' he cried, chasing her as she ran for the shore, her squeals of laugher encouraging him. He soon was upon her and swept her into his arms, carrying her, kicking and shrieking, back out into the water.

'Dump her,' Elmo called, wanting to see his sister punished.

'That's not very nice,' Marietta told him and splashed water into his eyes.

As soon as he blinked away the salty water, Elmo made a beeline for Marietta, who was wearing a spotted two-piece suit with skirt-like shorts and a flattering halter-top. Even Martino had to admit his sister was looking her best that day. He found her silly though when she started begging for Elmo not to wet her hair. Of course, he did so instantly, pushing on her shoulders to dunk her.

'Look,' Gian murmured to him.

Martino gazed beyond Marietta's outrage and saw Taddeo holding Daniela. Her hands were locked around the back of his neck, their faces close. They made a nice couple, he thought. It was time they got together. His brother had harboured a crush on her for years.

'Kiss her,' Nardo demanded.

Laughter broke out around them and Martino couldn't help but join in.

The couple turned, and on seeing everyone watching them in amusement, pulled apart, though they were smiling broadly.

'Let's get away from the girls,' Gian suggested to Martino, and he agreed. They made their way to the other side of the jetty, where they stayed in the cool of the water for over an hour.

Then Nardo called to them. 'Hey, come in, you two. Soccer's on.'

Gian glanced at Martino, his expression overly apologetic.

'It's okay. You play. I'll go and … find something to eat.'

Martino padded up the shore, picking up his towel from the sand as he went.

As he dried off on the grass, wiping the sand from his ankles, he saw Monte strolling beneath the pine trees. He was alone. His shirt was off and Martino whistled to himself at the sight of his powerful upper body. He must spend a bit of time working out, Martino thought. Monte's chest was bulky yet firm above a small waist. His stomach looked tight, rock hard. Martino kept his eye on him and saw he was heading towards a girl in a yellow swimsuit. She was watching the sea, a towel slung over her shoulder. When he reached her, she turned and Martino was disturbed to see it was Daniela. Monte struck up a conversation with her and she seemed to respond almost automatically to his opening remarks with an enthusiastic laugh.

Martino's face darkened. Everyone knew that Taddeo liked Daniela. He observed them with interest and then saw them heading down to the water, walking so close that their shoulders were almost touching. Where was Taddeo? He strained his neck looking about and saw that he was among the group setting up the soccer game. Taddeo was taking charge, deciding who was playing on which team.

He looked back to the waterfront, but Monte and Daniela had disappeared. Feeling hungry after the long swim and sorry he wasn't joining in the soccer, he continued ambling along the grass and wandered over to where his mother and Nonna were sitting.

'Want some cheese, Martino?' his Nonna offered.

'Sure.'

Nonna cut him a generous piece. 'Why don't you take Maria with you to go watch the soccer?'

Martino glanced at his sister, who was hugging her yellow teddy bear, and saw her eyes light up on hearing Nonna's suggestion.

'Want to come Maria?'

'Yes please,' she practically shouted.

She brought her bear with her. They walked over to a grassy slope set back a safe distance from where the boys were playing soccer. He spread out his towel for her to sit on, protecting her from the ants, and she settled in close to him.

Together they watched the friendly match. Cappi had volunteered to be referee and, taking the job seriously, he was already engaging in heated debates with players. Even friendly matches were hotly contested, Martino thought, smiling to himself.

Nardo was highly skilled. His talent was apparent. With ease, he bounced the ball on the top of his foot, then flicked it up to his chest where it slid down the length of his body to the other foot. From there, he was side-stepping players that came at him, applying shoulder feints to look like he was going in one direction, only to take the ball in the opposite direction. He made the moves look simple. Martino found his skills impressive and wondered if he could master such control. He wished he could try.

'Are you sad you're not playing?' Maria asked him suddenly.

He looked down at her. 'Yes,' Martino replied. 'I want to play but, you know, my leg is bad.'

She nodded and leaned forward to examine his scar and irregular stretch of skin, then, using her strong hand, pressed her bear against it.

'What are you doing?' he asked, smiling at her.

'Yellow Ted will look after your leg,' she explained. 'Super bear.'

Martino stared, wishing he could strap it on … then had a thought. He could put padding on his shin to protect it … he could wear a shin guard. Would it be enough? He had never thought to try. The doctors had just said 'no' to soccer, but there had never been any discussion around taking precautions. He was older, the shin was stronger; maybe it was time. Excited, he grabbed Maria's bear and gave it a big kiss.

'Maria, you are a genius. You're right! I can wear something to stop it being hurt.'

'Are you going to wear a bear?' she asked, gaping.

'No,' he laughed. 'A shin guard.'

'What's a shin gad?' she asked, pronouncing it incorrectly.

'Let's hope I can show you. Come with me.'

He took her by the hand and they returned to their mother, who was smiling calmly, a wine glass in hand. When he had her attention, he put the idea to her.

'Martino, you know what the doctor said,' his mother said, shaking her head.

'But he didn't say anything about a guard.'

'Well, we can ask him about it soon.'

'Please, Mama. I want to play today. Just five minutes. Just to try it with a shin guard. Just five minutes. Please?'

His mother took a breath, preparing to dig in, when Maria spoke up: 'Say yes, Mama. He wants to play.'

She gazed at Maria's pleading eyes. All her friends and Nonna had stopped talking and were looking at them, listening.

'I guess you could try it. Five minutes. Just five minutes,' his mother relented.

Martino yelped with joy and picked up Maria in his arms and swung her around. He set her down, seeing her eyes were bright with laughter.

'Now show me a shin gad,' she said.

'Yes!'

Excitedly, Martino ran off, asking every boy of soccer playing age at the picnic if they had one. When one was unearthed in a training bag, Martino ran over to Maria and strapped it on, showing her how it was done.

'See, it covers my bad leg. Think it will stop my leg being hurt?'

She punched her fist against the front of the guard. 'Did it hurt?'

'Not one bit,' Martino told her.

She smiled.

'Think I'm ready?'

Maria gave a single nod.

'Thanks, doc.' Martino looked over at the game. The ball was being kicked with force between the players, who ranged in age between fifteen and twenty years.

'Go on,' Maria urged. 'Just try.'

He nodded and ran into the thick of play. Gian stopped running. 'You found a guard, then?'

'Yes. Worth a try …'

Gian smiled encouragingly.

Martino saw the other players had come to a stop too, and were looking at him with interest.

'It's okay. Just for five minutes,' he yelled for all to hear. 'Just giving it a go.'

'We'll take it easy on you,' Nardo announced, and there were many murmurs of agreement from the others.

'You sure, Martino?' Cappi queried, gazing at his leg. He knew the extent of the damage that had been done and how long and agonising his recovery had been. Cappi couldn't help but express concern.

'I'm sure.'

'All right. Take the kick in,' Cappi told Taddeo, who had the ball.

Play recommenced.

Martino was running. He found he was instantly breathless, not from exertion, but from joy. He couldn't believe it was happening. He was actually chasing a ball, pursuing it with an instinct that felt natural.

His first touch of the ball was electrifying. He passed it to Gian. A good pass. The ball hadn't touched his shin. He continued. He ran, he kicked, then he tackled, softly at first, then harder. *Whack.* The ball thumped against the guard. The skin there was a little tender, felt fuzzy, but seemed to be okay. He stopped to check his leg. It was fine. The skin was intact. Five minutes turned into ten. Many more minutes later, he heard clapping. He glanced in the direction of the applause and saw his father. He had Maria perched on his shoulders, where he used to sit. Their smiles were radiant.

'Look, Papa. I'm playing.'

'It is good,' he called back. 'Now go score a goal!'

Martino didn't score a goal, but he had in his heart. A

tremendous goal had been achieved that day. He could play without damaging his shin. To think, it had been little Maria who had shown him the way.

Afterwards, all the red-faced players agreed that they needed a swim to cool off. Martino removed the guard and went with them, their young athletic bodies moving rhythmically as they ran beneath pine trees to reach the sea.

As they neared the shore, Taddeo pulled up short in front of him, forcing him to halt too. Martino wondered what had stopped him. And then he saw what his brother was seeing. Only a stone's throw away, sitting together on one beach towel, engaged in a long, slow kiss, was Monte and Daniela.

Martino wondered what Taddeo was going to do. He stole a sideways glance and saw his brother was furious.

As sweaty bodies plunged into the water in front of the couple, their kiss came to an end. It was then that Daniela looked around and saw Taddeo staring at her. Shock registered on her face and she leapt to her feet, rushing towards him, but he held up a hand, commanding her to stop. Trying to comply, her feet rammed into the sand, causing her to stumble. She waved her arms and found her balance.

'I didn't mean …' she stammered, trying to explain.

'I thought you hated Monte. After what he did. Don't you remember the cat, the kittens?'

Martino did. Daniela had loved those kittens. At the refugee camp in Germany, Monte had drowned them in a rage, but that had been so long ago—in another time and place.

'He was a child. He was angry with us for not letting him play. You and your brothers never gave him a chance. He was alone. We were too hard on him.' Her words came out in short emotional bursts.

Taddeo was mortified. 'You're going to stand there and defend him, defend that monster?'

'He's not …' she said too quickly, then peered back at Monte, who was facing the sea. She scanned his evenly tanned, slender back, his superbly toned arms, his longish, damp hair. Her eyes seemed to like what she was seeing.

'He is, Daniela,' Taddeo practically shouted to regain her attention. 'People don't drown cute little kittens just because they're feeling left out!'

Daniela looked as though his words had slapped her.

Martino studied Taddeo's face and saw him looking at the girl in a way he never had before. It was as though she had become repugnant to him.

Fear was in her eyes. 'I loved those kittens,' she cried suddenly, her lips forming a pout that demanded he forgive her.

'I know. The saddest part is … I thought for a long time, I thought you loved …'

Martino knew what he wanted to say but he didn't finish.

Instead, Taddeo flung at her: 'You kissed him. You kissed him.' He shook his head and turned away, striding back beneath the cover of the trees, hurt and bitterness stamped on his face.

Martino hesitated before following him, calling, 'Taddeo, you okay?'

'No. Why would she do it?'

'I don't know. Monte is hard to work out.'

'Monte is easy to work out. She's a pretty girl. He kissed her. What I can't understand is why she kissed him.'

'I don't know, Taddeo, but I do know she loves you.'

'How can you know that?' Taddeo was distressed.

'I know because I heard her say it, just then as you walked away.'

Taddeo stopped and looked at him. 'She said that?'

Martino nodded. 'Don't give up on her. Some things are worth fighting for.'

'Thanks, Martino. But it will take me a long time to forget that kiss.'

Chapter seventeen

December, 1956
Stafford, Brisbane

A new Christmas tree, straight out of a box, had been put up. A green, plastic tree, with perfectly shaped branches.

'What are we going to decorate it with?' Martino asked.

'Leave it to me,' Nonna said with a wink.

'What are you going to do? Can I help?' Maria knelt by the tree, gazing up at it.

'Yes, you can be my helper,' Nonna told her.

On waking the next morning, Martino walked into the living room and, on seeing the tree, began to smile. Tied to its branches were shiny wrapped lollies, making it sparkle all over.

'Good idea, Nonna,' he shouted.

Nonna came out of the kitchen, wiping her hands on her apron. Maria was following, her clothes dusty with flour. 'You saw it?' Maria beamed.

'Yes. It's perfect. Can I take one?'

Maria peered about. 'All right. One. Take one. But don't tell.'

In the days leading up to Christmas, it became a family game to steal the lollies without Nonna seeing. Maria declared herself the Christmas tree guardian and kept a close watch on it. Strict on everyone, Martino was flattered that she kept giving him permission to take a lolly.

'You are good to me, little sister,' he told her. 'You have one too.'

'I did. One every day!'

On Christmas Eve, their father, having consumed a few glasses of red wine, decided it was timely to make a few announcements.

The family sat around in the living room, Martino and Nardo content to sit on the floor. Nonna was seated in the middle of the sofa with a glass of homemade liqueur in her hand. Maria curled up beside her. His mother was wearing a dark blue wraparound dress. Her hair had been cut short, which accentuated her large, brown eyes and slender neck.

'As you know, Nardo has graduated from high school. Usually, we would expect him to get a job, but his results were very good. We've decided to send him to college.'

Martino was surprised. College! He had not thought it was an option. He glanced at his brother, thrilled for him.

His father continued, 'He will study accounting. Well done, Nardo.'

Accounting … Martino suddenly had a thought. 'Papa, I'm good at maths too. Any chance that when I graduate …'

'No,' his father cut him off, then quickly explained: 'We don't have enough money to pay for two to go to college. Only one, and I'm sure you wouldn't want to hold Nardo back. He's worked hard.'

I work hard, Martino thought, but dared not voice it. He was happy for Nardo, and of course didn't want to hold him back, but he wanted the same opportunities for himself. That was fair, wasn't it?

'Finish junior high school, Martino, then we'll look for an apprenticeship for you. Perhaps you can join me in the panel beating shop.'

Martino's head snapped up. What was he saying? Panel beating! No, never, was his first reaction. Martino had been forced to spend a large portion of his school holidays helping his father in the workshop, and he had hated every minute of it. It was gruelling work, hot and relentless. It was not for him.

'I don't … I don't …' But how to say he didn't like what his father had to do every day? He couldn't say it, but there was no way in the world that he wanted to be a panel beater! He bit his lip, looking desperately to his mother for support.

'It's a conversation we can have another time,' she said smoothly. 'For now, let's congratulate Nardo.' She started to clap and everyone followed suit. Their father waited for the clapping to subside, then went on.

'As you know, Marietta has been working hard at the dressmaking factory. She has been told that she will get a pay rise, starting after Christmas. Well done. We are very proud of you.' The family applauded. 'Marietta says they are often hiring new girls, so Isabella, there's a good chance you can work there too when you finish junior high school.'

'Yes, Papa,' Isabella said. A slender, graceful girl of eleven, she peered at Martino and her eyes told him that she, too, didn't like what was being planned for her. Martino felt an ally in her and gave her a look of understanding in return.

'As for Taddeo, we all know he has been accepted into the Australian army. He has just learned he'll be transferred to Melbourne for his training.'

'Melbourne!' Martino shot to his feet. 'You're leaving us, Taddeo?'

'He's a young man. It's time he saw a bit more of the world, hey Taddeo?' his father answered for him.

'Yes. Melbourne should be interesting,' he replied. 'And the army will give me a chance to finish my education,' he added pointedly.

'It is wonderful for you,' Nonna muttered.

The family broke into applause once again. When it stopped, their father, not yet done, cleared his throat.

'And Martino,' he continued.

Now what? He had not expected a speech or an announcement about him. What could it be? Martino's eyes were fixed on his father.

'Martino, I have checked again with the doctor. It seems this year, you can start playing soccer at a club.'

There was clapping, but he hardly heard it. He was stunned. Just like that? After all these years? Permission to play! It was outstanding news.

'Best Christmas present ever,' he declared, and everyone laughed.

'Now, about Christmas presents. I've decided to give one early. Wait here.'

Their father ran up the hall and returned a few minutes later, walking slowly with a large, heavy, gift-wrapped box in his arms. He placed it down carefully. Martino sized it up with his eyes. What could it be? He couldn't guess.

'Go on, family. Open it,' his father urged.

Martino joined the others at tearing the red wrapping paper, and Marietta screamed when she saw what was beneath it.

'It's a television,' she shrieked, jumping up and down.

'I thought we might like to plug it in and watch a Christmas show tonight.' Their father smiled. 'What do you think?'

'Yes!' Martino cried. He couldn't wait to see it. He had seen televisions in the shop and through the window of a neighbour's house, but never up close.

'Okay, Taddeo and Nardo, give me a hand with it. We can put it in the corner over there.'

The black and white television was set up and, after some manipulation with the antennae, reception was established. Eagerly, they sat around and watched as their father turned the clunky channel knob, clicking it around to a Christmas show. Martino, eyes alert, watched singers in fashionable clothes belt out Christmas carols. He hardly heard what they were singing. He was too busy marvelling that the box was presenting moving pictures and it was in their living room. It was theirs! How could they be so fortunate? He couldn't wait to tell his high school friends.

On his way to bed that night, he glanced back at their Christmas tree, covered in empty lolly wrappers, sparkling by the glow of their new television. It made him smile. He was happy and content.

Not long after the television came another addition to the household. Of all their purchases, it was one that made his father most proud. He had bought a Dodge. It had taken all his father's mechanical skills to put it on the road. Even so, each morning Martino had to go outside with the whole family to help push the car from behind to clutch start it. Martino often saw their neighbours peering out their windows or looking up from their gardens to smile in amusement at them as they shouted and pushed the old car.

Things were certainly starting to improve. Their home had become a real home. And yet, it had not come easily to them. Their father had worked hard for it, as had their mother, and Martino was never allowed to forget that.

Although it was the week after Christmas and most businesses were closed while families went down the coast to enjoy summer holidays at the beach, Martino's father continued to slave away in the panel beating shop. Martino and Nardo went with him, expected to help.

Martino found it torturous. He was too aware of all the fun his school friends were having. He knew of their summer plans. And so he resented being forced to go to work with his father, waking at dawn, eating a quick, cold breakfast, then push-starting the Dodge to make their way to the hot and stuffy workshop. His father, intent on his labours, barked short, vague instructions at him, expecting him to understand his needs or to read his mind to comply.

'Fetch me that,' his father snapped for the tenth time that day.

'What?' Martino queried, tired of all the guessing.

'Hurry, Martino. I don't have all day.'

'I don't know …'

Then Nardo picked up the closest tool to him and handed it over.

'Thank you. Your brother seems to know. You need to pay attention. You should know what I mean.'

But Martino didn't know. He didn't want to know either. The workshop was hot, that's all he knew, and he longed to be out of it. He didn't like the man his father was at work. In the workshop, his father was stressed and impatient and short with him. It was awful.

He knew his father had sacrificed much for them to have a home and a television and a car … perhaps too much. He started to believe that he'd trade it all to have his old father back, the one who had time to tell them stories and jokes. Work had sapped the joy out of him and Martino didn't know if he would ever get it back.

The next day, Nardo managed to escape going to the workshop. He told his father he had to order books for college. Martino envied him his good excuse. Wretchedly, he went with his father, knowing he would have to do twice as much without Nardo there to help. It was Friday. Together, they spent many long hours of physical work and, as always, Martino was eager for it to end. When they finally finished up late in the afternoon, his father said he had to go to the pub to meet someone. Martino was displeased about the proposed detour as he just wanted to go straight home, but didn't dare complain. His father parked the car on a slope so they could get it going again by way of a hill start. When they reached the door of the corner pub, his father turned to him.

'Wait here. Want a drink?'

'Lemonade?' Martino requested hopefully.

Surprisingly, his father nodded and returned in a few minutes to hand him a cold, frosty can. Martino grabbed it gratefully.

'I won't be long. Stay out of trouble.'

Martino sat on the footpath in the shade and sipped at his drink. A mutt of a dog had been tied to a post nearby. Partly in the sun, the dog was hot and panting uncontrollably. Eventually, after watching him for some time, Martino took pity on him and wandered over to it. He poured some lemonade on the ground in front of the stressed animal. The dog sniffed at the liquid then lapped at it.

After the owner came and took the dog away, Martino went to the pub window and peered in, looking for his father. He saw him perched on a bar stool, talking to his friend in Italian. But what shocked him was that behind his father was a man who had obviously had too much to drink, staggering around like a jester, making rude faces at the pair of Italians and laughing at their strange sounding language. At least one other person at the bar found the drunk's antics amusing and started to chuckle. But Martino could see his father, who had become aware of the comic, was far from amused.

Turning fully around, he addressed him directly. 'Get lost,' his father said gruffly in English.

The drunk, dressed in linen pants and a wine-stained striped shirt, did not respond to the demand but swayed on his feet and grinned stupidly.

'What?' The drunk pretended not to understand his father's clearly spoken English, winning a couple of laughs from onlookers. 'Did ya speaka da Englesh?'

Being a panel beater, his father had fists of steel. Martino watched as he clenched one of them and swung it without hesitation. The swipe sent the intoxicated clown wheeling to the ground with a busted lip. Calmly, his father stood, finished his beer in one swig and walked out, his friend following close behind.

'Come on, Martino. Let's go now,' he called. Martino leapt to his feet and hurried to keep up with him. As they walked briskly to the car, Martino kept glancing at him, wondering. It had not occurred to him that his father might have been experiencing bullying too. He had thought it was only happening in the schools. As they continued along the footpath, side by side, Martino felt that perhaps he had been judging his father unfairly for his temper and tiredness. His father had every right to be that way. What future did he have but to keep slogging away in the panel beating shop? Without the language, his prospects were limited. At least working for himself he would be financially rewarded.

As he felt his father's rage pulsing beside him, Martino started to unlock his compassion. Unlike him, his father had not had a chance to learn much English. Learning the language had made all the difference. His father had said it would. How right he'd been.

Chapter eighteen

January 1957
Stafford Brisbane

'Mama, do you know where my blue shirt is?' Martino called out.

'Why do you need it?' his mother said, coming into his room.

'It's sign-on day at Thistles. Today they are having a barbecue for it. Everyone is going—the whole club. There will be friendly games and raffles and free soft drink!'

Martino was really looking forward to it. It would be a good chance to meet the coaches. Nardo, Elmo and Gian were still players at the club, and he had seen Tommy, his old friend from Stafford State School, training there. He couldn't wait to be a part of it all.

'That is on today? I didn't know,' his mother said, joining him at the cupboard. 'Ah, here it is. Right in front of you!' His mother reached in and slipped it off the hanger. As she handed it to him, a car horn honked from outside.

'Oh, that's my ride,' Martino said, slipping on the shirt and doing up the buttons. 'It's a friend from school and his older brother. They offered to take me.'

He hurried from his room towards the front door, but his father was blocking his way in the hall. 'I've just been out the back,' he said ominously.

'And ...' Martino felt rising panic. Oh no, not now, he thought.

'I put my finger deep into the soil and guess what?'

Martino shook his head, though he knew exactly what his father was about to say.

'All dry. You're supposed to be keeping it watered,' he bellowed.

'Sorry about that, Papa. I'll water it when I get back.'

'No. You'll water it now.'

'But my friend is here. We're going to the club for sign-on day.'

'Your friend is going. You're watering the garden. You can sign-on tomorrow. Sign-on is all weekend.'

Martino's panic was spiralling into despair. If he signed on tomorrow, he would miss the barbecue. All the serious players would be there that afternoon. No one signed up on the Sunday. His father had always been strict when it came to chores, but surely he wouldn't let him get off to a bad start to his first soccer season?

'But Papa ...'

'No buts. Get down there now and do your chores. If you'd done them like you're supposed to, you'd be going. It's not my fault you're lazy.'

Martino cursed inwardly. He was not lazy. His days now consisted of delivering ice to homes before school and pumping petrol at the local gas station after school. On Saturday mornings, he sold drinks from a tray in the new Stafford cinema. All the money that he earned went straight to his mother for spending on the housekeeping. Saturday afternoon and Sunday were his time off, if he had finished his chores around the house. Why had he forgotten to water the garden? He hated gardening. Hated it.

He heard his mother telling his friend to go on without him and, fuming, he went down into the yard and watered it.

As he stared blankly at droplets dripping from the passionfruit vines, he felt his resentment building. He worked hard; he deserved a break. His Australian friends didn't do half the work that he did, and they got to keep whatever pocket money they earned. It wasn't fair.

The following day, Martino begrudgingly signed up at the club in an empty room. At least there was no queue, he thought.

He was then given the date for the tryouts. When that day came, he made sure the backyard was over-watered and attended the session early, meeting Cappi there, who wanted to lead him in a warm-up session. Cappi was full of last minute advice, telling him not to hold back, to give it everything he had if he wanted to be selected for a high division.

At last, his age group was called.

'Good luck,' Cappi said, slapping him on the back as he took the field. Martino saw Gian and Tommy. They were looking nervous, checking out the other players around them to see what kind of competition they were up against. Then the players were divided into teams for a game in front of the coaches. There were several substitutes, such was the high number of boys trying out. Martino nervously adjusted his shin guard. Playing social soccer with his friends and brothers was one thing; club soccer was another. It was going to test his shin to its limit.

As play commenced, he took Cappi's advice and played with all his heart; turning tricks, beating opponents and having shots with his right and left foot whenever he could.

'Good work, Martino. Good pass,' he heard Cappi shouting from the sidelines. His praise was helping to spur him on. He kept up the intensity, chasing the ball down like a hungry dog, sprinting for all he was worth.

'Who's that?' one of the coaches inquired, pointing at the slim, dark-haired boy.

The assistant coach looked at his sheet to match a name to the number the player had on his back. 'Last name Saforo, age thirteen. Saforo! That figures. His brother plays with us in the seniors. He's good, a striker. But this kid is fast …'

'He's short and there's not much meat on him, but he seems to be an all-rounder. Never seen such speed. He would do well to win the ball for us in midfield and take it up the park.'

'Look at him run! Italians are natural!'

'They're born with a ball at their feet. Sign him. And I don't mean in the under-14s. We need speed like that in the under-18s.'

'Right you are.'

Martino was stunned when the coaches called him over, offering him a place in a higher age group in first division. Were they sure? Did they have the right player? He cast his eyes around, wondering if they had made a mistake. But Cappi assured him the offer was real.

'I was standing near the coaches and heard them talking about you. Martino, they loved you. They were very impressed. It is a great achievement to be offered such a spot at your age. You have to take it.'

'But Cappi … what about my leg?'

'What about it? It is fine. You are older now. The skin has toughened. The shin guard will protect it. All you need do is play. Stop your worrying and play.'

Martino couldn't stop smiling as he rode his bicycle home. In his bedroom, he found Nardo studying.

'How did you go?' His brother glanced up from his book. 'Judging by your face, you got picked. I knew you'd be fine. Under-14s is a good competition. Did Gian and Tommy make it too?'

'They got selected, but I didn't make that side,' Martino said, dropping his training bag to the floor.

Nardo heard the words, but the expression on Martino's face did not relate. If he didn't get picked, why did he look so happy? 'What then?'

'I made the under-18s!'

Nardo stared for a few seconds, taking it in, then he was smiling too. 'You're joking. That's brilliant! Wait until you tell Papa.'

What followed was a wonderful two years of soccer for Martino at Thistles Football Club. The first year, his side won the premiership and grand finals. Martino brought home two trophies and placed it on the shelf next to Nardo's four trophies. The second year, his side enjoyed the same level of success and he came home with two more trophies. Nardo was also coming home with trophies, though he had shifted clubs to play at Azzurri, an Italian-based outfit. They were starting to need a longer shelf.

Tryouts for the following season opened a door for Martino that he could not have anticipated in his wildest dreams. When he returned from the club after dark, his family was sitting in the living room, watching television.

'Well, soccer star. Still in the under-18s?' his father asked, getting up to turn the television volume down.

Martino, looking dazed, stammered, 'I've been picked.'

'Picked? Yes, of course.'

'Picked for what?' Nardo urged.

'There was a scout at the club. He came and saw me after tryouts. It seems La Trobe Football Club has invited me to play for them next year. They're going to pay me—two pounds a game.'

Nonna covered her mouth with her hands, while his mother came to her feet and embraced him.

His father threw up his hands in celebration. He knew Martino's team had done well, but he had just been playing at the local club. He did not know it could lead to a paid position. 'How is it possible?' he mused out loud.

'I know. I'm only fifteen and I'm playing under-21s and being paid to do it. It is my dream. It is as you said it would be, Papa. Australia has made it happen.'

His father nodded, his eyes were lit up with pride. 'Now I will have two soccer games to watch each weekend: your game and Nardo's at Azzurri,' he said. 'They are good reasons to have a break from panel beating, yes?'

'Yes, Papa,' Martino responded, glad to see him happy.

By the end of that year, Martino was playing senior football for the Bardon-based club in first division. Such a promotion meant it was only a matter of time before he would have to face his brother on the field. When Azzurri and La Trobe entered the Tristram Shield competition, both clubs made the semi-finals, pitting brother against brother.

'So, Mum, who are you going for?' Nardo asked, chewing on a slice of crusty bread at the dinner table.

The family laughed as their mother overacted her confusion, placing her hands on her head in mock despair.

'Says here in *The Courier Mail* newspaper that the game will cause some friction in one family home thanks to a brotherly duel,' Nardo said, handing his father the newspaper.

'Let me see,' he said, poring over the name 'Saforo' printed in the sports section of the state's leading newspaper. 'You've made the paper! Saforo. Would you look at that. Who would have thought? Give the boys some wine—oh no—sorry. You boys are in training for the big game. No wine,' he teased.

'One glass won't hurt, Papa,' Martino whined and the family laughed as their father happily poured him and his brother a generous glass each.

'To the brotherly duel,' he toasted and the boys drank heartily.

On the morning of the game, Martino was advised by his coach that he would be marking his brother on the field. Even though he had half expected it, his nerves intensified once it was confirmed. His brother was highly skilled and stronger, being taller and broader. Yet, he reminded himself that he was faster, nippier, with reliable accuracy. In the backyard, when they contested each other, Nardo would often resort to force to get his way, because he could. Having rules and a referee to uphold them would make for a different and fairer scenario. Even so, Martino didn't think his team could beat the superior Azzurri side. His side was made up of young and fit players with talent and potential, while Azzurri had experienced players, several of them having represented Australia at some stage. He would give it all he had, especially when it came to marking Nardo, but in the back of his mind he knew it wouldn't be enough.

They took to the field and the whistle blew. Nardo immediately found his brother in the mid-field, where they met each other with uptight grins before launching into serious play. Martino couldn't shake him, and as such couldn't open himself up to receive the ball. Nardo knew him and his tricks too well and so he battled to outmanoeuvre him. However, speed was his weapon and Martino managed on a few occasions to slip around his brother and gain possession, only to lose it seconds later when Nardo came thundering down upon him, using his size and experience to gain the upper hand.

The brothers competed ferociously with each other, giving the crowd much to cheer about. Their personal level of play was at their best for the season.

The first half score was locked at one to one. The winning goal was scored in the last minutes of the game, an indicator of how close the game had been and how much hope had been kicked back and forth. Martino watched the ball fly into the net in agony. He was exhausted. With so little time remaining, they were unlikely to break another gridlock to equalise again. He and his team didn't have the energy for it. The last minutes were just down a countdown to their official defeat.

La Trobe was knocked out of the Cup. It seemed youth and passion had been curtailed by skill and experience, as he had believed it would.

In the dressing room, taking off his boots, socks and guards, Martino discovered a small trickle of blood issuing from a slight, shallow tear on his shin. It wasn't deep enough to have him concerned, though it did show how hard he had tackled during the game. His shin was still a weakness for him. He had to remember that.

As soon as he got home, he went into his room. His leg was sore and he wanted to rest. He lay on his bed, trying not to think about the game. It could too easily have gone the other way, he thought, sulking.

Sometime later, Nardo strolled in and sat on his bed. It was just the two of them sharing the room, now that Taddeo had gone to Melbourne. Martino couldn't look at his brother. He was waiting for him to gloat about the win and wasn't in the mood to take it. With such an expectation, his brother's next words came to him as a shock and he had to ask him to repeat them.

'How about playing with me at Azzurri next season?' his brother said for the second time, his smile broadening.

'What do you mean? How would that be possible?'

'Are you kidding me, Martino? You were incredible today. My coach thought so too. They think you're good for me. You fire me up. How about it? Want to attend tryouts and see what happens? I think it's a sure thing that you'll be selected.'

'You know I would love that. Azzurri is Italian. It is the best there is. Of course, I want to play there.'

'Then you will. Come on now,' he said, coming to his feet. 'Nonna's been slaving in the kitchen to cook something special for dinner. She knew one of us would be celebrating and the other would need cheering up. Food can do both!'

Martino smiled. 'I think two are celebrating now,' he said. 'Thanks, Nardo. I mean it. Thank you.'

While he was overjoyed that soccer would take on an exciting new dimension at Azzurri and he was looking forward to the season, the rest of his life was proving much more difficult to sort out. The year's end had brought on his graduation from junior high school and his father was determined to have in the workshop full-time. The conversation that his mother had said could come later was now upon him and he found himself being forced to be blunt.

'But what else will you do, Martino?' his father wanted to know. 'You are not like Nardo. He is good with the books. But you … you are not suited to work behind a desk. You need to work with your hands. Come, this you won't regret. It will be good for you.'

'No, Papa. Panel beating is not for me,' Martino told him repeatedly, assuredly.

Martino was disappointed that his father didn't seem to be aware of his potential. Changing schools in his formative years had not aided his academic cause, but he could do mathematics, he could problem solve, he could apply himself to books if he had the compulsion. He certainly wasn't about to sentence himself to a life in a panel beating shop. He had seen what such work had done to his father.

'I thought you would want to work with me. We have always got along well. We could spend more time together. You could come to the tavernetta and have a drink with me on Friday nights after work. It is solid and honest work. You will feel good about yourself at the end of a week. Bulk up your muscles. It would be good for you.' His father went on and on. Every mealtime, his father espoused the benefits of panel beating, none of which Martino believed. He hated working there. There was nothing his father could say that was going to change his view. How to make him understand that?

Eventually, his father stopped trying to talk him into it and they reached a stalemate, neither budging from their uncompromising stance.

The standoff made for quiet, sullen nights at the dinner table. Nonna tried her best to cheer them. She created amazing meals and served them up with flasks of red wine. But it did not help to ease the tension.

Then one early evening, when Martino was coming up from the backyard after watering it, his father met him on the back stairs. 'Sit down. I have another proposition for you. Maybe this one will better suit you.'

Martino sat on the step, not sure he was going to like it. He braced himself for yet another argument.

'Martino, I was talking to my friend at the pub last night. He says he is looking for an electrical apprentice. I mentioned that you've finished school and he's keen to meet you. How would that be?'

His father was sitting rigidly, the muscles across his back and shoulders were clenched tight. Martino was just as strained as he was.

A cross breeze caressed them. He looked up, casting his gaze over their fence to his neighbour's backyard, his eyes settling on a tree overloaded with green mangoes. He closed his eyes to clear his mind and focus on what his father was proposing. An electrician … working with your hands, moving about, problem solving and using maths—he liked the sound of it.

'All right, Papa. I'll do it. I'll meet him.'

'Good,' his father said, relaxing a little. 'A trade is a good thing. You'll see!'

Martino was not so sure, but working and living at home with his disgruntled father had become unbearable. He felt he had to meet him halfway. Besides, being electrician did hold some appeal. And so, he started work.

Chapter nineteen

Two brothers wearing the sky-blue jersey on the same team was a novelty. The name 'Saforo' started to mean something in Brisbane soccer circles. The level they were playing was attracting crowds, many coming from Brisbane's strong migrant community. Some games, especially those against a Greek-based club, were pulling up to 10,000 spectators.

Martino was overawed to be playing before such crowds. The games were whipping up much excitement and fever from their supporters, putting extra pressure on him to perform. After the games, he was even more amazed to have fistfuls of money stuffed down his shirt by rich Italian businessmen. The more goals he scored, the more money he collected. Festive banquets were regularly laid out for the players, making him feel like a star.

'Can you believe this?' Martino asked his brother, retrieving the notes that had been shoved into his shirt.

Nardo was peeling a prawn and had a beer in front of him. He had already grabbed the money and tucked the cash into his pockets. 'It is the dream, brother,' he said, dipping the prawn into a creamy tomato sauce. 'Make sure you try the prawns. They're fresh off Bobby's trailer.'

Martino had the sense he would never want for anything again.

One night when he and Nardo went to Fortitude Valley, otherwise known as 'little Italy' to meet some friends, they were shocked by the attention they received. Café and restaurant owners on seeing them walk by came running after them, begging them to come in for a free coffee or meal.

'You play soccer like the boys back in Italy. Your skills are second to none. Come in, have a glass of wine—on the house!'

Martino looked at Nardo, who was grinning. 'This is hard to believe,' Nardo said to him.

'What should we do?'

Nardo shrugged. 'Let's go eat.'

The brothers were also popular at the soccer parties regularly held at the club. Martino enjoyed them immensely. Music of the day, with songs from Elvis, Johnny O'Keefe and Bill Haley and His Comets, blared away while young people danced, drank, smoked and flirted.

Gian had also come across to Azzurri. He played for a lower division but he was at the club most weekends and didn't miss any of the soccer parties. Elmo, Francesca and Marietta also loved the social events and turned up whenever they could. It was a vibrant scene and Martino, known by just about everyone, was feeling on top of the world.

Azzurri did well that first year, but it was the following year that the first division side took out the competition, topping the ladder in 1961.

The club celebrations were elaborate and went on all weekend. At the end of the celebratory binge, Martino was exhausted and for a while just wanted to stay home to avoid being congratulated.

Yet the celebrations for Martino did not end there,

One Saturday afternoon in February 1962, Martino had just finished getting dressed to go see a movie with his family at the Stafford cinema, when there was a knock on the door. Marietta ran to answer it.

Martino poked his head into the hall to see who it was.

In walked Elmo.

Martino gave him a bright hello.

Then he heard his father calling out. 'Elmo ... what a surprise. Do you need to borrow a tool or some wood again?'

'No, no, Papa. Nothing like that. You see,' Marietta said, taking hold of Elmo's hand. 'Mama, Papa, Nonna ... we have something to tell you.'

Martino stepped into the living room where his family was gathered. His father, sensing the importance of the announcement, got up and turned the television off. For a moment, Martino couldn't understand what was happening. Why were Marietta and Elmo holding hands.

Then his sister uttered breathlessly, 'We want to get married ... with your blessing, at our local church.'

'I've come to ask for your permission, Sir,' Elmo added, appearing unusually awkward.

Marietta was wearing a red dress with a full skirt. A long dark ponytail hung down over her right shoulder across her breast, contrasting starkly with the dress colour. She looked radiant. Martino could see she was crossing her fingers at her sides.

Nonna came in from the kitchen and sat down. 'A family wedding?' she murmured, her hand to her chest.

'Is this true? We'll be brothers for real,' Nardo said, looking pleased.

Brothers? Martino smiled. To think, Elmo, who had always felt like part of their family, would become a part of it. He had not seen it coming, though as he ruminated upon it, he could recall seeing Elmo dancing with Marietta at the soccer parties. And he had seen him buying ice cream for her at the last beach picnic. It was starting to make sense.

'Of course, you have our blessing,' his mother was saying, kissing them both. 'It's wonderful news. Yes, a wedding! Does Bianca know? Why, I always thought it would be Taddeo and Daniela uniting our families, but here you two are! I thought you were just friends ... I didn't know things had become serious between you. Such a beautiful couple! It will be a lovely wedding …'

'We will visit Elmo's parents tonight to tell them,' Marietta answered. 'We've been serious for a while. Just were keeping it a secret because, you know, our families are close. We wanted to work things out before letting you know.'

'Happening right under our noses, that's why we didn't notice,' Nonna commented dryly with a smile.

'And Maria, we want you to be the flower girl. Would you like that?' Marietta turned to her sister to ask.

Maria had been doing a jigsaw puzzle on the floor and had been listening to the exchanges with great interest. 'Really? A flower girl?'

'I will make you a beautiful dress,' Marietta promised her. 'Whatever colour you want.'

'Pink. My favourite colour is pink!'

'What do you think, sir?' Elmo redirected his focus to his future father-in-law. 'Will you grant me your permission to marry your daughter?'

Martino had no doubt as to his father's response. He peered over at him expectantly, and saw him choked up with emotion.

'My daughter marrying the son of Roberto? Of course, of course,' he bellowed, embracing Elmo heartily. 'I welcome you into our family with open arms. We must have a big wedding. A big one. This will be the happiest day of my life.'

* * *

That big, expensive wedding took place six months later, on a chilly August day. Martino stood at the back of the church, placing him well to see Marietta as she stepped out of the car, making her grand arrival. She was wearing a brilliant white, long-sleeved, laced bodice that pinched at her thin waist only to flow out into a long satin skirt that swept the floor. With her were her bridesmaids, Daniela, Francesca and Isabella. They wore sky blue, knee-length dresses and pillbox hats. The shade was not unlike the colour of the Azzurri jerseys, Martino couldn't help thinking. Maria was the last to hop out of the car. She was wearing a pale pink tulle dress and holding a bouquet of yellow and white flowers.

Marietta took her father's arm and the ceremony began. Martino looked on, aware his mother and Nonna were weeping in the front row. He couldn't help but be moved by the service. His sister was getting married. And it was to Elmo!

An hour later, the newly wedded couple emerged from the church to meet and be congratulated by their guests. Eagerly, the photographer moved in to catch those first shots of the husband and wife.

During the orchestrated photography, Martino sought out his brother, Taddeo. How he had missed him. Taddeo looked handsome in a grey suit, and he told him so.

'You look fine too,' Taddeo returned. 'I believe I must congratulate you on the soccer. I've heard all about it.'

'It was a great win,' Martino responded, but was tired of talking about it. 'How about you? Playing soccer?'

'No, hockey!'

'Hockey? Who would have thought?'

At that moment, they were summoned to be part of a Saforo family photo. Moving in towards the bride and groom, they brushed past the bridesmaids, and Taddeo and Daniela exchanged a glance. Daniela's eyes were hopeful, a smile at the ready, but Taddeo's expression remained fixed and cold. He was unresponsive. She walked away, her head down.

'Still haven't forgiven her? After all these years?' Martino asked as the photographer rearranged the bride's dress for the shot. He was surprised. Taddeo had always been the soft and forgiving one.

'No,' Taddeo confirmed, then cast his eyes about.

'If you're looking for Monte, he's not here. He's moved to Sydney, doing what I don't know,' Martino told him and saw his brother visibly relax.

'Where's Daniela living now? Is she working?'

'Last I heard, she was heading down south, looking for secretarial work. I'm not sure how far south that took her, but I know she's not in Brisbane. Only up for the wedding, like you. Why don't you ask her for a dance at the reception?'

'No,' he said abruptly.

'Smile,' the photographer instructed.

Martino smiled and prodded Taddeo to do the same. The photographer clicked away.

Martino glanced over to see Nardo with his arm around his fiancé, Rose, a spirited girl of Irish heritage. She was always at the club watching Nardo play soccer. It was odd having her in the family photo on the steps of the church. Their family was growing!

Just as his smile was starting to feel strained, the photographer dismissed them as he wanted to assemble the parents of the bride and groom for his next photograph.

Wandering off, Martino stayed with Taddeo and they meandered round to the side of the church where they found a quiet spot away from the throng. Their youngest sister followed them and approached from behind.

'Taddeo, you're here. How long are you staying?' Maria asked, giving him a quick hug.

'For a whole week. I have brought you a present for doing well at school. Mama tells me you are very clever.'

'A present? Where?'

'I will give it to you tomorrow. Are you liking the wedding?'

'It was a bit boring in the church, but I like it now.'

'Me too,' Martino agreed. 'Now for the fun part. Will you dance with me, Maria?'

'Of course, I will,' she giggled. 'Though I think you will have too many girls asking you to dance.'

'But I will dance with you first,' he promised. 'Okay?'

'Okay.'

That beautiful wedding was soon to be followed by another.

* * *

Two months later, on a perfect spring day, Nardo and Rose tied the knot. While Rose was not Italian and his mother had hoped for an Italian wife for Nardo, she accepted that the girl came from a nice Catholic family and had strong family values, and as such, made for a suitable match.

For Martino, it was a joyous time as it meant seeing Taddeo again, twice in the space of eight weeks. While Taddeo grumbled about the expense of the airfares, Martino could tell he was pleased to back in Brisbane among his family and friends. It was nice, he thought, to have his family all together for the celebrations, for they were starting to go their separate ways.

After taking their marriage vows, Marietta, and then Nardo, moved out of the Stafford house to live with their respective spouses.

For the first time in his life, Martino had a bedroom to himself. He should have been grateful for the extra cupboard space and privacy, but he just felt lonely in the large room. It was strange not having his brothers there anymore.

And he was even missing Marietta. Her absence meant he had been given a new loathsome role: chaperone to his seventeen-year-old sister, Isabella. It was a task that Marietta had once fulfilled, but now fell to him. Wherever Isabella went, he had to accompany her, especially as she was pretty and attracting many male admirers.

What was worse, if he took a girl out to the movies or to a

café in the Valley, his mother made him take Isabella with him. Someone had to protect the honour of the girl he was with, his mother explained. Those dates were usually arranged by his mother, keen to set him up with nice Italian girls. And there was one girl his mother seemed particularly keen upon.

'Come on, Martino ... what is wrong with Natalia? She is a good girl.' His mother sighed while her son sipped at a spoonful of tomato soup.

'That's the point, Mama. I don't want a good girl,' he grinned, earning a clip over the ear.

'I don't want to hear that talk from you. You will find a nice girl and take her out. It is time you started thinking about marriage. Soon you will finish your apprenticeship and get a good job. You will have enough money to support a wife.'

'But, Mama ... I'm only nineteen. I'm too young to be taking girls seriously. All the other boys my age are just having fun. They aren't thinking about marriage.'

'Fun! Fun will only get them into trouble,' she warned.

Martino kept his mother happy by taking out the girls she lined up for him. But he mostly had eyes for other girls: Australian girls, who didn't require chaperones or have early curfews. He admired their form fitting dresses, with above-the-knee hemlines and plunging necklines, in bold colours and prints. They wore them with high heels and matching headbands and handbags. He loved the lipsticks they wore and the smell of their perfumes. He liked how they did their hair in the latest styles.

Those girls accepted his invitations to dance with him and, being fit and agile from soccer, he had mastered some smooth moves. His ability to throw a girl over his shoulder and from one side of his body to the other side meant he was never short of a dance partner. But taking such girls on dates was proving tricky under his mother's scrutiny. She had banned him from taking out girls she deemed unsuitable and, given that he was living at home and his mother was aware of his weekend movements, he had to find all kinds of excuses to get out without having Isabella thrust upon him.

One day during that summer, he decided to take a girl whom he had a crush on to the beach. He had his own car, a V-dub, and when he learned that Isabella and Marietta were already planning a trip to the coast, he decided they would make for a good cover. He would tell his mother he was taking his sisters, then on the way he could pick up his date.

When he hopped in the car with his sisters, he straightaway put to them the cheeky request. 'Is it all right if I pick up my friend Sally on the way?' he asked them.

'Sure,' the sisters agreed.

'Don't tell Mama,' he reminded them.

'We won't.' Marietta smiled.

Their mother waved them off. Martino then drove to a house in the next suburb and picked up a pretty, blond girl, wearing a pink short-suit and dark sunglasses.

As soon as they arrived at the beach on the Gold Coast, Martino and his date separated from his sisters, arranging to meet up late afternoon for the drive home. Martino could hardly take his eyes or hands off Sally, who flirted with him outrageously. He took her for an expensive lunch of fish and chips. Then they walked along the beach, holding hands, stopping to kiss every now and then. At the end of the date, she agreed to meet him at a dance at the Cloudland hall that Friday night.

All had gone well, all had gone to plan.

But later at home, Isabella accidentally let slip that Sally had been in the car.

'Sally ... who's this?' his mother demanded to know.

The trio fell silent. Marietta and Isabella looked desperately to Martino for an acceptable reply. When none was forthcoming quickly enough, their mother guessed they were trying to shield her from the truth. She was stung by their deception and lashed out.

'Sally ... not Italian?'

'No, Mama. She's just a girl ... a girl I know, that's all,' Martino mumbled.

His mother, appearing flustered, charged downstairs. Mere seconds seemed to pass before his father came thundering up the front steps, down the hall and into the living room, ordering his daughters to get out of the house.

Then he let fly. 'How could you? You were meant to be looking after your sisters. Instead, you show them no respect! Putting your harlot in the same car. Tell me, did you stay with your sisters or abandon them to fend for themselves on the Gold Coast?'

Martino, not wanting to answer for his guilt was all over his face, managed to wince apologetically.

At this, his father grabbed him by the shirt and pushed him up against the wall.

'Papa, she was a nice girl,' he tried.

'You have lipstick here,' his father pointed, roughly shaking his collar. 'How could you?' Then his father pulled back his fist and hit him, hard in the stomach, then again, and again. Martino tried to lift his hands in self-defence. He'd never seen his father in such a rage.

After the short but intense beating, his father, panting hard, stomped out of the house, got into his car and drove off.

Slumping to the floor, hands clutching at his ribcage, Martino struggled to take an even breath. Before long, Marietta, Isabella and Maria rushed to him, wanting to tend to him. Isabella felt responsible and kept apologising.

But Martino didn't blame Isabella for a second.

'That's it. No more,' he vowed. 'He's gone too far.'

With effort, he pulled himself up and staggered to his room, where he fetched his training bag and started stuffing into it his clothes and soccer trophies and whatever else he saw that belonged to him.

'What are you doing?' Isabella squealed, starting to panic. 'You can't leave. Don't leave me here,' she begged. 'Without you, I won't be able to go anywhere!'

Martino zipped up the bag and swung it over his shoulder. 'You'll just have to get creative and take your chances like me, or stay home,' he said to her.

'But Martino, they want to choose a husband for me.'

'I know, Isabella. It is the same for me and I can't take it anymore. I need to run my own life. I have to go.'

'Don't go,' Maria said, so sweetly that Martino stopped in his tracks.

He looked at the girl, who would always walk with a limp. She had long brown hair and lovely eyes in an angelic face. He bent down to be eye-level with her.

'I have to go, sweetheart. I'll miss you.'

'You will visit,' she insisted, wrapping her arms around his neck.

'I don't know if that will be possible after this,' he said, giving her a hurried kiss. 'Take care.'

'Martino ... Mama will be devastated,' Marietta pointed out earnestly, but Martino ignored her. He was angry. He raced to his car, tossed his bulging bag on the backseat, started the engine, then jogged back to the house where he poked his head into the downstairs laundry. His mother and Nonna were there, chatting and sorting the washing.

'Well, I'm out of here. Time to move on,' he announced. 'Don't worry about me. I'll be just fine. See you Mama, Nonna,' he said, giving them each a kiss on cheeks taut with shock. 'Bye Isabella, Maria and Marietta,' he sang to his sisters, who had followed him down.

He then sprinted to his idling car.

'Martino … come back. Don't go!' his mother cried, running after him. Her hands reached out to grab hold of him, but he was nimble and determined and her fingers slipped on his shirt. He slid into the driver's seat and accelerated.

'Martino. Don't break your mother's heart like this. Come back inside and talk about it,' Nonna shouted.

Frantically, his mother and sisters gave chase, breaking into a canter to follow the car, now chugging up the road.

'Martino,' his mother screamed, her voice shrilly with despair. 'Please …'

Martino glanced back in the rear-view mirror. He saw his mother and sisters standing forlornly in the middle of the road, their faces strained as they repeatedly called his name, pleading for him not to go. He spied his Nonna back at the gate, standing defeated. His heart skipped an uncomfortable beat and he swallowed hard, but he did not stop the car. His ribs were sore from the beating he had received from his father, reminding him why it was time to move on. His father still lived the Italian way … he did not. Most of his life had been spent in Australia and he thought like other Australians. He had to break free.

For a couple of blocks, he harboured twinges of guilt, then, considering his newfound freedom, started to brighten. He was looking forward to a life of greater independence: no more chores, gardening, curfews or chaperoning. He could do what he wanted, when he wanted. His head felt light with just the notion of it.

As he drove around Stafford, he finally came to the idea to seek out his old friend Tommy. He was living in a share house in New Farm, and Martino knew it would be fine to crash on the couch there for a while.

He found the house easily, having visited it a couple of times, and walked up the rickety stairs. They needed a good painting. Briskly, he knocked on the door, which was wide open.

A voice from within called for him to come in.

He wandered down the long hall to the main living room. There he saw three young men sitting on the couch, shirtless. Beer bottles were on the table. The ashtray was full of cigarette butts.

As he entered, his eyes met Tommy's and his friend smiled.

'Saforo! What brings you into our humble abode?'

'I need a place to stay,' he said simply.

'Well, of course. You are most welcome. We have a spare room. The rent is cheap. Cheaper when split four ways. We'd love to have you. Want a beer?'

'Sure do.'

Time to get the party started, he thought.

Chapter twenty

April 1963
Brisbane

Usually at the end of the soccer parties when the club closed its doors, Martino would make his way home.

Not that party. Not that night.

Now that he was his own person, answerable only to himself, he decided that instead of going home at ten o'clock when it was winding up, he would keep partying. To satisfy his thirst for excitement, he glanced around at who was still keen to kick on and attached himself to a group of Italians—the type his mother would have classified as 'bad company'. After chatting to them for a while, he willingly clambered into a taxi with them.

'So where do we go to find action this time of night?' he asked.

One of the young men laughed. 'Oh, Martino. You are going to love this.'

The taxi pulled up in a dark street in Fortitude Valley. They alighted and walked up to an ordinary looking door on the side of a building. Opening it, they walked up a smoky stairway to enter a room decked out with gaming tables and a small bar in the corner.

'A casino?' Martino asked, turning to the young man next to him.

'Feeling lucky?'

Martino found the hidden, illegal establishment fascinating. Digging into his pocket for a wad of cash that had been given to him after scoring a goal that day, he converted the money into chips and went to work, and with very little effort doubled the amount he had arrived with. Such easy money. His father had preached that money had to be hard earned for it to be valued. How wrong he was! Martino was valuing his winnings very much.

He visited the casino again the following night and had some more luck. Too easy! He was hooked.

He started smoking, drinking, gambling … all the fun he had been missing! And no one was there to tell him he couldn't do it.

'Where do you go after the parties?' Nardo had asked him on one occasion.

'Why? Want to come?' Martino's eyes promised much excitement. Nardo hesitated, curiosity eating away at him.

'Nah, Rose wouldn't let me stay out that late,' he said.

'The joys of being married, hey?' Martino laughed.

'So where do you go?'

'Up town. It's good. If you ever get permission, I'll take you.'

Nardo smiled longingly. 'Don't like my chances. Glad you're having fun though.'

Martino found that gambling suited him. He loved taking risks and feeling the high associated with a win, while losses were shrugged off as temporary setbacks. Knowing his parents would not approve of him participating in such activities made them more alluring. He had lived under his father's strict conditions for too long. He was starting to be his own man and he liked it—a lot.

On one occasion, he was having a lucky night and his winnings were high, when there were shouts from the front of house. A flash of blue uniforms caught Martino's eye and he stood away from the betting tables, shoving his winnings into his shoes. The police charged in, demanding everyone stayed where they were. Martino was put in cuffs and pushed into the back of a police car. It was hard not to feel guilty.

He spent the night in the watch house and the next morning

194 ~ Michelle Saftich

was given one phone call. He called Cappi, who came straight away to bail him out. When he climbed into his car, Cappi handed him a newspaper. There on the front page was the headline: 'Illegal Casino Raided'.

'Oh no! No, no, no.' At the bottom of the article were the names of all those arrested. His name was there, clearly in print. He cringed at the thought of his family and friends seeing it. Devastated, he closed his eyes.

Cappi shook his head at him. 'What were you doing in a casino, Martino? You are too good a boy for that.'

'I don't know, Cappi. It seemed like a fun thing to do at the time,' he muttered, mortified.

Cappi shrugged. 'I guess you are young and finding out what life is all about. Just take it easy. You have had so much success in soccer and you have a good job. Everything you ever wanted. It is all going right for you … you worked hard for it and I'm happy for you. Don't throw it all away just for fun, hey? Think about it.'

'I will,' he said. He thought about it as Cappi drove him to his share house at New Farm. Martino knew his life was going well, better than he ever expected, but he also liked going out with his friends and having a good time. He wanted the fun to continue and didn't see why it had to interfere with his soccer and work. His Australian friends worked hard and partied harder. He wanted to do the same.

Later, Isabella told him that his parents had been shattered to see his name in the newspaper for being arrested. She said their father had tossed the newspaper across the kitchen table, cursing at him and threatening to kill him. His mother had started crying, worrying he had become a criminal. She was anxious about what the community and their friends would think. But Nonna had stood up for him, saying he was just finding his way. Give him time, she had advised.

Martino was sorry to hear it. Shaming his family name was

not what he had set out to do. He wished he hadn't got caught. For a while, he feared that his father would hunt him down and rage at him again. Weeks went by and such a confrontation did not eventuate. He soon learned he had nothing to fear. The next time their paths crossed was at the soccer club. Martino was walking out of the dressing room, holding his bag, when he looked up and saw his father standing on the hill rising from the field. Martino knew his father saw him, yet he simply turned his head away. That hurt. Martino didn't want that. He had always been close to his family. It wasn't right for him and his father not to be talking. While he stood there wondering if he should approach and apologise to him, his father spun on his heels and walked away. The moment was lost. Perhaps it was for the best for a while, Martino thought. There were still too many things they would argue about. What his parents wanted for him was not in line with what he wanted. He didn't want to marry the first Italian girl he agreed to go steady with. Not when he knew he was popular with the girls, that he could afford to date many before settling on one, just like his friends were doing. That felt right to him.

His coach at Azzurri had relegated him to the bench as punishment for his public arrest for illegal gambling. For the past few games, he'd been lucky to get a five to ten-minute run on the field. The other players were making fun of him for it too. Nardo was angry with him, though he didn't say anything about it. He could just tell he was disappointed with him. Feeling guilty and ashamed, he no longer felt comfortable at the club and was starting to get annoyed with it all. He did one thing and it seemed everyone knew about it!

A few weeks later, Martino phoned his friend Gian. They met in a pub, both ordering a tall glass of beer.

'Saw your name in the paper,' Gian said almost at once.

'Didn't think you read the paper,' he teased.

'So, how's life?'

'Getting better all the time. I'm taking off to Sydney.'

Gian was surprised. 'When?'

'At the end of the season.'

'For how long? What's taking you down there?'

'Sydney's the place to be,' Martino told him. 'I'm going to try and get work down there, live there for a while. Play for another club. I want a change. You should come with me. There's a group of us going.'

'I don't know. I've only been working in this job a short while. The pay's good. I'm seeing this girl ... well, kind of.'

Martino understood, but was disappointed. 'Fair enough.'

'Told your parents?'

'Not yet. Think I'll just send them a postcard when I get there.'

'Your poor Nonna,' Gian said. 'Martino, I can't believe you're going to walk away from Azzurri. It's doing so well. They've just moved to Spencer Park. It's all happening there!'

'I know. I just need to do something different. Get away from Brisbane.'

Gian smiled wanly, then reached out. 'Is everything okay, Martino?'

'Sure, sure it is. I just want change, you know how it is.'

'I'll miss seeing you around. I'll miss watching you play!'

Martino shrugged. 'Well, Gian, if ever you're in Sydney, look me up,' he said, wanting to end the conversation. He finished his beer and stood. 'Promise me.'

'Sure thing. Good luck to you,' his friend said, standing.

They embraced and parted company once more.

Chapter twenty-one

November 1963
Kings Cross, Sydney

The brightly lit Coca-Cola sign spread across a busy intersection welcomed them.

Martino was in the front passenger seat of a carload of twenty-something-year-olds. Arriving in Sydney, they had driven straight to Sydney's notorious Kings Cross. They had been on the road for fourteen hours, travelling in Martino's V-Dub, their suitcases strapped to the roof racks.

The late-night buzz outside the car was everything Martino thought it would be and he found himself smiling in anticipation.

Girls in mini-skirts and high heels were clicking up the neon-lit footpaths. Horns were honking. Men were standing on street corners, smoking cigarettes. One older woman, heavily made up, draped in silk robes with her hair teased high above her head, leered at him. Martino found her quite frightful.

The street presented little cosy coffee shops, bars and nightclubs. He knew that tucked away in the side streets were brothels and illegal casinos.

On the radio, Elvis was belting out 'Girls, Girls, Girls'.

Parking the car, Martino and his four fellow travellers checked into the Americano Hotel, depositing their belongings, then didn't waste any time in hitting the streets, keen to explore. They drank in the bars and ended in a nightclub, struggling to find the hotel again when the club closed and they were sent on their way. Martino thought it was the perfect start to his new life in Sydney.

When it came to acquiring work, he had no difficulty given he held an electrician's licence. Such licences were in short supply and so he was able to walk straight into a job, immediately taking the helm as leading hand at a construction site in charge of thirty-five workers. He couldn't believe it.

His fellow travellers soon went their separate ways, in search of work and permanent lodgings. Martino spent days getting to know the big city before deciding he wanted to live near the beach. He was drawn to Sydney's famous beachside suburb of Bondi and found a spacious room at a guesthouse. He had to share it with a Canadian backpacker. It was the kind of place that attracted young international, interstate and country lodgers, willing and ready to have a good time.

Martino's new roommate Simon advised him to lock his bag in the cupboard in their room and to follow him.

'I know a cheap place to eat. Great food! Come, you'll see,' he said in his strong Canadian accent.

Martino followed him down the stairs just as two tall, thin blondes in swimsuits were making their way up. He stared back, raising his eyebrows at the Canadian.

'They staying here?' he inquired hopefully when they were out of earshot.

'Marty, you have no idea what it's like here. Girls like that everywhere, all day, all night. It's heaven around here. You're never going to want to leave.'

Martino started smiling. He was a long way from Stafford now.

They devoured big, juicy burgers at a nearby bright and flashy food outlet and then crossed the road to the beach. Girls in two-piece swimsuits of all colours were lying on beach towels or tackling the surf in the sea. A couple of girls were tossing a Frisbee back and forth. Men were toned and sun tanned and were either sleeping off hangovers on towels, chatting up girls or trying to catch waves on boards. It was quite a scene. They hung around for a while, taking a quick dip, then returned to the guesthouse.

As soon as they re-entered, Martino felt a party atmosphere. Music was playing from a room upstairs and laughter could be heard rippling down the stairwell. He trailed the sound and joined the non-stop party.

Martino allowed himself to be carried away. For the next six months, he rarely slept in his own bed, with wild parties being held every night and an assortment of girls coming and going.

The pace of life was much faster than in Brisbane, but he had no fear of it. He wanted to embrace the city experience, and revel in it as much as he could.

At night, he dressed in a sharp suit with thin necktie and went out to the clubs, often spending an hour or two on the dance floors. Late one night, he was dancing in a club when he found himself being pulled into a high-hanging cage by a go-go girl. All eyes were on them and Martino felt compelled to put on an energetic dance show. Out of the corner of his eye, he saw security move to intervene as it was not club policy for patrons to enter the girls' cages, but then he saw the manager halt them. It seemed the manager thought he was adding to the party atmosphere and didn't want it to stop. Being given the green light, he went on with his show to the cheers of the crowd below.

As well as clubbing, he found he was being increasingly drawn to the gaming tables. Late at night, he sought out small underground casinos, seeking greater thrills at higher and higher stakes. Whether it was in a hand of cards or by casting some chips on the roulette table, he liked to take a punt. He was naturally lucky, but his fascination for numbers had him working to stack the odds in his favour. The thrill of the win was intoxicating and big money could be acquired all too quickly. Unfortunately, the unsavoury hobby was taking him into the seedier end of town, where criminal activity was rife and he was not wise enough to it. He needed to learn. After a significant win on baccarat, he was approached by a fellow whom he rightly assessed could help to show him the ropes, and he willingly became his avid student.

'Nice playing,' commented the young man, who was fair-haired, tall and lean. He strictly adhered to the fashion of the day and, Martino soon learned, he could muster the right amount of charm to sweet talk his way through any precarious situation. He was not French, he just went by a French name to impress the girls and impress them he did, long before they learned his name. He was, in fact, an Italian from Fiume, and like Martino had learned as a refugee that survival sometimes meant having to break the rules.

'My name's Francois,' he had said, introducing himself. 'Your luck seems to be in tonight.'

'Thanks. I'm doing all right,' Martino responded modestly. He too was wearing his hair in the latest style, with a curl that swept his forehead. He was slim and fit from years of playing professional soccer and tanned from his months at Bondi Beach.

Francois continued to watch Martino gamble for a couple of hours and by the night's end put a proposal to him, one that was too alluring to ignore. It would see Martino quit his well-paid managerial job on the construction site and give up his enviable lodgings at Bondi. Instead, he moved into a flat at Potts Point with Francois, with the aim of launching a career as a professional gambler.

Martino knew it went against everything his parents had ever told him. He had been raised to be honest, hardworking, responsible and solid. His choice to pursue gambling represented none of those things. It frightened him, but the fear was intoxicating. If ever there was a time in life to take risks and go against what was expected of him, now was that time.

As soon as he moved in, Francois readily went to work, teaching him a range of street skills, for he was an expert in living off his wits. Martino had learned that the French-named Italian had not worked a day since his arrival in Sydney.

'So how much is the rent here?' Martino inquired nervously, taking in the more luxurious surrounds of his new pad.

'Don't worry about it,' Francois replied.

'What do you mean? I can't let you cover it.'

'Oh, I cover it all right. I cover the old landlady upstairs'

'What are you saying?' Martino did not believe he had heard correctly.

'I give her what she wants in bed and we get free rent.'

Martino found himself laughing. 'I see. What about cooking?'

'We don't cook. How many girls do you know who work in restaurants?'

'A few.'

'And I know a few. We just call on them at their work on a rotational basis. Trust me, they'll look after us.'

Martino smiled. 'Sounds good.'

'And the Italian Club will never turn you away. They put on a free feed for the new migrants. I've been a new migrant for months but they don't seem to mind.'

'Seems you have it all worked out.'

'I sure do. Look at this list.'

Martino read through a list of casinos with times marked against them. 'What happens at these times?'

'Sandwiches are served,' Francois grinned and winked.

'Lunch?' Martino was laughing hard.

'Yes. Stick with me and we'll never go hungry.'

'I'm beginning to see that.'

'What about drinks?'

'The girls pay for those.'

'What girls?'

'The girls we meet who will do anything for us to show them a bit of attention.'

'I like it.' And he did—too much.

The duo hit Kings Cross and had a ball, mucking around, gambling at illegal casinos and taking a punt on the horses at the track. When it came to the horses, Francois always seemed to have inside information. They couldn't lose.

While Martino still had his trusty V-Dub, they often got around on a Lambrarta motor scooter, parking it anywhere and everywhere all over town. One day, as they approached the scooter, Francois whispered to Martino, 'Keep walking.'

He did as instructed, noting the policemen inspecting the vehicle. Were they being issued a parking ticket?

'No. I stole it months ago,' he replied casually. 'Don't worry. I'll get some new wheels.'

Martino shook his head. His friend had no shame. It should have worried him but it didn't. He was having too much fun and learning skills he thought essential to survive.

The pair eventually found work as part-time waiters at the Chevron Hotel, serving drinks on trays at weddings and fashion shows, simply so that they could sneak a feast on fine food while meeting loads of beautiful women. With another function looming, Martino and Francois were asked to go downstairs into the cellar to bring up more cartons of champagne for chilling.

On entering, Martino noticed a new shipment of boxes. He examined them curiously and tore one open. 'Hey, Francois. Look at this stuff. Pink champagne! Let's take a couple of bottles,' he suggested.

'Forget the bottles, let's grab a couple of cartons,' his friend advised.

They hid the boxes of bubbly behind the hotel's rubbish bins and came back for them after their shift.

What followed was one of the biggest parties to be hosted in the Cross in a long time. Word about the party spread, bringing a vast variety of street life of all backgrounds. Bongo drums played, luring in the crowds; the pink champagne flowed and flowed; potato chips were circulated. Martino started on champagne, then switched to beer, then was handed a strange cocktail in a hollowed-out pineapple. It was a long, sensational night of despicable fun. In the small hours of the morning, Martino fell into bed with a woman and when they were done, he found himself being pulled into a nearby bed by another.

The next morning, he awoke with a hangover, the like he had never experienced. Dressed only in his underwear, he was alone in a bed in a grubby motel, though the perfume on the sheets told him he had not been alone. He staggered up. His head swam. What had happened? He had very little memory of the night after a certain point. He felt ill. What time was it? A glance at the clock gave him a shock, for it was three in the afternoon. He dressed, located his shoes, slipped them on, then set out to make his way home.

Francois wasn't in the apartment and Martino was glad. He didn't feel like talking. He sat on the couch, closing his eyes to his pounding head. He awoke to see Francois standing over him.

'Marty, put on your suit, the silver-blue one. We're going out.'

'No, Francois. I can't do another night. I'm going to bed.'

'Sleep tomorrow. There's one more casino I'm yet to show you. I've been saving the best for last. This one is for the high rollers and very swish. I believe they are serving seafood tonight. We can't miss it. Trust me, all the other casinos are nothing in comparison. Here ...' Francois handed him a shot glass filled with an amber liquid. 'Take a swig and you'll be back in form.'

Martino tipped the contents down his throat and the pure alcohol spread warmly across his chest. It did the trick: one taste and he craved more.

'What are we waiting for? Show me the way.'

Chapter twenty-two

October 1964
Sydney, Kings Cross

The room was larger than most, with plush, soft carpet and velvet-lined wallpaper. The ceiling was high and ornate, the windows large and covered in heavy curtains. It had the smell of money and reeked of high society. Everyone was well dressed: the men in suits, the women in flowing dresses of silk, satin or velvet. Jewels sparkled at soft throats and gold watches caught the light and glittered on male wrists alongside the shine of gold cufflinks.

Martino was offered a glass of champagne but didn't take it. It was too soon after all that pink bubbly. He thanked the drinks waiter and approached a gaming table.

'What do you think? Nice place?' Francois asked him, holding an almost empty champagne glass. He had downed the drink in two swigs.

'It's nice,' he agreed.

'See him. That's the owner. Italian.'

Martino, disinterested, looked over and was startled to see a familiar face. It couldn't be. How could he have come to own a place so swish in the centre of the Cross?

'Martino … you look like you've seen a ghost.'

'No, I … it's nothing. I thought I knew him. Francois, I'm not feeling well. Too big a night last night. I think I'm going to head back.'

'No way. You're not missing this. You think it easy to get into a place like this? I had to call in a few debts to get the door open for us. Stay, enjoy, have a bet.'

Martino did not want Francois to know he had recognised the owner, for he would use any connection, no matter how remote, to his advantage and he did not want, not even for one more second, that person back in his life. He turned away, hoping beyond hope that he could stay hidden in the crowds. He glanced back over at the owner, but then his eyes rested on another face and he knew her straight away. She was holding Monte's arm, hanging off him, laughing at his joke.

Daniela and Monte ... it was a shock to see her there. She was exquisite in a glamorous, figure-hugging dress of white satin. A string of pearls embraced her dainty neck. Her blond hair was cascading down her back in waves; her high, full fringe parted to the side. Moist, ruby red lips whispered in Monte's ear and she started to float away from him, but he suddenly gripped her arm tightly and pulled her back, causing her to wince.

Martino felt a rush of protective anger. He had hurt her.

He watched as Monte continued to hold her firmly and then, with what appeared to be a concerted effort, she forced a smile. Her lips spoke again and he released her, but not before he muttered angrily in her ear. Frowning, she stood still, stiff as a board, her eyes misty then solemnly blank.

Martino stared at her face and saw a mark on her cheek ... he was drawn to move closer to inspect it. He wandered much closer ...

'Why, can it be? Martino? What brings you to Sydney and crawling into my little establishment?' Monte sang out to him.

'Martino ...' Daniela said his name softly, wistfully and, when she turned her face in his direction, he saw there was fondness in her eyes. 'Are you here alone?' she asked expectantly and peered around ... for who? Taddeo?

'I'm alone.'

'Strayed far from the nest, haven't we? Like to play then?' Monte inquired, indicating the gaming table.

'Sometimes.' Martino bristled under Monte's close scrutiny, knowing he was seeing the dark circles beneath his red eyes.

'Like to party, do we?' Monte commented, his face lighting up.

'Sometimes,' he replied again.

Martino had edged close enough to the dazzling couple to see a shadow on Daniela's cheek: a bruise, concealed by heavy foundation make-up, but he could see it.

'What happened to your face?' he asked directly.

She was immediately embarrassed and her hand flew to cover her cheek. She shot a furtive glance at Monte, worried. Her reaction confirmed what he suspected and he felt another stab of anger.

'She wasn't careful,' Monte replied for her, and Daniela lowered her gaze.

'How's your family?' she said suddenly, lifting her eyes to Martino with a flash of confidence, defiance …

'They're well. Taddeo's in Melbourne in the army. He's in administration, in stores.'

Monte's arm snaked around Daniela's waist and yanked her sharply against his side. She tried to keep her expression neutral, but Martino had detected a spark of interest in her eyes.

'And your mother?' she asked swiftly, not missing a beat.

'She's waiting on babies from Elmo and Marietta. They're very happy together.'

Monte turned to Daniela and said curtly, 'Go out back and check the waiters are doing their job …' then forcibly he added, '… my sweet.'

Daniela smiled coldly and did as instructed, gliding through swinging doors at the rear of the room to the kitchen.

'I bet she's the only trophy you've got, and you're having a hard time defending it,' Martino remarked dryly, staring icily at Monte.

Monte's face grew dark. 'Where's your trophy? No girl on

your arm? Oh, you mean those little soccer trinkets you and your brother like to collect. Well, let me assure you, it's more fun polishing mine.'

Martino was struggling to suppress his disgust. Monte was unquestionably handsome in a black suit and thin silver tie. His longish hair was slicked back and his black eyes were cold in an arrogant face.

'At least we earned ours,' Martino mumbled. 'So, this is your place … your father must be proud.'

Monte shook his head with a hard laugh. 'I suppose you're going to run and tell on me, like you always did!'

'So, he doesn't know? Figures. Your secret is safe. I don't go home much these days.'

'What are you doing in Sydney?' Monte threw at him.

'Stuff.'

Monte raised a brow. 'I see. Well, enjoy your night. Feel free to stop by anytime and do some stuff here. I'd like to acquire more of your … coinage.'

Martino smiled coldly. 'You mean steal it? No, thanks. I was just leaving.'

'Don't go just yet. Stay for the show.'

A spotlight had appeared on a curtain in the back corner. The curtains drew back and revealed a beauty: classical, but sleek at the same time. She reminded him of a Siamese cat with smoky green eyes and long, black, silky hair that extended out in full waves around her face, then dropped down almost to her waist where it kinked outward at its ends in the latest flip style. Her shapely, slender legs stretched on forever down into tiny, sparkled platform shoes. She was exotic, sexy, sophisticated—the kind of girl he was more inclined to run away from, so powerful was her effect. Then she sang and he was mesmerised. It was a voice that did not falter; its timbre was warm, soft and mellow, the notes were hit effortlessly.

'She's something else, hey?' Monte said to him, handing him a glass of whisky.

Martino took the glass. 'She's … good,' he admitted.

'I'm half in love with her,' Monte confessed. 'But of course, I have Daniela.'

Martino watched the girl finish her song. He was so caught up in the performance that he didn't notice Monte wandering off. At the end of the song, he applauded with the others, becoming aware that Francois had since joined him.

'You know the owner,' he stated, smiling with avid interest.

'Yes, I know him.'

'That's very fortunate for us. We can come here often. I like it here—more money!'

The girl began to sing another song, that time leaving the stage to wander around the club, visiting tables to sing to people directly. Patrons smiled, touched by her close presence. She had a magical quality that settled over the crowd, spreading love, calm and peace. She neared the bar and her eyes lifted to meet Martino's steady gaze. Their eyes locked and she proffered him a flirtatious half smile. She then retreated, meandering back to the stage, where she finished her sultry song and the curtains closed.

Strong, raucous applause rang out.

'She smiled at you,' Francois observed.

'Just part of her act,' Martino explained it away.

'Sure, it was. You're handsome and available. She was interested.'

'Don't even tease me about it. She's way out of my league.'

'I don't think so, my friend. You're just the right match for her. Now I'm going to hit the gaming tables.'

'Francois, I know the owner and I can tell you now that I don't trust him. Leave with me and forget you ever saw this place.'

'Forget this? Not likely. I'm hooked. There's money to be made here.'

Martino all but sighed. He wished his friend would take his advice, just for once.

'Suit yourself, but remember, you've been warned. I'm going home to sleep off my hangover.'

Martino began to walk towards the front door, when blond hair and white satin filled his vision.

'Lovely to see you again,' Daniela said and, surprisingly, rushed forward to give him a brief embrace and a light kiss on his cheek. He felt her hand secretly press something into his palm. His hand closed around it and he kissed her back, his lips brushing her on the cheek, the one without the bruise.

'Take care,' he whispered to her and she darted away.

Downstairs, outside, by the glow of a streetlight, he opened his fist to see a tiny crunched up piece of paper. He unravelled it.

Help me, it read simply.

Oh God, what trouble was she in? Dating Monte, it would be a lot. He stared at the two powerful words for a second longer and then shoved the paper into his pocket.

He couldn't ignore it. It was Daniela, the girl he used to follow around in the refugee camps. She had been the eldest of the girls while Taddeo had been the eldest of the boys. Together, they had watched over all of them. She had been kind and pretty—always pretty. And … she was Gian's sister. Gian. If he knew his sister was locked into an abusive, inescapable relationship with Monte, he'd want to kill him.

As he walked, the cool night air cleared his head and he started to form a plan. He had to get Daniela out of Sydney, as far away from Monte as possible. And he knew exactly what would draw her away. The bait was obvious. Besides, he needed help if he was to do it right.

When he returned home, he dug around for his address book and found a phone number he had never called. He went downstairs to a pay phone and dialled, despite the late hour.

A gruff male voice answered and it took some minutes for his brother to come to the phone, but he did eventually.

'Martino?' Taddeo's voice was thick with concern.

'Everything's fine. The family's fine. It's about something else—or should I say someone else.'

'What are you talking about? Do you know what time it is? Are you drunk?'

'For once, I'm not. Listen, Taddeo, I just ran into Daniela. She needs you, bad.'

There was a long pause and Martino heard his brother suck in his breath.

'All right. Go on. Tell me what you're talking about.'

By the end of the conversation, Taddeo had been talked into taking special leave to come to Sydney. He would come that weekend. Martino was not surprised. Taddeo had a soft heart and would always come to a person's aid, especially if it involved a girl as beautiful and as special as his first love.

The following day, Martino slept in and awoke feeling refreshed and fully recovered. Francois was not in the apartment. He figured his flatmate had probably met up with a girl and spent the night out. He went down the road to a coffee shop and ordered a fried breakfast. Afterwards, he did some laundry at a laundromat. In the afternoon, he found himself putting on his sports gear and running around a nearby field, suddenly wanting to re-address his fitness. As he jogged, his mind wandered back to the night before, and instead of thinking about Monte and Daniela, he was surprised to be dwelling on the singer who had performed. Had she really smiled at him?

When Francois suggested they return to Monte's casino, Martino did not argue. He was hoping that the entertainment was a regular act. Besides, he should really keep an eye on Daniela until Taddeo turned up, he thought.

They were allowed entry without any problems.

'Good evening, Martino.' The woman at the desk smiled at him as he walked through. He was surprised she knew him by name. No doubt, Monte would now be alerted to his arrival. He peered about but could not see Monte or Daniela.

He watched Francois betting heavily. He won a few, lost more. Martino drank whisky and waited.

Sure enough, at around the same time as on the previous occasion, the singer was introduced. This time Martino took note of her name: Medina. He liked it. She even sounded exotic.

Once again he found his heart racing as the sexy singer sauntered around the tables, nearing his post against the wall. Medina sang to people as she went, draping a scarf across men's shoulders or sliding it across their eyes, later tying it seductively around her wrists as she wandered around. She approached the back of the room, drawing nearer to Martino and then she was before him. He was afraid to take a breath.

Slowly, she uncoiled the scarf from her wrist and handed it to him. He took it, smiling. She blew him a kiss. The crowd clapped wildly. She flew back to the stage, the song promptly ended and, all too quickly, the curtains closed.

Martino couldn't believe he was holding the perfume-filled silk cloth in his hands.

'Told you,' Francois said, laughing at his friend's stunned expression. 'You have the sexiest admirer in Sydney. Lucky bastard!'

Martino shook his head and stuffed the scarf into his pocket. He would have to find a way to return it to her … perhaps he could ask her out. Was he mad? A girl like that! He shook his head. He would need more than luck to win her over, he thought. But he couldn't stop thinking about her. She had given him the scarf. Did it mean anything? Did she want him to ask her out? Did she admire him or was that just Francois' crazy imagination?

The singer did not reappear and so he took his leave early, not wanting another run in with Monte.

The next day he was still thinking about Medina as he rose early and dashed down to his V-Dub to pick up Taddeo from the airport. He was late and Taddeo was already at the luggage bay, waiting for his bag to slide down the chute.

'Martino,' he cried on seeing him, and they embraced.

Taddeo was wearing jeans and a collared shirt. His fair hair was cropped short, army style. Martino was also wearing jeans but with a white T-shirt. His hair was short at the back, longer at the sides and front.

'My bag,' Taddeo suddenly exclaimed and reached forward to grab it.

'Got it? Good. Let's get out of here. I'm parked illegally out front.'

'You would be,' Taddeo commented with a sly smile.

The car was parked right out front and had not been seen by a parking inspector. Elated, Martino slid into the driver's seat and pushed open the passenger door. 'Jump in.'

The two brothers were in high spirits as they drove through Sydney, Martino keen to show off the city. He drove around streets that afforded glimpses of the magnificent Sydney Harbour before heading back into Kings Cross, where he intended to buy his brother lunch. He parked in a side street and they walked around the block and up to the main road, where they found a strip of coffee shops. They chose an alfresco café and sat at a table on the footpath, beneath a large red umbrella. A waiter was at their side instantly and took their coffee orders. Taddeo then placed his bag at his feet and, as soon as his fingers released it, a skinny, pasty teenager lurched from nowhere and snatched it. He would have made away with it, but Martino had spied him a while before and stuck out his foot to trip the thief up. He stumbled and lost his grip on the bag, which Martino reclaimed.

The boy glanced left, saw Martino about to backhand him, and he fled in surrender.

'Hold on to your bag,' Martino told his brother with a smile, handing it back to him.

'I see I have to.'

'The Cross has some desperate types.'

'Like Monte.' Taddeo looked murderous.

Martino grew serious. 'We have to get Daniela away.' He reached into his pocket and took out the crumpled note. He gave it to Taddeo, who opened it.

'I'm guessing she wants to leave him, but is afraid he'll kill her if she does,' Martino said.

'And she's probably right. He would.'

'What can we do about it?' Martino was as lost as he sounded. It was not going to be easy.

'I say we just get her straight to the airport and she'll fly back to Melbourne with me.'

Martino smiled. 'Nice idea ... but even if she did go for it, he'd track her down,' Martino pointed out. 'And when he finds out it was you who took her away, both of you will be in deep trouble.'

'But how would he find her? How would he know she was with me?'

'He's smart, rich and well connected. He'd find her. He's not the type to let things go, or let girls who he believes he owns just walk away.'

Taddeo nodded, considering his words. 'He does get fixated— doesn't like to lose. So, what can we do?'

At that moment, their coffees arrived and the waiter handed them a food menu.

'Thanks,' Martino said, taking it from him. 'Hungry?'

'I could eat a burger.'

'Two burgers with everything on it,' he said to the waiter, who had just deposited the coffees.

'Sure thing.' The waiter retrieved the menus and hurried away.

'So, do you have a plan?' Taddeo queried, taking a sip of his black espresso.

Martino shrugged. 'Maybe, if we had something on him ...'

'That shouldn't be hard. Didn't you say he owns an illegal casino?'

'Police won't care about that,' Martino guffawed. 'They know about the casinos—they're on the take. But I'm sure he's up to his neck in more than that. If we had something on him, we could tell him to leave her alone or else.'

'You want to threaten him with something? I don't know about that.' Taddeo was clearly nervous.

'We'd have to have something concrete to do it. Threaten to take it not just to the police, but to the media and to his father. He's always cared about what his father thinks of him.'

'I guess so. We could follow him round with a camera,' Taddeo suggested.

'Not us. We'd be seen in five seconds and he knows us. No, if we're going to follow him, we'd have to hire someone professional to do it.'

'I don't know.' Taddeo shook his head. 'It all seems wrong.'

'He'll never let her leave. Not unless we can threaten him.'

Taddeo nodded. 'All right. I'll go along with it for now and see. But I don't like it. I don't like any of it.'

'My flatmate Francois will know a guy. He always knows a guy ...'

'Fine. I've got some savings. I send a lot home to our parents, but I put some away, just in case.'

'Good. All right. Leave it with me. I'll find someone and we'll see what we uncover.'

Taddeo sipped at his coffee. 'So, we don't grab Daniela until we've got something on Monte?' He was disappointed. He wanted to get her away right then.

'No, but she may know how to help us. How about we both visit the casino tonight? I think she'll be happy to see you.'

Taddeo wasn't so sure. They hadn't spoken in years. 'You sure it's a good idea to let Monte see me here?'

'No, but I think it's a good idea to let Daniela see you here.'

Taddeo's mouth twitched. 'All right. It's just … we've got to do this right so no one gets hurt.'

There was a long silence as they sipped at their coffees and thought about Monte. They both weren't looking forward to him being back in their lives.

'After lunch, let's go shopping. We'll get you a new suit. Trust me, you're going to need it for this place,' Martino advised.

Chapter twenty-three

October 1964
Sydney, Kings Cross

Fashionably dressed, Martino and Taddeo walked into Monte's illegal casino.

A jazz band, comprising three young men in striped jackets, was playing and couples were dancing seductively with each other on the dance floor. Girls with beehive-styled hair and wearing dresses of silk or taffeta were being led by their partners, clean shaven and reeking of aftershave.

Taddeo couldn't believe his eyes. 'This place is something else,' he said with a long, low whistle. He didn't usually drink much, but Martino kept replacing his empty glass with full ones and so he was quite animated. Every few minutes, he darted hopeful looks at the back and front doors, willing Daniela to walk in.

'Give it time. She'll be here. It's Saturday night,' Martino told him.

The band stopped to take a break. Quieter music started to play.

Martino was also casting hopeful eyes in one direction, towards the stage. Would Medina perform? He kept his eye on his watch and saw that right on ten o'clock her act was introduced.

'Let's get a bit closer to the stage,' Martino said to Taddeo. 'She's good, this singer.'

The curtains slid apart. Medina was wearing a short black dress and long black boots. Her hair was teased high in a bouffant and her legs, long and creamy, were strolling back and forth across the small stage in a confident strut.

'Wow. Who's she?' Taddeo's eyes were wide. 'She's smokin' hot.'

'That's my future wife,' Martino joked.

'You'll need to get a real job to catch a girl like that.'

The comment stung. Martino took a swig of his drink.

'A girl like that, well, she could pick any man in the room ... and a girl like that, well, she'll go for the bloke with the most expensive sports car.' Taddeo's words were starting to slur.

'Last drink for a while,' Martino mumbled. Though his brother was right. He couldn't imagine those long, gorgeous legs gliding into his V-Dub.

Medina was stepping down from the stage, weaving through tables, singing to patrons, when suddenly a large, red-faced man pulled her down on to his lap. She continued singing but tried to rise and move away. His thick, hairy arms clamped around her.

Martino made to move towards them, but Taddeo gripped his arm and held him firm.

'Security's got it,' Taddeo advised, indicating with his chin a tall, well-built man in a black suit swiftly rushing to the singer's aid. The suited man bent down and whispered in the patron's ear. The big man swung his fat head round, saw the security guard, noted his bulky chest and shoulders and obligingly dropped his arms to release the girl.

Medina did not miss a note. She shifted from the lap and returned slowly to the stage. Her song came to an end and the applause erupted.

'Smooth,' Taddeo said, clapping his hands.

'And we now know how sharp security is in this place,' Martino said.

The curtains closed. Only one song tonight—a shame. Perhaps the incident with the patron had upset her more than she let on. His eyes swivelled back to the bar, but he felt a thump on his arm. Taddeo was hitting him.

'She's here.'

Sure enough, Daniela was walking in from the back door, her

eyes scanning the room. She was wearing a gold, figure-hugging, sleeveless dress. A matching sparkling headband was straddling her blond hair, which had been teased out in a wave around her.

Taddeo was taken aback. He had not expected her to look like that.

'Glad you're wearing the suit?' Martino asked him.

He nodded, unable to tear his eyes away from her. Then she spotted him.

Their eyes held for the longest time.

She began to move, weaving through people, taking her time. When she reached Taddeo, she held out her hand, touching his elbow lightly. Her eyes did all the talking. Glistening with emotion, they were expressing love, loss, sorrow and begging forgiveness all at once.

'Hold back,' Martino whispered in Taddeo's ear. He could see his brother just wanted to wrap his arms around her. 'Monte's here.'

'I thought you were in Melbourne,' she gushed. 'You shouldn't have come here.' She glanced back anxiously and saw Monte. He had seen them and was coming their way.

'I know, but I had to see you,' Taddeo said earnestly.

'I've missed you dreadfully. I've made so many mistakes,' she said as fast as possible.

'We want to get you away. I want you to come with me. I can look after you. I can keep you safe,' Taddeo hurried to tell her.

'He would come after me and he …'

'Ah, Taddeo. You're in Sydney. How interesting,' Monte said. 'Martino, seems you can't stay away. Your friend Francois is here also. He likes to gamble hard.'

'Yes, he does,' Martino said, staying calm.

Taddeo and Daniela were looking uncomfortable.

'These two are just catching up. Been a while,' Martino went on.

'Can I get you a drink?' Monte asked, snapping his fingers at a nearby waiter. He dashed over, presenting a drink tray. 'Scotch, champagne, wine?'

'Thank you.' Martino took a glass of amber liquid and drank deeply from it. Taddeo refused.

'So, Taddeo, in town long?' Monte inquired, his eyes boring into him with malice.

'Not sure yet. My brother is showing me around while I'm on leave.'

'Is he? Glad to see that he's including all the top sights on his tour,' he said, pulling Daniela close to his side.

'Yes, Sydney is more beautiful than I had heard,' Taddeo said, his eyes fixed on Daniela.

'Be sure to have a bet. You and your brothers always were fond of taking risks. And good luck.' Monte strolled away, taking Daniela with him. They left the room, striding out the back door.

'We could follow,' Martino put to his brother. 'And if they see us, we can just say we hadn't finished telling Daniela all our family news.'

The brothers charged through the rear door, which led to a dimly lit hall leading to another door. It opened to a dark back alley. They scanned the shadows for any sign of Monte and Daniela, but they must have got into a waiting car. They were already nowhere in sight.

Instead, only metres away and searching for her car keys within a mesh purse was Medina.

'They've gone,' Taddeo said, disappointed.

'I know. I doubt he'll let her back here for a while.'

'Damn. Did you see the way he grabbed her hand?'

'I know, I know.' Martino was distracted, watching Medina, who had located her keys and was throwing her bag on the front seat of her car.

The singer looked up in their direction. He wanted to call out to her, say hello or something, but Taddeo was talking at him. 'You're right. She does want to get away from him. She mentioned making mistakes ...'

Suddenly the sound of running footsteps approached them. They looked to the street corner and saw Daniela, her heels clicking fast on the pavement as she hurried towards them.

'Taddeo! I had to come back,' she called, scurrying up to him breathlessly.

'Where's Monte?' Taddeo placed his hands on her shoulders to steady her.

'He told me to go home and put me in a taxi. I ordered the driver to drop me around the block and I ran straight back. I was so afraid you would leave and I wouldn't have a chance to see you again.'

She threw her arms around him. Taddeo peered over her shoulder at Martino, looking perplexed.

'Where is Monte?' Martino was compelled to ask again, for all their sakes.

'I think he went back in round the front, looking for you,' Daniela said, her voice high with concern.

'We've got to go,' Taddeo urged. 'Security would've seen us go out the back.'

'I'm parked at the front,' Martino warned. 'I don't think we can walk Daniela that way. There's security on the door who'd recognise her.' Martino rubbed the back of his neck. He didn't like it. The alley way was dark and quiet; anything could happen there. They had to move.

'I can drive you someplace if you like,' a voice offered.

Martino turned to find Medina leaning on her car, gazing directly at him.

'We can't accept ...' Martino started, not wanting to involve the girl in anything related to Monte.

'It would help. We need a ride now,' Taddeo urged.

'Oh, hello Medina. I didn't see you there. That's kind of you,'

Daniela said. 'These are old family friends of mine. We came out from Italy together.'

'Don't worry. I won't tell Monte if that's what you're worried about,' Medina said smoothly. 'Where can I take you?' She opened her car door.

'You two know each other?' Martino asked.

'Sure. We're both here all the time. Medina is a resident singer,' Daniela explained.

'Coming?' Medina raised a brow.

Daniela nodded and hurried over to the red Ford Fairlane, sliding into the backseat. Martino and Taddeo exchanged a quick glance. 'Why not?' Martino relented.

Taddeo climbed in beside Daniela, leaving Martino to take the front passenger seat. In the front, he was so close to Medina that he felt suddenly shy. Every time he glanced sideways, it was to take in the sight of lovely, long legs and a dress riding high, just covering her mid-thighs. It was too much. Sweat broke out above his upper lip.

'You might want to keep low, Daniela,' Taddeo said, and she ducked her head as they pulled out on to the main street.

Medina glanced back. 'You've taken on a lot, dating that one,' she commented, sympathy in her tone. 'Rich and nice to look at, but …' She shook her head and Martino saw anger flash across her face. Her lips pressed together. 'Where can I take you?'

There was a long silence.

'We can go back to my apartment,' Martino suggested. 'I'll get a taxi in the morning and get my car.'

'All right,' said Medina. 'Where do you live?'

Martino's heart was racing. Keep calm, he told himself. She's just another girl and he knew how to talk to girls. He knew what she wanted to hear, yet his mind was not thinking clearly. He didn't know what to say. What was she asking? Where he lived. Yes. He could tell her that.

'I'll direct you,' he said, and was annoyed to hear his throat was tight. He tried to clear it. What was wrong with him? The girl was affecting him, too much. It was a first. 'Turn right at the end of the street,' he managed to say.

When they arrived at the apartment building, Medina found a park out front. 'Nice place,' she observed, gazing up at the brick building awash with orange light.

'You are …' Martino cleared his throat again. He was nervous as hell. 'You're welcome to come up. Have a drink.' His offer sounded clumsy and he expected her to turn him down.

'Why not?' She smiled.

And just like that, the most beautiful girl in Sydney was coming up to his apartment. With Daniela on Taddeo's arm and Medina taking his, Martino began wondering what had led to such good fortune.

In the apartment, Martino poured them all a drink of whisky on ice with a dash of water, and even went to the extra effort of adding a slice of lemon to the drinks, which he served up in heavy crystal glasses. He silently thanked Francois for always having their liquor station well supplied.

Taddeo and Daniela stepped out on the dark balcony, sitting close together on a low two-seater sofa. Martino remembered how frosty Taddeo had been towards Daniela at Marietta's wedding. They had a lot of catching up to do.

Leaving them to it, he turned his focus back to Medina, who had perched on the leather sofa in the main living area. Martino strolled over and sat opposite, putting some space between them to keep a clear head. She sipped at her drink; his eyes were drawn to linger on her lips.

'Thanks for driving us,' he began.

'My pleasure. It's given us a chance to meet. You seem to like my show.'

Martino liked her bold opening. 'I do.' He smiled. 'You sing at other venues?' he asked, wishing he could see her somewhere other than at Monte's establishment.

'I used to, but once I sang at the casino, well, the owner there wanted me exclusively. He pays very well. I work as a receptionist during the day.'

Martino didn't like the idea of Monte having her to himself in any capacity.

'You know it's not safe for girls like you to be in places like that.'

'Girls like me. What kind is that?'

Martino knew he had to choose his words carefully. 'You're a classy singer. You should be on Broadway.'

Medina's laugh had a soft ring to it. 'Broadway is a long way from here. This place pays my rent.'

Monte nodded. 'You live in an apartment?'

'Yes, with my sister. What about you? What do you do?' Medina asked, leaning forward, the ice clinking in her drink. Her shift in position meant that Martino could now see the deep curve of her breasts, and he fought to lower his gaze.

'Usually I'm an electrician and a soccer player. Right now, I'm kind of taking a break.'

'A break? Okay.'

'You've got a beautiful voice,' he said, changing the subject.

'Thanks. If only I could overcome my nerves.'

Martino was surprised. 'You, nervous? I don't believe it. You look so calm, so in control!'

Medina laughed. How he liked the sound of it. 'I'm anything but calm. Look at my hand next time—it shakes on the microphone.'

'It's dark, no one notices. Everyone loves you.'

'Do they?' Medina smiled and looked at him pointedly.

Martino took a sip of his whisky. He turned his gaze to the balcony to see how Taddeo was getting on, and saw him and

Daniela kissing passionately. Going well then, he thought, feeling pleased. He had always wanted her for Taddeo. It seemed right.

'She better hope Monte doesn't find out,' Medina said, glancing behind at the love-locked couple. 'He isn't the forgiving type.'

'What do you know about him?' Martino asked, moving over to sit beside her. Her green eyes lifted to meet his and suddenly their faces were close, so close their noses were almost touching.

'He's a snake. A crook. He buys protection at the highest level. A person's life means nothing to him. I've seen things, heard things ...'

'Yet still you sing for him?' Martino said, his tone clipped. He wished she didn't. He couldn't believe he was jealous of the arrangement.

'Not for him. For you, perhaps?'

Her eyes were misting as she studied his lips. She inched her mouth closer to his. It was too strong an invitation to ignore. He kissed her. Soft lips parting beneath his. She tasted like whisky, her lips cool from the ice. He warmed them with his own, pressing and kneading against them.

Their long kiss was interrupted by a sound behind them. They reluctantly parted and peered back to see Daniela and Taddeo.

'Sorry,' Taddeo said. 'I've got to see Daniela to a taxi. Are they easy to flag down out front?'

'I've got to go too,' Medina said. 'I can drive you home or wherever you need to go.' Medina rose and Martino stood with her. He was sorry she was leaving.

'I guess you could drop me off. It's only a few blocks away,' Daniela said hesitantly.

'Fine, let's go.' Medina picked up her purse from the coffee table.

'We'll see you off,' Martino offered.

Medina stood close to him in the lift. He breathed in her

perfume, wanting to store it to memory. They walked through a carpeted foyer and stepped out on to the street where a cool breeze was blowing.

Medina turned to Martino. 'Thanks for the drink,' she said.

'Anytime,' he said hoarsely. She kissed him but he continued it, shifting his hands to slide from her waist to the small of her back where he pressed her against him. It felt so natural having her there. A moment later, almost cruelly, she pulled back and gave him a warm smile.

'Can I call you?' he had to ask, afraid to let her go without securing a chance to see her again.

'I'd like that.' She slipped out a card from her purse and handed it to him.

'Dinner or lunch?' Martino proposed uncertainly, popping the card in his jacket's pocket.

'Anything—you decide.'

The girls climbed in the car, and Taddeo and Martino stood on the footpath to wave them off. The engine started and they were motoring away.

'I want to kill him,' Taddeo said quietly.

Martino put his hand on his brother's shoulder. 'Easy now. We'll sort him out. I'll talk to Francois tomorrow and we'll get someone trailing Monte straight away.'

'Daniela said we have to be careful. He has a lot of minders.'

'Don't worry. The kind we'll be hiring will have done this before.'

'How did you go with the singer?' Taddeo was interested to know.

'All right, I think. I hope.'

'I think she's taller than you,' Taddeo said, rubbing the top of Martino's head.

'Get out. It's impossible to know for sure. Her boots had high heels.'

Martino talked to Francois the next day, who gave him the name of a friend who might know of a detective. The friend then put him on to another friend and then finally, he was given the name of someone who could help. A large sum of money exchanged hands and a detective was hired.

In the meantime, Martino took Medina out to lunch and, a couple of days later, wined and dined her in one of Sydney's most expensive restaurants.

Every time he saw her, he wanted more. He didn't like being apart from her. His need for her was driving him insane. No girl had ever occupied his thoughts so intrusively. He was glad Taddeo was in town and helping to distract him, or he felt he would be calling Medina all the time, something he knew must not do. A girl like that would be used to being chased. He had to play it cool. Not seem too eager.

At last, their private detective Leo called for a meeting. Martino and Taddeo met him at the alfresco coffee shop with the red umbrellas. Leo was a dark, reedy man, with greasy hair combed back from his narrow face. Unshaven, he wore tight dark jeans and an oversized, grubby shirt. The trio ordered coffees, then Taddeo launched, firing a series of questions, eager to ascertain whether the week of surveillance had yielded any results.

'I've got photos of him meeting with men known to deal drugs, but nothing exchanged hands. He's very careful, this guy. Gets others to do his dirty work for him. I'll keep on him. He's bound to put a foot wrong sooner or later.'

'Keep taking photos of everyone he meets. We'll connect him to something big, I just know it,' Martino said, though he was worried. It could take months to pin dirt on him. Taddeo was getting anxious and Martino didn't want him taking matters into his own hands. He didn't think he was shrewd enough to outsmart Monte.

'I'm going back to Melbourne next weekend. We need to have something by then,' Taddeo prodded, drumming his fingers on the table.

'I won't let him out of my sight. I'll have my coffee and be on my way,' Leo told them, tapping his foot.

'He hasn't noticed you following him?' Martino was unsure. Monte had a way of knowing things, always did. He found it hard to believe that even a capable ex-cop like Leo could remain undetected.

'He saw me a couple of times, but I pretended to be a junkie.' Martino smiled. It was a believable cover.

'Thanks. We appreciate you doing this.'

'No worries. I'd like to see you get this guy. He's not very nice.'

'We know,' Martino stated coolly. 'Well, we'll meet back here next Saturday. Same time?'

'Unless I get something beforehand,' Leo replied. 'I'll call you if I do.'

After their coffees, Taddeo said he wanted to go uptown to buy some new clothes. He'd only packed a few shirts. The brothers separated. Martino was keen to return to the apartment. He was thinking about the next dinner date he had organised with Medina and wondered if she would be amenable to more than a few kisses … Could he bring her back to his apartment?

He had a quick shower and changed into his black suit. He was combing his hair when he heard the apartment door open and click shut. 'Taddeo? Francois?' he called out.

'It's me,' he heard Francois respond. Then he heard the clinking of ice and the distinct gurgling sound of whisky being poured.

'Starting hard a little early?' Martino laughed, entering the living room, and was shocked to see a grim-faced Francois, pale and shaken. He was sitting on the sofa, the whisky glass visibly trembling in his hand.

'What's up?' Martino asked, concerned. He had never seen his friend that badly shaken.

'They just dug up Parlo. He was murdered, his body put under concrete,' Francois spat out in a rush.

'God … why? Who did it?' Martino collapsed in the nearest chair and sat back, aghast. Parlo was a gambler, a good one. He was part of a group of gamblers who Francois and Martino sometimes hooked up with. 'What happened, do you think?'

'We've been found out.'

'Found out … doing what?' Martino was confused and immediately on edge. 'Doing what, Francois?'

'Some of us have been running a bit of a fiddle in a casino.'

'What? Are you crazy?' Then Martino had a horrifying thought. 'Which casino? Which casino?'

'Don't worry, you're out of it. You know the casino owner, so we didn't want you involved.'

Martino felt his heart beat faster and his palms grew clammy.

'You got caught cheating in that fancy casino uptown?' Martino didn't want to take it in.

'Yes.'

'Do you know who owns that place? Do you have any idea of who you're dealing with? Why I wanted to leave that night you took me there? No wonder Parlo is under concrete!'

'I know. I'm sorry. You're right. We shouldn't have taken that place on.'

Martino took a deep breath and exhaled slowly. 'All right, Francois, tell me this: does he know you were involved?'

'He has all our faces. After we cleaned up and cashed in all our chips, the owner came over and handed us a glass of champagne—complimentary—to celebrate our big win. He told us to look at the camera and they took a photo. We didn't know they were on to us at that point and we felt we had to play along. Then they asked us to give the money back. We laughed and when we saw they were serious, we fought our way out of the casino and ran for it. Parlo didn't make it out. We couldn't go back for him. I thought they'd just beat him up—teach him a lesson.'

'Francois, listen to me. You've got to get out of Sydney. These guys won't stop there. They don't just let people take from them and get away with it. They took that photo for a reason. Monte knows you. He knows your first name and he knows we are friends.'

'I know, I know. I know how it works. But I'm not running. Look, it'll blow over. They've got blood for it and we'll never go back there. We got the message. I'll just stay low for a while. Keep to the horse races and stay away from the casinos.' He tried to smile, to look relaxed, but his face was tight, anxious.

'Francois, you are my flatmate and believe me, there's no love between that casino owner and me. They'll come for you, for their money and just because you know me. Please, I've got a bad feeling. You shouldn't have messed around with these people. You need to leave town now!'

'A few of us got greedy. We got bored. I don't know. Stupid. Very stupid.' He drank the remaining whisky in his glass in one gulp and stood to pour another. 'I can't believe they killed him,' he said, thinking of Parlo as he refilled the glass. 'He was engaged to be married.'

The two fell quiet, remembering their lively, risk-taking friend, a Sicilian. It was hard to imagine him gone, a corpse encased in concrete. A fiancé left in tears.

'The cops won't do anything,' Martino commented.

'No.'

'Are you going to leave town?'

'I'll think about it. You might be right. I should pack.'

'Tonight Francois. Pack tonight.'

Francois finished his second drink, then started making a

few phone calls, wanting to account for the rest of the group and give them a warning about what had happened to Parlo.

Martino slipped on his shiny black shoes and left the apartment. He was worried about his gambling friends, especially Francois. It had him wondering, with a constant twist in his gut, what Monte would do to them if they were to whisk Daniela away? For the first time since Taddeo had arrived, Martino felt like they were in over their heads. No matter what Leo dug up, Martino believed that Monte would somehow find a way around it.

Uneasy, he picked up Medina and took her out to an Italian restaurant. Even though she looked alluring in a short silver dress, his mind kept drifting to Francois and his troubles with Monte. At least Francois was awake to it and was streetwise; he would notice if he was being followed.

'Something wrong?' Medina asked, her finger tracing the top of her wine glass.

'Sorry. Got a few things on my mind. How's the pasta?'

'Soft,' she said. 'Want to try some?'

She held up the ravioli on the end of her fork and he opened his mouth to receive it. As he chewed, he realised how beautiful she looked that night. Her hair was loose, teased out down her back. He admired the shape of her slender neck, the curve of her breasts, the promise in her eyes ... He really wanted her back at his apartment.

'Want to get the cheque?' she suggested and smiled.

It was silent in the car. Martino caressed her hair and pressed light kisses against her neck as she drove. Soon she pulled up outside his apartment, her breath ragged.

'Shall we go up?' she murmured thickly.

'Maybe we should just stay here a while,' he replied and they kissed, their lips hungrily tearing at each other's. Where else could he take her? With Monte hunting Francois, he didn't think it safe to take her to his apartment. But he didn't want to insult her or scare her off by suggesting they find a hotel. Oh, he wanted her so bad.

When the kiss finally subsided, Martino peered over at the doorway to the building's foyer and he clamped eyes on an unexpected sight. Leo was coming out of the lift, his face ashen, a camera clenched in his hand. What was he doing there, at his apartment building?

And then the only possible answer hit him and he started to panic. Where Leo was, Monte was.

Chapter twenty-four

November 1964
Sydney, Kings Cross

'God no!' Martino exploded and pushed open the car door.

He turned back to address Medina firmly. 'Whatever you do, do not leave this car. In fact ... go home. I'll explain later.'

Medina was instantly alarmed. Not listening to him, she flew out of the car. 'What's wrong? What's happening?' she begged to know.

'Will you just listen to me ...'

Leo then spied Martino on the street and sprinted over to him. 'Call an ambulance.'

'Why? What's happened?' Martino's legs went weak.

'Acid bomb. Unit 23 level 5.'

Leo did not know he was giving Martino his own address. 'Look, I've got to go. He might've seen me,' Leo mumbled, looking ill.

'Who might've seen you?'

'Monte,' Leo confirmed, then shook free of Martino's grasp and ran down the street.

Martino turned to Medina. 'Can you call the ambulance?'

'Yes. I'll call it.' Sensing the urgency of the situation, she raced across the road to a pay phone booth.

Martino had to go back to the apartment to help Francois. For all he knew, Monte was still there, but he didn't care. He had to do something.

Not bothering to wait for the lift, he took the stairs, leaping up them two at a time until he reached the fifth floor. The door to his apartment was eerily ajar. Martino's heart was pounding, hurting his chest, confusing his breathing ... On approach he heard rasping shrieks of pain. He pushed open the door and bolted inside, ready to defend himself from whatever he would confront, but the room was void of people except for Francois, who was lying on the floor, his hands groping at his face that seemed to be sliding off. The smell of burning flesh was acrid. He wanted to heave, but knew he did not have the time. Forcing himself to stay strong and focused, he ran to the bathroom, grabbed a towel and soaked it in water. He then returned to his flatmate and wrapped his head with the wet towel, ignoring his howls of agony.

Within minutes, the sound of an ambulance was whirring outside.

'Here's help. Just hold on, Francois. Help is here. You're going to be all right,' he told the writhing man who was making God-awful noises—grunts and groans and guttural cries.

The paramedics took over and the police arrived shortly afterwards. Martino played dumb. He had just arrived home and found his flatmate in that state. No. He had no idea what had happened. Yes, he would come down to the station for questioning. No, he'd been on a date with a girl and only just come in.

He accompanied the police and made a formal statement. The police cordoned off the apartment, put a police guard on the door and booked a detective to come in at first light. Released in the early hours of the next morning, Martino returned to the apartment to find Taddeo sitting in the foyer, waiting for him.

'Where have you been? What the hell happened?' Taddeo was on his feet. He was grey in the face.

Taddeo had been up to the apartment, where the police guard had prevented him from entering, but not before he had smelled the pungent stench of acid and burning flesh. A glance inside and he had seen the carpet severely marked, burnt. Furniture had been tipped upside down. The bloody bath towel had been left in a heap on the floor. Taddeo had not known what to think. He had feared something had happened to Martino. The police wouldn't tell him anything.

'Sit down. I'll explain everything.'

'You think Monte threw the acid bomb?' Taddeo had his doubts. He usually had others do his dirty work.

'He enjoys that kind of thing. He knew Francois was my friend, so it made the payback personal.' Martino felt guilt rising like bile at the back of his throat.

He didn't like thinking about his flatmate: that charming face, those eyes that could coax anyone into bending to his will, those lips that were always shaped in a smile that promised mischief, that had kissed the lips of many girls … and then the smell and sight of the acid searing through his skin, ripping it from his face.

'We need to speak to Leo,' Taddeo stated.

'I'll call him.'

Leo agreed to meet them at his studio. Martino and Taddeo climbed grotty stairs at the back of a fish and chip shop to enter a large but run-down apartment. Leo was waiting for them and ushered them in.

Three pairs of bloodshot eyes surveyed each other. None of them had slept. Tired and anxious, they took a seat on the old, faded brown sofa.

'Want to tell us what happened, what you saw? What you caught on film?' Martino asked the detective in a soft voice.

'Everything. I saw it all. I followed Monte to the building, saw what apartment he went in. The neighbouring apartment was unlocked. The occupant was in the shower. So I walked through to the balcony and climbed across to the other balcony. When I looked inside, I saw Monte talking to a man. They talked for less than a minute, then acid was flung in the poor bugger's face … heard him scream … I'm still hearing him.'

Martino knew what he meant. He too could still hear Francois' shrieks.

'Take photos?' Taddeo inquired, and the brothers stared at Leo, waiting, hoping.

'I took them through the glass. I had to be discreet so I don't know what I got, if anything,' Leo confessed. 'Let's hope I got lucky. I'll develop it now. After you pay me a development fee.'

Martino handed him money. Leo then ducked into his bathroom, which had been transformed into a darkroom.

The brothers waited in the lounge area. They waited over an hour for Leo to re-emerge. When he did, he shook his head apologetically. 'Sorry, I have a photo of Monte entering the building where his face is clear. As you understand, I couldn't use a flash and had to shoot from a low angle through glass. I kept clicking whenever I could. It's dark. You can see two figures, quite blurred … You can't see who they are. In one photo you see one figure with arms raised, and in another photo it shows a figure on the ground. Basically, I got nothing. All we can prove is that Monte was there around the time of the assault.'

It wasn't enough to prove anything. Martino and Taddeo hung their heads, cursing to themselves.

'Would you stand up in court …' Taddeo put to him.

But Leo was instantly shaking his head. 'I was paid to take photos, not point fingers. That guy is very well connected. I take the stand—I'm a dead man.'

Taddeo folded his arms across his chest, anger pulsing through him.

'I'll take the photos, what you've developed,' Martino said, wanting to examine them more closely.

'I'll get them ready for you.'

As Leo packed them up, Taddeo turned to him. 'Why take them? They're useless.'

'Ever played poker? Ever pulled off a good bluff?'

Taddeo studied Martino's intense face. 'You wouldn't?'

'I've got enough of a hand to bluff with. Are you in?'

Taddeo shook his head. 'Got another plan?'

'No.'

Leo returned and handed the photos over in a large envelope. 'Thanks.' Martino took them.

The brothers left. Martino took Taddeo to a rundown hotel and booked a room.

'We'll stay here for a couple of nights. Why don't you go take a shower and try and get some sleep? I'm going to go to the hospital to see how Francois is doing,' Martino told his brother.

'Okay. Just go to the hospital. No doing anything crazy like showing those useless photos to Monte. You've got nothing, and Monte's too smart to fall for a bluff. Got it?'

Martino nodded. 'Yeah. You're right. See you back here later. We can talk more then.'

'Martino, promise me you're not going to see Monte.'

Martino looked Taddeo in the eyes. 'I promise. I won't.'

* * *

He went via his apartment and asked the police to let him in to pack some clothes and personal items for himself and for his flatmate. He changed into another suit, then carried two full bags down to his car. Francois had a large amount of cash hidden beneath his mattress and Martino wanted to make sure it didn't go astray while he was in hospital.

It was a depressing visit.

First he waited in the hall while nurses conducted a check-up. Then, before he was allowed in, a senior nurse turned up and advised him that Francois would never see again. The acid had rendered him permanently blind and left his face partially disfigured. It made Martino sick to think of it. The nurse went on to explain that Francois was heavily medicated and accepting only family visitors. Martino was one of the few outside of family allowed entry.

Within minutes of Martino being seated by Francois' bedside, his friend confirmed that it had been Monte who threw the acid.

'Have you told the police?'

'No. He'll kill my family. He said as much before he did it. He said he knows where my sister lives.' His voice was flat, his face and eyes were covered in bandages. It seemed to pain him to talk but he wanted to.

'We'll get him, Francois,' Martino had responded in a harsh whisper.

'No. Get out of Sydney. Never come back,' he pleaded.

'I can't. I'm not finished here.'

'Martino, I like you. You've been a friend. I don't want you to end up like Parlo, or like me. Monte will come for you. Oh, he said to give you something.'

Martino felt chilled. He was shocked to think that Monte had talked about him, before tossing acid in his friend's face.

'It's with my things. The nurse said my clothes were in a bag. Can you see a bag?'

'Yes.'

'Look in the pocket of my jacket.'

Martino went through the bag gingerly. The stench of acid on the clothing was strong. He reached in the pocket and his fingers closed around a coin. He took it out and looked at it, already knowing what he would see: a penny with the year 1940 printed on it.

He felt sick. Monte had carried it around all these years. At that moment, fear really started to take hold. What kind of person held on to such tokens? He didn't feel safe. He held the penny tight and suddenly felt a boy of seven again. That penny meant something to him. It was his lucky coin, his welcome-to-Australia coin. It was good to have it back, even though it now carried the message of a threat, one he had to guard against.

He had come up against bullies most of his young life, but this bully had gone too far. Like the others, he had to stand up to him, and he would.

'What's with the penny?' Francois asked.

'He took it from me when we were kids. He knew it mattered to me then. He likes to take special things away from people.' Martino looked at Francois' face covered in bandages. He had taken Francois' pretty face away from him.

'You should get out of town,' Francois said. 'I wish I had.'

'Sure. Sure. I will.'

'You can stay for a while. My family are interstate and won't get here until tomorrow.'

Martino heard something in Francois' tone that he'd never heard before. Fear. Francois was afraid. His eyes would never see again and he was in the dark, literally. He couldn't walk out on him. He stayed a couple of hours, until the nurse requested it was time for him to leave. He had been glad to stay, to offer some comfort, to provide a voice in the dark. He somehow felt responsible for Francois' terrible injuries, believing their friendship had made him more of a target.

'Thanks for stopping by and for my clothes and, you know … the stash!'

'Not a problem.'

'Take care.'

'You too. I'll visit again soon.'

Martino felt for the penny, which he had tucked away in his pocket. He needed luck to be on his side. With the envelope of photos tucked beneath his arm, he returned to the car and drove straight to Monte's casino.

It was time to pull off a bluff.

Chapter twenty-five

November 1964
Sydney, Kings Cross

'Can I help you? A drink, sir?' An attractive woman in a tight sparkling dress had approached him. She was a hostess, paid to meet and greet casino guests, but also paid to spy, to ensure the right types were entering.

'I want to speak with Monte,' Martino said curtly, trying to keep his heart rate steady.

'Ah, Martino, isn't it? Yes, wait here.' She disappeared and returned a couple of minutes later.

Martino could feel stress oozing sweat all over his body.

'Monte is busy. He's being entertained,' she said with a knowing wink and glanced towards a far door.

'I see,' Martino said. 'I'm sure he won't mind sharing his entertainment.'

He sidestepped the hostess and strode into the main room, passing suits and swirling dresses, dodging waiters with drink trays. When he reached the door, a man of considerable breadth stood before him, barring his way.

'Let me pass,' he said to the burly security man, but he did not move.

The door flung open.

'Martino. I was expecting you. Come in. Come in. You know Daniela and Medina …'

The two women were seated on a sofa that took up a large part of the small room. The women's expressions were stern. They looked upset. Both were dressed in evening wear; Daniela in cream and Medina in soft lavender.

Martino stepped inside and Monte closed the door softly behind him.

'Nice of you to visit. How's your flatmate? Seeing the error of his ways? Or not seeing much at all?' Monte smiled a horrendous smile.

Martino cringed. How could anyone be that cold?

'I think what we need to say needs to be said in private,' Martino said. He looked with concern at Medina, wishing she wasn't there.

'Say what you have to say, then leave us.'

Martino hesitated, not sure he could pull it off. But he had to!

'I have photos and copies of photos,' Martino blurted out, staring intently at Monte. 'They show you entering my apartment building and assaulting my flatmate.'

'Do they? So why haven't you taken them to the police?'

'I want you to let Daniela walk away from here, from you, and for you to leave her alone. Otherwise, I will take the photos to the police, the media and to your family.'

Monte smiled. 'Playing the family card too? Well done. You've come along way for a Saforo. How do I know the photos exist? It was dark that night. May I see?'

'Here's a sample …' Martino showed the photo of Monte entering his apartment building, his face clearly visible.

'And I have more photos. The person who took these photos will take the stand if you don't let Daniela walk away.'

Monte smiled. 'Nice. I like it. But I don't believe you have anyone stupid enough to take the stand against me, and I think that photo is the best you've got. Which is nothing! Daniela is going to be my wife. And the only one going to walk away is you.'

'No. Tell Daniela to come with me, now.'

'Martino, how long have you known me? You know I don't like to be told what to do. It is time you were on your way. My security friend here will take you. He likes to take people for a drive. He's a very good driver. Have you seen the Blue Mountains yet? They are worth a visit,' Monte said softly.

Daniela began to cry. Medina put an arm around her.

'Please take my guest for a long, scenic drive,' Monte said to the guard at the back of the room.

Martino felt one strong hand clasp his shoulder and something sharp pressed against his lower back. The guard pushed him forward. He tried to resist, burying his feet into the carpet, but his shoes easily slid across it. The sharpness in his back intensified and he had to take a step. His mind was racing. There was no way he would get into a car. He knew if he did, he would never be seen again. But how to extract himself? The guard gave him one more shove towards the door when it burst open and Taddeo stumbled in.

Beyond the open door, Martino could hear chaos taking place. Glass was smashing, women were screaming and squealing, and there was the rustling of fabrics as people started scurrying away.

'What is going on …' Monte craned his neck.

To Martino, it sounded like a police raid. 'Taddeo? What's happening?' he asked.

Almost as in answer to his question, three men entered the room, strolling in, their faces grim. Martino couldn't believe what he was seeing. What were they doing here? The absolute last people he expected to see!

Ettore, Edrico and Roberto.

'Papa,' Daniela cried, running and flinging herself into Roberto's arms.

'Ah my pet. I should have known things weren't right. You hardly call your mother. I'm sorry. I should've come down sooner.' Roberto was blubbering as he saw Daniela's rush of tears.

'Martino, you okay?' his father asked. The guard holding him then let go and retreated.

'It's good to see you,' Martino said, meaning it. 'What are you doing here?'

It was Edrico's turn to address his son. He turned on Monte, his expression shifting between sorrow and rage.

'You've been mistreating Roberto's daughter? Running an illegal casino? Organising hits on people who owe you money?'

Monte smiled and took a low bow. 'I'm everything you thought I'd be.' Monte smiled calmly. 'A great disappointment.'

'You are more than that. You are a criminal, a thug and ...'

'Your loving son.'

'The police are in the foyer. They are going to want to speak to you.'

If Monte felt cornered, he didn't show it. Instead, he let out a sharp laugh.

'Your finest hour. Dobbing in your own son to the cops! You must be so proud. Thank you for coming all the way from Brisbane just to have me locked up. What you've always wanted and expected, isn't it? Well, why don't you add this to your list of disappointments.'

He did it before anyone could see or react. He took a handgun from his jacket, lifted it and fired one shot, slamming a bullet into his father's stomach.

For Martino, it was as though time stood still, with every action around him slowing down to be observed in agonising detail.

Ettore and Roberto yelled in helpless protest, reaching for Edrico.

Taddeo tackled Monte to the ground, disarming him as the police rushed in. A senior constable slapped cuffs on Monte and brought him to his feet.

Daniela was screaming so hard that the junior policeman moved to comfort her.

Medina huddled on the sofa, her face pale and partly hidden behind her long hair.

Monte, grim-faced and tight-lipped, was led out. Passing through the doorway, he threw back a final glance at his father lying on the floor, his expression pensive rather than remorseful.

Edrico's blood was flowing freely on to the carpet. A police officer handed Roberto a towel, telling him to apply it firmly to the wound.

Edrico looked up at his friends. 'The police have him?' he croaked and yelped as the towel was held hard against his torn stomach.

'Yes,' Martino heard his father whisper. 'He has been arrested.'

Edrico gave a single nod. He appeared to stop struggling against the pain, seemed more at peace.

'The ambulance is coming. Stay still and quiet,' Roberto said, though there were tears in his eyes.

Edrico gave his friends an apologetic look. 'I'm not young anymore,' he rasped. 'No pretty nurse for me this time.'

'Shush. I'll make sure you get a very pretty one,' Martino's father gushed.

'Tell Tazia … I'm sorry,' he breathed. 'He was our kid. He lost his brother to the war. He was never right after that. My fault. I was his father.'

'I'll tell her,' Roberto said. 'It wasn't your fault. You are a good man, Edrico. You've worked hard. Say hello to Italy for me, if you ever …'

Pain silenced him. Then life slowly slipped away from his grasp, taking his hurt, his words, his dreams with it.

Martino watched as his father and Roberto wept over their friend's body. He wished he could take their pain away, but there was nothing to be done or said at such a time.

He went over and gathered Medina into his arms. She buried her face against his chest and cried.

* * *

Much later, tired, drained and still visibly shocked, Martino and Taddeo sat with their father in a bar in Kings Cross, their lips burning against the alcoholic purity of their drinks.

Roberto had gone with Daniela to hospital, where she was being treated for shock. Medina refused any treatment, wanting just to go home to her parents.

Martino soon learned that Taddeo had called their father and told him everything about Monte's mistreatment of Daniela, the casino, the acid bomb. His father had then phoned Roberto, and Roberto had contacted Edrico.

Edrico had not been surprised to hear of his son's abuses of people and the law. He had chosen to fly down and sort it out himself, saying he needed to take responsibility for his son's actions. Ettore and Roberto had offered to go with him. They had caught the very next flight to Sydney and were at the casino within three hours of Taddeo's phone call.

'It was Edrico's first plane flight. He had the window seat. He liked looking out the window,' his father told them, his eyes misty.

'You want to go back to the hotel, Papa?' Taddeo asked, sounding concerned.

'Not yet.' He took another swig. 'Not going to sleep anyway.'

'I'm glad you're here,' Martino told him.

His father peered up and studied him, taking in his sharp suit. 'You look well.'

'I've been better.'

'You left on bad terms. I lost my temper. I was wrong. I expected too much of you. I had forgotten … You spent more of your childhood in this country than in Italy.' His father inhaled and exhaled heavily.

'Papa, we don't have to do this now. You don't have to say these things. I'm sorry I left the way I did.'

But his father was determined to continue. 'What I'm trying

to say is … your mother and Nonna want you back. Every day they blame me for your leaving. I would like it very much if you could come back home.'

Martino slid off his stool and walked around to his father and embraced him. He held him tight for a long time.

'I don't know if I'm ready to come back just yet, Papa,' he said sorrowfully.

Taddeo cut in. 'He's met someone.'

Ettore raised a brow.

'And she's not one to walk away from easily,' Taddeo expanded.

'Is that right? Dare I hope that she is Italian?'

'Australian born,' Martino told him, 'though I think she said her father was part Dutch, part Indonesian.'

His father nodded, holding his drink in a firm hand. 'And she's pretty, this girl, hey?'

'Very pretty,' Martino said. He wasn't surprised his father didn't see her at the casino given all that happened.

'Catholic?'

'No.'

'Okay.' He was quiet for a moment, then asserted, 'You like her, we will meet her.'

Martino was aware his father was trying hard to be more accepting, more accommodating. He could see it wasn't easy for him.

'Thanks. I'd like to bring her home for you to meet. But it's early days. Let's see how it goes.'

'Sure. When you're ready. But don't take too long. Your brother Nardo misses you! You, too, Taddeo. When you're released from the army, come home. And tell me, is there anything between you and Daniela? Your mother is hoping, you know.'

'I hope so.'

'Okay. Just both come home, when you can … Soon!'

The two boys nodded, wanting to.

'Now. I want to make a toast. To my dear friend Edrico … a man of strength and courage. I'll miss him for the rest of my days. Heck, I miss him right now. He was fond of a drink. He would have liked this bar very much.'

Martino drank, but his father didn't. He was staring off into space, his mind filling with memories. After a long while, he drank deeply, then said, 'Okay. Take me to the hotel now.'

Chapter twenty-six

December 1967
Stafford, Brisbane

It was almost Christmas. Martino stood on the veranda of the Stafford house, holding Donna's hand.

He had since learned that Medina had been only her stage name. He liked the name Donna. It suited her.

Nonna answered his knock. Martino saw her eyes peeping through the crack in the door, then heard her gasp of surprise. Next thing, the door was swinging wide.

'You've come home,' she said, elated. Then immediately complained, 'You should have warned us. I would have planned a lovely meal. Now I have only an afternoon to cook. What to do with you! Come here.'

Wrinkly hands cupped his chin and she kissed him on both cheeks, her expression softening as she did so.

'Sorry, Nonna. Don't worry about the cooking. I love anything you make. It's good to see you.'

'You love my cooking because it takes a long time and a lot of care, but we'll see, we'll see what I can do.'

'Nonna, I want you to meet someone. This is Donna.' He put his arm around her, bringing her forward. She had confessed that she was nervous about meeting his family and he could feel her tension.

'You are Donna! Beautiful Donna.' Nonna grabbed hold of the girl's hands. 'Finally! We hear about you … for three years! Now we meet at last. The singer from Sydney. So tall and slim. You are taller than my Martino. Contessa, Ettore, Maria, come quick! Look who is here. Martino and his Donna.'

Martino guided Donna into the house, walking her down the hallway into the living room. He remembered discovering the house as a boy, running from room to room with so much excitement. In the corner of the lounge area was the same Christmas tree that had once been decorated with sweets. Now its plastic branches were draped in sparkling tinsel, with the odd bauble hanging from their ends. Beneath the tree, a miniature nativity scene of hand-painted figurines had been set up.

His mother, wearing a floral dress with gardening shears in hand, hurried in through the back door. Ettore, dressed in overalls, was behind her. Maria, wearing jeans and a T-shirt, came out of her room, her limp obvious.

'Martino! What are you doing, surprising us like this? Look how we are dressed to meet you and your girlfriend. It is terrible.' His mother lightly scolded him in Italian, but Martino ignored her distress and embarrassment and kissed her on both cheeks. She smiled tearfully and kissed him back enthusiastically.

'How I've missed you! Now, let me go change. I can't receive your girlfriend like this. I just can't,' she said in Italian to Martino, smiling briefly at Donna before rushing to her room.

'Mama wants to dress up for you,' Martino explained his mother's sudden departure to Donna.

'Hello, welcome,' his father said in English to Donna, taking her by both hands and kissing her on the cheeks. 'Bella, bella. You are beautiful.'

'Thank you. Nice to meet you,' Donna said, smiling broadly.

'I will change ...' He indicated his overalls by plucking at the straps and followed his wife down the hall.

'And this ...' Martino said, putting his arm around the fifteen-year-old girl's shoulders, ' ... is my sister, Maria. She's my favourite because she never picks on me. You've grown tall while I was away.'

'Hello, Maria. Nice to meet you,' Donna said.

'Hello. I love your dress!' the teenager gushed. 'Did you make it?'

'No. I'm not that clever with sewing. But thank you.'

Donna was dressed in the height of fashion. She was wearing an orange pleated tent dress with white, low-heeled, sling pump shoes. Her hair on her crown was teased high and held back with a white headband, while the ends of her hair were flipped out.

Nonna appeared with a tray of glasses and a jug of cold juice. 'Sit down. Be comfortable,' she urged in Italian. She waved her hands towards the sofa, indicating for Donna to sit.

The couple sat side by side, and Martino poured the juice into the glasses.

Shortly after, his parents reappeared wearing their best clothes that would normally only be worn to church or the soccer. Holding Donna's hand, Martino came to his feet and she stood with him.

'Welcome, Donna,' his mother said in English, kissing the young woman on both cheeks. 'My clothes are clean now. I can kiss you!'

Martino felt his father's eyes upon him. 'You look well. You're a young man now. What are you? Twenty-four? Your hair's too long.'

Martino smiled, running a hand through his thick hair.

'Sit down. We'll join you,' his father continued. 'This is a big surprise. We did not expect you.'

'It's been a long time. I've missed you all. And I wanted you to meet Donna.'

'It has been too long,' his father agreed. 'We have been wanting to meet Donna for a very long time. We are happy you're here, at last! Been working hard?'

'Yes,' Martino responded proudly. 'I have a good job at Claude Neon. Just been made manager.'

'Manager? I am pleased to hear it. I told you a trade would serve you well.'

'We haven't seen you since Isabella's wedding,' his mother cut in. 'Taddeo has been home three times since then.' She appeared miffed and wasn't letting him get away with his prolonged absence.

'Sorry, Mama and Papa. We've been busy,' he tried to explain.

'Holidaying in New Zealand, I hear!' Nonna smirked as she carried in a plate of assorted cheeses and cold meats from the kitchen. 'Martino, ask Donna if she wants a glass of wine. I know it's only mid-afternoon, but this is a special occasion.'

Martino translated for his Nonna, who was staring at Donna awaiting her response. Donna looked uncertain. 'Go on. Nonna would love to drink wine with you,' Martino advised her.

'All right. Yes. Yes, please,' she said. Nonna understood that and scurried off to find a good bottle.

'How is everyone?' Martino wanted to know. He had made it home for Isabella's wedding. He hadn't taken Donna to it, as she had long before booked an important singing engagement that weekend at a show at the Opera House. He had been pleased to see Isabella was happy with her choice of husband. He was Italian, but she had met him independently of her parents. That wedding was over a year, ago. He had had very little news since as he rarely called home.

His father replied quickly, 'Nardo is doing wonderfully. You remember how last year *La Fiamma* newspapers named him the best and fairest soccer player in Australia? Well, they gave him a free trip to Italy with spending money. He took Rose three months ago. They visited Trieste and took the most beautiful photos. We'll get him over to show you. Anyway, just last week, Rose tells us she's pregnant. Look at the timing ... conceived in Italy, perhaps?' His father seemed pleased about the possibility and chuckled loudly.

'They had a beautiful trip,' his mother said, rolling her eyes.

Martino was impressed and a little envious. His brother had always stuck at things, done well. His success in soccer was extraordinary and he had married, gone to Italy, now was having a baby.

'And his accounting business is doing very well. He has many Italian families as clients. Everyone comes to him to do their books. He's bought a big house—a brick one,' his mother added. 'You should see his lawn!'

'And he has a rose garden,' his father put in.

Martino nodded. 'It is good,' he said, seeing his parents waiting for him to respond. 'I couldn't be happier for him.'

'So how are things with you?' Nonna asked, coming in with a dusty bottle of wine and handing it to his father to open.

'We are doing well. I'm a manager now as I said, and I help to manage Donna's singing career. I book her at clubs and restaurants,' he said.

'You must be a good singer,' his mother said to Donna. 'You two have been seeing each other a long time ...' she prompted, raising a brow.

Nonna came into the living room, carrying the wine glasses.

'Yes. It has been a long time,' Martino agreed and smiled at his mother, knowing he was about to tell her what she was expecting to hear. 'I will make an honest woman of her,' he said in Italian first to his family. Then said in English, 'We want to be married and we want you there, at our wedding.'

Nonna understood the English word for 'wedding' and cried with joy. She grabbed Donna's hand. Speaking a mix of English and Italian, she stammered, 'You, wonderful girl. You have made my Martino very happy. I never thought I'd see the day ... Married at last and to such a beautiful girl. Beautiful. What beautiful children you will have.'

Martino looked to his parents, who were smiling.

'Congratulations!' his father said, kissing him and Donna.

His mother followed suit. Her smile was warm and genuine. 'Any chance you will settle in Brisbane?' she had to ask.

'Please, Martino. Come back and live near us,' Maria pleaded.

'We'll see. Perhaps we'll move up here one day,' Martino conceded, though it was a conversation that he was yet to have with Donna. Her family was in Sydney and she was close to them. He wouldn't want to tear her away. 'Who knows what will happen?' he said in Italian.

Then Nonna was pouring the wine. 'To Martino and Donna,' she said.

Martino peered at Donna, who was smiling. 'To us,' she said, and they clinked their glasses.

* * *

They were married the following year in a church in Sydney on a Sunday in February, 1968. Gian was the best man and Donna's sister was her bridesmaid. It was a small and simple wedding, with the reception held in the backyard of Donna's parents' house. Martino thought she had never looked more beautiful in her tight fitting laced dress and long veil. He was absolutely delighted to have his parents and Nonna travel to Sydney for it. While they were in the city, he showed them around the majestic harbour, which had them remembering and telling stories of their beloved portside towns of Fiume and Trieste.

The parting from them was even more painful than Martino had prepared for. He had enjoyed having them stay. It seemed he was missing his family more than he knew.

'Please visit more often,' Nonna begged of him, and he agreed that he would.

A year after the wedding, Donna told him that her parents were moving to the north of the state to a coastal town, chasing the sun and a change of scene. The town was only a two-hour drive from Brisbane.

Martino smiled.

'I know.' Donna smiled back. 'Now we can both be near our families. I know how much you've been missing them. Shall we do it? Move up?'

Martino wrapped his arms around her. 'There is a lot to leave behind. I've a good job, you have plenty of work booked …'

'You will get work in Brisbane. And I've been thinking, I wouldn't mind a break from the singing.'

Martino gazed into her green eyes. 'If you are okay to move, I would love to.'

They bought a house on a corner block in a western Brisbane suburb about half an hour away from Stafford. Martino loved the area because it was green and hilly. It had a nice feel.

Wanting to go into business for himself, as his father and Nardo had done, he started seeking electrical work from the Italians he knew from his early years in soccer and gaming. When a request came for him to wire up an illegal casino in Fortitude Valley, he accepted it. He took the work gladly. Starting up was difficult and he had to take what was on offer. He was touched when Donna offered to help him get his business off the ground and started going door to door, handing out his business card and introducing herself as having a husband new to the area and looking for work.

Though building up his business absorbed a lot of his time and focus, there was something he longed for above all else. His return to Brisbane was never going to be complete without it. He wanted to play soccer again with Nardo. His brother was player and coach at the Italian-based club at Spencer Park. He wanted to join him.

As soon as was practical, he met up with Nardo and asked if there were any spots on the team available. He had been playing in Sydney and was still match fit.

'For you, Martino, there will always be a spot. Come on. I've missed having you pass me the ball. You could always find my feet!' Nardo told him, slapping him on the back. 'Show me you've still got it.'

For Martino, running on to the field at Spencer Park before a large crowd was a real homecoming. He loved it—how he had missed it. Soccer was in his blood, it was who he was, but playing with Nardo was sensational. It was Italian-style soccer at its best. Now he was home in every sense.

A couple of years passed, and in 1971 Martino found cause to be extremely proud of his brother. Nardo had decided he would no longer take to the field as a player, but put his energy into coaching. That year, he surpassed all expectations as coach. He guided the club's senior team to achieve a successful trifecta, claiming the Queensland Cup, the premiership and the grand final. Martino couldn't believe it. It was a dream run and he and his family and their friends were there every step of the way to cheer Nardo on.

The year of success was also a happy one, personally, for Martino. It was the year that Donna gave birth to their first child, a girl, who they named Natasha. The following year, a second girl was born to them. They called her Linda, after a name in Donna's family.

Martino was content. He was near his family and having one of his own. His parents were thrilled to be near their granddaughters and all was well.

The years started to pass in relative peace. His business thrived, his babies grew up and started school. He sent them to the nearest state school, not wanting the Catholic education for them. Too many bad memories of strict, mean nuns!

Donna took up art classes and began to paint. Her works were soft and delicate, like her, he thought. She held art exhibitions and people came and bought her watercolour paintings.

Martino stayed with his brother at the club, applauding success after success. In 1976, Nardo's senior team again celebrated a trifecta of wins. In 1977 and again in 1978, he led the side to take out the national cup.

They were heady times, with lots of celebratory parties being held at the Italo-Australian club, a large building located opposite the football club. Martino and Donna attended the games. They brought their daughters, dressed in pretty frocks. After the games, they headed up to the Italian club to celebrate the wins with the other club supporters; wins which were all too common under Nardo's guidance.

At the end of that season, Martino was invited to step up his involvement with the club. The invitation came by way of Nardo, who had driven out to the western suburbs and knocked on Martino's door to put forward an offer. It was summer and the air-conditioner was on high. Martino was surprised to find Nardo on his doorstep and welcomed him in.

'What brings you here?' Martino asked as they sat in the living room. Martino regarded his brother, who was wearing a brown suit, cream shirt and had his thick hair combed to one side. He easily filled the sofa, having always been a large man, but Martino noticed that he sat tall, confidently, with shoulders back and head high. Success was sitting well on him.

Glasses of port between them, Nardo soon put forth the proposition.

'I want you to coach a team in the southeast league,' Nardo said ardently. 'Give up the boots. We can coach side by side. I'll be in national league, you in the state's southeast. What do you say?'

Martino, sporting sideburns and wearing casual shorts and a polo shirt, peered over at Donna, who was playing dominoes with their two daughters.

'I think it's a wonderful idea,' she said. 'You'd make a fine coach. You need a new challenge.'

'Listen to your wife, Martino. You need it. Remember when

we used to play together on the same team? Now we can coach together at the same club!'

Martino was smiling. He, a coach? Why not? 'All right. Let's do it.'

It was a spectacular year of soccer. Nardo took the team to the grand finals and was named runner-up Coach of the Year in Australia, while Martino's team won its premiership.

The end of season party was held at the Italo-Australian club. Martino walked in to the expansive, smoky room with Donna on his arm, his prettily dressed daughters in tow. An accordion player was whipping up music on a small stage next to a crowded dance area. He saw couples dancing and twirling in amongst children who were spinning and sliding. It looked like mayhem. Many players and families sat at tables, eating huge plates of pasta or thin slabs of veal, served with vegetables or salad. They passed around baskets of garlic bread, many hands taking slices. Jugs of beer and soft drink were being carried away from a long bar, held high overheads so as not to be knocked and spilled by the tightly pressed throng.

'What do you think of all this?' Martino asked his wife.

'I love it,' she replied.

'Want to get up and sing?'

'No way. My singing days are behind me.'

'Happy in Brisbane then?'

'I'm happy wherever you are.'

They kissed, high on love and wine and celebration.

When the next season began, Nardo and Martino thought their success would never end. Martino idolised his brother, thought he had the magic touch, and he was feeling confident that coaching was in his blood too. What he could not have known was that their most tumultuous season was about to begin, and that it would be followed by a tragedy that would rock their family and the entire Brisbane Italian community. Martino did not, could not feel it coming. He started that coaching season in good spirits. He hired Gian as his team manager and, with his old friend by his side, he was the happiest he had ever been.

But right from the start shadows began to appear, marring their dream run. Nardo's team was battling. The club, having spent too much money on players in previous years, was sinking into debt and had been forced to sell off some key players. Other star players were unable to play due to injury.

Martino started opening his door to Nardo regularly. Beginning to buckle under the stress, Nardo was turning to him for advice, talking with him until midnight, trying to work out different strategies that might overcome the problems associated with the weakened line-up. Martino brought out the dominoes and used them to represent players, manipulating them in patterns on his coffee table as they discussed tactics. They tried all kinds of player combinations, but nothing was working.

Martino watched in sorrow as Nardo's team lost game after game. He felt for him. His brother was not used to losing and he was suffering. He decided to go to a training session to see if he could help him. That night, while he was there, the club president turned up and interrupted the session, pulling Nardo aside away from players' eyes.

Martino wandered to the end of the field and saw his brother and the president engaged in what looked like a heated exchange, though he couldn't hear a word of it. After the president left, Nardo strolled to a seat in the grandstand and slumped into it. When Martino joined him, he was pale and shaking his head.

'What did he say?' Martino asked.

'I've just been issued a warning. If I don't turn things around and have a win in the next two games, I'm sacked.'

'Sacked?' Martino's voice rang out in shock.

'Shhh. Keep it down. It won't help the players to know that.'

Martino lowered his voice but pressed on furiously, 'You've

given this club years of service and more success than they'd ever dreamed of. Two Phillips Cups, for crying out loud!'

'I know what I've done. All they care about is now. And now, I'm losing.'

'They've given you nothing to work with, and there's been a run of injuries.'

Nardo wiped his face with his hands. 'Let's not talk about this now. Come on. Players are waiting. And given the pressure I'm under, we better put in a great training session. Can you help me?'

Martino nodded. 'Of course, I will.'

Nardo and Martino divided the players into two groups and trained them hard. The team left exhausted. Martino was helping Nardo to pack up the cones when he spied a figure walking towards them across the dark field.

'Nardo,' he said, indicating the person approaching.

As the man drew closer, Martino was surprised to see it was his father. He never attended training. He hoped there was nothing wrong.

'It's all right,' his father assured them. 'I just want to have a chat. It is about soccer. Everything is okay.'

'Sure, Pa. What do you want to talk about? Must be important to bring you out here late at night,' Nardo commented.

'It is to me. I have a favour to ask on behalf of someone. A favour for Cappi.'

'Cappi?' That was the last name Martino had expected his father to say. 'What favour? What about him?'

'Well, it would mean a lot to me and to him, Nardo, if you could give his boy a run in the topside. His son plays reserves, but he is better than that. If he could just get a run, be given a chance …'

'No!' Nardo spoke quickly and harshly.

'But he is Cappi's son. Can't you just take a look at him?' their father pressed.

'I've seen him and the answer is no! He's not up to it. I don't care whose son he is. I have fathers asking me all the time to give their sons a run. This is not the amateur league. This is no Redcliffe picnic match. I'm under all this pressure to perform, to win games ...'

'You are not on such a winning streak right now. What would it hurt to try a new player?'

Nardo looked pained on hearing his father's words. His recent run of losses was a sore point.

'I am trying to turn that around,' Nardo cried, sounding exasperated. 'The last thing I want ...' Unable to finish for anger, he slammed down the cone he was holding and stalked off, heading towards the car park.

Martino saw his father's expression darken with disappointment. 'What can I tell Cappi?' he muttered sadly.

'I know his son, Reggi. Sharp looking kid,' Martino piped up. 'Maybe I can take him aside and see what he's got.'

His father glanced up, surprised. 'You'd do that?'

'Sure. You can tell Cappi that I'll take a look at him. Cappi's done a lot for me. This is the least I can do.'

His father exhaled a breath of relief. 'Thanks. That would be good. Thank you.'

'Nardo will calm down. He's under a lot of pressure right now.' Martino felt a need to excuse his brother's temper. His father didn't know about the president's warning.

'I know. I understand. It wouldn't be easy for him right now. I wish I didn't have to ask ... but it is Cappi!'

The next training night, Martino left Nardo with the senior side and ran over to watch the reserves. He spotted Reggi and saw that like his father he had intensely black eyes and a serious manner. He was clearly enjoying his soccer, his feet owning the ball, mastering it. His passes were smooth, comfortable, effortless and on target. He had short bursts of speed and flexibility. His first touch on the ball was admirable. Martino wanted to know more. He asked the coach if he could borrow the young player and he was released to him.

'Take the ball off me and see if you can have a shot between those two cones,' he told Reggi.

'All right,' the player replied quietly. And when Martino gave him the nod, he charged at him. Martino felt his strength, observed his speed and examined his technique. He did eventually wrest the ball from him, but then struggled to get around Martino's defensive moves. However, he got off a shot regardless, only just missing the target.

'Close,' Martino told him. 'You weren't balanced to take the shot on that leg. You should have taken it with your left foot.'

Reggi nodded in agreement. He was nervous and keen. He wanted to impress.

Martino saw his eagerness, and saw something of himself in him.

'Look, my brother says you're not ready. I think you need just a bit more experience and a few tips. How about you train with me every night this week and have a game with my side in southeast league on Saturday morning?'

'I play Reserves Saturday night.'

Martino shrugged. 'Young guy like you—two games in one day shouldn't hurt. Get your fitness up.'

Reggi nodded. 'Why do this for me?'

Martino thought about Cappi and remembered him training him on the oval, helping his leg to recover after the car accident. Cappi had been a friend to him and to his family. That had something to do with it. But it was more than that. He actually liked the kid.

'You want to be a soccer star? Play topside?' he put to him.

'More than anything.'

'Why?'

Reggi gave a shy smile, reluctant to share his personal thoughts.

'Why?' Martino asked again in a softer tone.

'I don't have much in common with my old man. He's very Italian, you know? But the one thing we agree on—we both love soccer.'

'You're doing it for him?'

'No. I'm doing it for us.'

Martino smiled and got it. He understood more than Reggi could ever know.

'All right. Let's start now. We do the same exercise, but this time, you shoot with your left foot, all right?'

Reggi smiled and nodded. 'Okay.'

'After that, we talk tactics. I know what my brother's team needs and your skills might just be what's missing.'

After training, Martino joined Nardo to help pack up. They were silent for the first five minutes as they gathered up the balls into the sack, then Nardo erupted.

'What do you think you're doing with Reggi? I told you he's not good enough.'

'He's not without talent.' Martino shrugged. He had expected his brother to attack him about it and was ready to feel a few lashings of his pent-up stress.

'They've all got some talent. They've all got great fathers: rich fathers, fathers that make all kinds of promises if you give their kids a run, but I can't operate like that. We play to win.'

'You're not winning.'

Nardo clenched his fist and swiped it at his brother, but Martino caught the punch in his hand and held it. Nardo was surprised at Martino's strength, forgetting that during the week Martino worked as an electrician, lifting heavy ladders and the like, while he worked behind a desk, crunching numbers.

Martino spoke slowly and clearly. 'At this point in time, you could take a risk on a young player who is showing promise. The players you've got now, they haven't got it.'

'It will be different this Saturday,' Nardo promised him, lowering his fist and wiping sweat from his upper lip.

'Will it? Let's make a deal. If you lose this Saturday, the following Saturday you give Reggi a twenty-minute run. Deal?'

'If I lose this Saturday, I have to win the next or I'm sacked. You remember I told you that, right?'

Martino nodded solemnly.

'Oh, to hell with it. You're right. It's all over anyway. Deal.' Nardo strode away, his head hung low, his shoulders hunched.

Martino felt sorry for him. He didn't want to be adding to his stress, but he actually believed that Reggi could help. He hoped his hunch was right.

Martino trained with Reggi during the week, training him hard, and at the end, sweaty and doubled over, Reggi thanked him.

'I really enjoyed it,' he said as he panted for breath.

'You did well. Great, in fact. Look, if you do get a run in the topside, you have to give it your all, you understand? It will be your one chance to impress my brother.'

'I will. I want to do it.'

'Good. Okay, see you on Saturday morning.'

Reggi took his leave, sprinting across the field.

Martino took off his sweaty shirt and swapped it for a dry, clean one in his sports bag. He glanced up at the stands and was startled to see a lone figure sitting there.

'Martino.' His father rose and started walking down the steps. He jumped the fence and strolled to him on the field.

'You're starting to make a habit of coming to training.' Martino smirked.

'I see you're training Reggi.'

'Yes.'

'You said you'd take a look at him and now you're training him. Is he any good?'

'Yeah, he's good. He's just as good as Nardo at the same age.'

His father seemed stunned to hear it. 'That's great news. I don't like to interfere or put pressure on Nardo if he's not any good, but if he is, well, I can ask Nardo again. Do you think Nardo will give him a game?'

'He might get twenty minutes, Saturday week.'

'Saturday week,' his father said, considering it. 'That your idea?'

Martino nodded and was taken aback to see his father's eyes fill with tears.

'What is it?'

'There are things you don't know about,' he said, shuffling his feet. 'But perhaps you're old enough now to know about such things. You should know ...' his father mumbled, searching for the words. 'Cappi didn't just help Edrico, Roberto and myself escape from prison. We ... we were on the edge of a sinkhole—a big, gaping hellhole in the ground. And the Yugoslavs were pushing us one by one into it—to certain death. It was a mass execution.'

His voice was soft and reluctant. He fell silent for a moment, seemingly remembering the horror of it. 'It is impossible to describe what it was like—the look on the men's faces as they were pushed. I still see them, all the time.' After a couple of breaths, he continued.

'Then Cappi showed up, with one pistol and some half-baked ruse to get me out of there. Before we knew it, he'd started a rebellion and he saved the whole group of us. And the thing is, while he was there, saving our lives, the Yugoslav soldiers were at his parents' farmhouse trying to arrest his brother.'

His father stopped. His eyes filled with anguish, but he pushed on with his tale. 'Cappi's brother and father fought back and they were killed. Shot dead, in front of his mother, Lisa. That happened thirty-five years, ago, and it still feels like yesterday.'

Martino was shocked to hear it. 'I did not know this,' he said.

Yet his father was not finished. He was still remembering. 'Cappi's father opened his home to us and gave us refuge for a year—all of us. And he lost his life on the day his son saved ours. I can't forget that. I can't. And so, when Cappi came to me and said ever so casually over a couple of beers one night, "Hey Ettore, any chance Nardo can give my son a game in the topside?" ...'

His father's voice had cracked and his eyes were awash with unshed tears.

'One game! He asked for a soccer game. The first time in thirty-five years he's asked me for anything from me, and all that time I've been waiting, trying to think of ways to repay him. Nothing ever coming up, because Cappi never asks for anything. He is always giving, never taking. But he asked for that. And Nardo refused it.'

'He's under a lot of pressure ...'

'I know. But you are training him.'

'Yes.'

'You can convince Nardo to give him a run. I know you will. You're a good man, Martino. I know we've had our differences in the past. But now you've got your own electrical business, a nice house, a beautiful wife and two daughters. You've done me proud.'

He patted Martino on the back. It felt good.

'I'll see you at Gian's wedding, Sunday week. And tell your wife I've booked the first dance with her,' his father said, finishing up.

Martino found his smile at last. 'I'll tell her that.'

'And Martino ...'

He looked up expectantly.

'Is Reggi really that good?'

'Yes, He is.' He laughed. 'Lucky for Nardo, hey?'

His father nodded, well pleased. 'He's in good hands.'

Then he was walking away—tall and strong, with thinning black hair. Martino watched him go, admiring him. He was seventy years old and still working as a panel beater, still working six days a week. He walked slowly up the hill and took the corner. Martino picked up his training bag, feeling light of heart. His father had said he was proud of him, words that any son longed to hear. And yet he was proud of his Pa too:—proud of how hard he'd worked, proud of his sense of honour. God, he felt more than pride ... he loved the man and always had. To think what he had gone through in Fiume, facing his own death, seeing others killed! He had been through a lot and given a lot, and was still living to repay his debts. He was a good man.

Martino decided he would do whatever he could to help his father pay back Cappi. He wanted to. After all Cappi had done for him, it would be his pleasure.

Chapter twenty-seven

July 1979
Brisbane

The game on Saturday got off to an abysmal start.

The opposition scored in the first fifteen minutes. Nardo paced the sideline, chewing gum, looking anxious. Nothing was going to plan. At halftime, no one wanted to be in the dressing room. He was enraged, shouting about every fault his eyes had detected in the past forty-five minutes of play.

The team went out—fired up, but unable to deliver. Another two goals were scored against them in what was seen by all as a devastating loss for the club.

'The sports journalists will have a field day. They'll attack my every decision,' Nardo said to himself, and he wasn't proven wrong.

After the game, Nardo didn't want to face anyone. He left without saying goodbye to the players or his family.

The following Saturday, Nardo paced the dressing room, sweat glistening on his forehead. Everything rested on that day's match. A loss would see him sacked. He chewed gum and changed his mind several times as to whom he would play and in what position.

Martino approached him minutes before the match was due to start. 'Just stay calm,' he told him. 'Look, I know you don't need me to go on about it, but last Saturday I played Reggi as striker for me, and he scored a hat trick. It was easy for him. He can find the net!'

'It was just southeast league,' Nardo said tersely.

Martino felt as though he'd been slapped, but he gritted his teeth and went on. 'Even so, even though it was just southeast league, he's got it. He can score. Trust me.'

'I lose this game … the season's over,' Nardo said. 'It's all over. Everything I've worked for. My reputation in ruins.'

'Reggi can win it for you. But look, if you don't believe me, don't worry about it. The deal is off. It's your call. This game means too much to you. But just remember, Cappi had your back once … Just saying.' And with that Martino stalked off, his breath coming hard and fast. He had said what he wanted to say. The decision was in his brother's hands. He had to hope he would listen and take a chance. The way he saw it, Nardo had no choice left but to take a risk.

Nardo heard Martino's choice of words. 'Cappi had your back …' And they echoed through his mind in a faraway memory. Greta camp. A boy with a knife. He hung his head and cursed. Martino had a point.

Back in the grandstand, Martino found Donna and his daughters and sat with them. To the far right, he saw his parents sitting with Nonna and Maria and their friends. Cappi was among them.

'Hey, Martino!'

He turned to see Taddeo and Daniela passing people in the stands to reach him. He leapt to his feet.

'You're here! When did you fly in to Brisbane?' He slapped Taddeo on the back and kissed Daniela, who happily sat next to Donna. Daniela looked as lovely as ever, dressed in a blue pants suit. The women greeted each other as old friends.

'We flew in yesterday, spent the night at the Stafford house,' Taddeo replied.

'Just up for Gian's wedding, or will you stay on a while?'

'Just for the wedding. We'll go back Monday.'

The players were starting to run on to the field and Martino's eyes were drawn to them. He searched their faces, sized up their builds, and eventually spied the shortest of the pack, Reggi, and felt a rush of relief and renewed affection for his brother. He had listened—and what was more he was starting with him, which meant if he performed he could earn himself a full game.

Come on, Reggi, he thought.

The whistle blew and Donna, still sitting on his right, took his hand. 'I'm as nervous as you,' she said, knowing all about it. 'Come on, Reggi,' she whispered, willing him to perform.

Nardo's team was jittery. They couldn't settle and the ball was everywhere but where they wanted it. The opposition was calmer, on top of it, dominating, pushing up the field. Nardo couldn't sit still. He was on his feet, living every moment of the game. Then bang. The ball was sliding beneath the post, the Italian keeper unable to get a hand to it.

They were one down and only two minutes in.

Nardo was white in the face. He stopped pacing and plopped down on the bench. Martino felt his temples begin to throb. 'Come on. Turn it around. Settle down.'

Half an hour later, the Italian team found their rhythm but they were struggling, their confidence was low and they weren't taking chances. Nardo could hardly watch. Reggi, still on the field, was always putting himself in the right spot up front, but was not being fed the ball. The team, not knowing him, were not trusting him with it. It was a debacle.

At halftime, with the score still one-nil down, Martino rose to his feet.

'Where you going?' Taddeo asked.

'I have to do something,' he replied, and hurried away. His feet took him around the back of the stands where he found the door to the dressing room. He entered. Nardo was shouting. Extreme stress had him fired up.

'Hey, Nardo,' he called across the team.

His brother looked up, stunned to be interrupted.

'Mind if I have a few words?' Martino inquired, a light glint in his eyes.

Nardo sighed and shook his head. 'All right. You've got one minute. Make it snappy,' he said and leaned against the wall, looking defeated.

'I just wanted to say: great first half. You were starting to settle. Mid-field, you need to start bringing the ball out wide and shoot them low across the centre to Reggi. You see Reggi—he's short—see. He's not going to win in the air, but he's fast—he'll get there first. And see those feet. Go on, look at them!'

All the players gazed down at Reggi's black boots.

'He has the best left foot that I've seen in years. In fact, the last time I saw anyone shoot like him, it was when I played with my brother here. So, trust him. Get the balls up front, keep them low and watch him win it for us. You all can do it. You've just been unlucky the past few weeks. Unlucky! Now I'm going to go back out there and watch you boys turn it around. Don't do it for yourself, do it for your coach. He's given you so much over the years. Given you his life. He believes in you. So, now's the time to give back. Okay, that's my one minute.'

The players clapped, smiling, responding. He peered up at his brother and saw Nardo had been moved by his words.

'All right, you heard my brother. Go out there and turn things around.'

The players returned to the field, looking at Reggi somewhat differently. Martino had compared him to Nardo—no small compliment. They were keen to see if he could live up to such high praise.

Almost as soon as the whistle had blown, the mid-field had secured the ball and pushed it up front, slotting it low to Reggi.

Martino, sitting next to Donna, had his heart in his mouth. "Come on. Show them, Reggi. I know you can do it," he said to himself.

And being young and confident and believing in himself, Reggi, despite being well back from goals, spun on the ball and slammed it, hard and fast and right on target.

The cheer that erupted confirmed what Martino's eyes had just seen. Reggi had scored a cracker of a goal, less than one minute after the referee had started the second half. The goal changed everything. It was the confidence boost the struggling team needed, and now they had a striker who they believed in. They could win it and they started to fight for it.

The set moves Nardo had drummed into them started to come to life. They were playing smoothly, playing as a team, eager to get the ball up the front, to slide it across to Reggi.

But time was ticking and the score was stuck on a draw. They needed another goal. Nardo prayed for it. And then, with ten minutes to go, every eye in the stand was watching the ball being run down the wing, saw it cross to Reggi. Most people sprung to their feet as the new, fresh striker dropped the ball to his feet and took a shot with his left. It curved; the goalkeeper stretched his arm, hoping to get a hand to it, but it couldn't be stopped. The ball dropped into the far corner of the net.

Nardo ran to the sideline, screaming, arms up in the air. His manager was hugging him, the fans were jumping and shouting and cheering. It was bedlam.

Martino gazed across the stands and saw Cappi electrified with excitement on his feet, flashing an enormous smile, and his father was patting him on the back, laughing and nodding and wiping at his eyes. In that moment, Martino took a deep and steady breath of peace. All was well with the world, with his father's world.

Finally, the referee blew the full-time whistle. The elusive win was secured and the celebrations could begin.

The first to cross his path after the game were his mother, father, Nonna and Maria.

'What a game!' his father said.

'I've never cheered so much,' his mother said, smiling at him. 'It was wonderful to see Reggi score.'

'It was the best outcome possible,' Martino agreed, accepting kisses from his mother, sister and Nonna. 'I will go and congratulate Nardo.'

'Yes, tell him how happy we are. It's great to see him break that losing streak,' his father said.

At the dressing room, the players welcomed him in, smiles everywhere.

'You did great, fellows,' he told them, shaking hands with a few of them. 'Where's my brother?'

'He's upstairs in the box with the president,' the midfielder responded. 'He was summoned.'

Martino saw Reggi taking off his boots. He bent over to speak to him directly. 'Nice one. I knew you'd do it.'

Reggi smiled. 'Thanks. Thanks for knowing!'

'No problem.'

Outside the stand was emptying out, people drifting up to the clubhouse, over to the Italian club or up to their cars. He knew Donna and his girls were at the clubhouse. He would meet them there soon. Looking to the back of the stand, Martino spotted Nardo and the club president in the glass sealed box, and so sat down to wait for him. Ten minutes later, Nardo came and gingerly sat down next to him.

'All done? President happy?'

When Nardo didn't respond, Martino glanced sideways with a prickling of concern. 'What did he say?'

'Too little too late.'

'What?'

'It means I take a walk anyway. They've bought a player from overseas. They want one of them to play and coach.'

'No!'

'They've been lining it up for weeks. The warning was just to buy some time and try and push for a win in the meantime. He arrives this Tuesday.'

'They can't sack you—you!'

'They have, they can and they just did.'

'But everyone's up there celebrating. They won't want you gone. The players will protest.'

'The players are under contract. They'll have to accept it. Look, I can't go up there. I'm not in the mood for celebrating and can't tell anyone just yet. I'm going to go home.'

Martino was shocked. 'I'll go get Donna and we'll come back to your place ...'

'No. I really don't feel like company. Thanks, but no.'

'Sure. Look if you want to go out for a drink later, give me a call.'

Nardo nodded absently. It looked as though his whole world had just been ripped out from beneath him. He came unsteadily to his feet.

'Nardo ...' Martino stood and looked him in the eye. 'With you gone, there's no point me staying. I'll resign from coaching too. We'll find another club, you and I, coaches together. I have business connections in Fortitude Valley, the types who follow soccer and could help us fund a team. I know they will. And we'll take Reggi with us.'

That made Nardo smile wanly. 'Reggi ... you were right about him. Top player. All right, we'll talk about next season, another time. Right now, I don't even want to look at a soccer ball.'

'Understandable.'

Martino walked with him and saw him to his car. He then went up to the clubhouse and spread the word amongst the players that Nardo wasn't feeling well and had gone home.

He found Donna and his daughters with Taddeo and Daniela, and Gian and his bride-to-be Simone.

He broke the real news about what had happened to Nardo and they were suitably stunned.

'God, if you can sack someone after all that success, no one's safe,' Gian observed. 'Looks like my soccer management days are over.'

'Nah. We'll find another club,' Martino said.

'Well, shall we get out of here then?' Taddeo asked.

'Yes, why don't you all come back to our place? No point staying here now.'

They parted company to walk to their cars.

In the carpark, Martino looked at his wife and pulled her close. 'You know, with the soccer season being cut short, we'll have more time together.'

'That's true,' she said, starting to see the bright side.

'Perhaps we could do a trip.'

'A trip?'

'You know … go to Italy or something.'

Donna squealed her delight and wrapped her arms around his neck. 'I'd love that,' she said, kissing him hard on the lips.

Dinner was had at their place. They talked about Nardo and his run of bad luck. Gian and Simone left early, given their wedding was taking place the following day.

Taddeo, who had consumed a lot of wine, accepted an invitation for him and Daniela to sleep over. Martino dragged out a spare mattress and the couple slept in their lounge room.

That night, Martino took a while to surrender his mind to sleep. It had been a long and taxing day, his thoughts still reeling from Nardo's sacking. Sleep claimed him just after midnight. At three am, the phone rang.

He was instantly awake and alarmed. The phone never rang at that hour. On the other end of the receiver, he heard Nardo's quavering voice. 'Martino, come quick to the Stafford house. There's been a fire.'

'A fire?'

'It's bad. Just come.'

Chapter twenty-eight

Martino hung up the phone and swung out of bed.

'What's wrong?' Donna was alert and sitting up.

'There's been a fire at my parents' place. Nardo wants me over there. I'm going … I'll wake Taddeo.'

He struggled to pull on clothes as his mind was racing ahead of his fingers. He grabbed his keys and quietly crept into the lounge room.

'Taddeo,' he called into the darkness.

Taddeo and Daniela both woke.

'Come with me. There's trouble.'

The drive took just under twenty minutes, and during that time Martino imagined all kinds of scenarios, the worst being that Nonna, at age eighty-six, might not have made it out of the house. He braced himself for such dreadful news.

But the reality was much worse.

The exterior of the house was black where flames had licked out windows. Inside was a charred mess of burnt walls and furniture and melted plastics. Four fire engines were stationary out front and firemen were surrounding the house, still hosing down smouldering embers. Neighbours were gathered in the street, looking on the scene sombrely, with expressions of dazed disbelief.

Next to an ambulance, three bodies beneath white sheets were laid out on the front grass.

Martino stared at them. Why weren't they moving? Why

were their faces covered? Why weren't the paramedics treating them? He was confused and distressed.

Nardo was only a few feet away from the bodies, his hands thrust in his pockets, his face stony.

'What … where …?' Martino found his voice as he reached his brother. Taddeo was behind him, stiff and silent.

Nardo spoke slowly, his words heavy with fresh grief and shock. 'Mama, Nonna, Maria,' he said simply. 'The smoke got to them. Found in the hallway.'

'And Pa?'

'In hospital … not likely to make it.'

Martino heard the news, but the words were coming at him from a far distance, as though his mind and senses were trying to retreat from them. He had gone very cold. He crossed his arms across his chest and stared at the sheet-covered bodies.

There lay his mother, little sister and grandmother. The word 'no' came loud and clear in his mind, but he did not voice it. He could not deny what his eyes were seeing.

'I was waiting for you. I thought we should go to the hospital together.' Nardo was speaking from far away again, but he understood.

'Yes, we must,' Martino mumbled on lips that hardly felt his own. He was floating from his body, feeling separate, removed. It was so cold.

'Are you ready?' a policewoman asked.

The three brothers climbed in the back of a police car and were driven to the hospital.

'Have you called Marietta and Isabella?' Taddeo thought to ask.

Nardo nodded. 'I phoned them. They will make their way to the hospital.'

They did not speak again.

The doctors who met them had no hope to offer. 'We're very

sorry. His outlook is not good. We don't expect a recovery. You should prepare yourselves and say your goodbyes.'

The brothers were shown to a room where their father lay. They approached his bed cautiously, hardly able to take in what was happening, what had happened.

Their father opened his eyes. His chest and arms were wrapped in bandages. There was a drip attached to his arm.

'The others …?' he wheezed hoarsely. His expression was one of overwhelming concern. He was in a state of panic and high anxiety, though he could hardly move.

Tears welled. Nardo cleared his throat and replied firmly, 'They all got out. They are all doing fine. They are in the women's ward. They're alive.'

Martino felt his father's eyes turn to him, wanting confirmation.

Martino nodded. Taddeo did too.

Hard as it was to lie at such a time about such a thing, Martino wanted his father to pass away in peace.

His father's gaze softened in relief. He took a ragged, deep breath.

'What happened? How did the fire start?' Nardo asked.

'I got up in the middle of the night and had a cigarette,' he said, his voice raspy. Worry and guilt were in his eyes. 'When I woke up … there were flames and smoke everywhere … We ran to the front door but couldn't …' He coughed violently, then settled, though he seemed to be fighting back pain. 'The door wouldn't open. It went black. I must've passed out. But they are alive, that is good … How's the house?'

'Just needs repainting. We'll get Roberto to do it,' Martino said flatly.

His father slightly relaxed. He seemed to like the idea of it.

But it was another lie. The house had been completely gutted. Martino and his brothers didn't have the heart to tell him.

'It's a fine house, Pa,' Martino said, as his father closed his eyes. 'You did good.'

Ettore Saforo died later that day, believing his family was well and safe and his house still stood intact. He died in peace.

Investigations later revealed that ash from a cigarette had fallen on to the carpet near a can of kerosene, which had been used for cleaning Ettore's work overalls as well as for filling a kero-heater. It had quickly ignited flames.

The wedding was cancelled. Gian and Simone could not celebrate after what had happened. Instead, funeral plans were put in motion.

The funeral was held on a rainy, dreary day. More than one thousand people attended. Many came from the Italian and soccer communities. They dressed in black and they filled the large church, their talk dropping away to silence as they entered, their eyes resting on four coffins at the front.

Among those invited to address the crowd was Roberto. Finding it more comfortable to speak in Italian, he did so. He read from a prepared speech.

'I've known the family for thirty-five years. Ettore was a hardworking man, a devoted husband and a good father. He came here to Australia from Fiume. He came here from Italy. We came out together on the ship with hopes and dreams of finding work, of rebuilding our lives. We came to Australia, wanting to make ourselves a new home. And we did. Ettore did. He gave his family the home they longed for. He watched his children grow up, and I know how proud he was of each of them.'

Roberto stopped to gulp. He was finding it difficult.

'Contessa was a beautiful, strong woman who loved her family very much. She too worked long hours to ensure her children did not want for anything. She met adversity with a sense of humour and had a sense of loyalty that gave her many long-term friendships. She was a proud mother and grandmother. Her own mother, Rosa, who we all knew fondly as Nonna, kept the family united with her strength, courage and wisdom. Nonna always knew what to say at the right moment. Young Maria may have come into this world with challenges but she was blessed with a big heart. She loved her family dearly and looked up to all her brothers and sisters. She never had a bad word for anyone,— only a smile.

'They will all be missed.

'On a personal note … Ettore was my friend. He helped me get through some very hard times. He was a good man, an honourable man. He leaves behind friends who will miss him, who can't thank him enough for all he did for them in life. I will miss him.'

Roberto took his seat.

The tears turned to wails as the funeral progressed. There was not a dry eye to be seen anywhere.

Martino felt empty inside. He had always sensed that his parents and Nonna were there for him, watching over him, even if it was just from the stands of a soccer field. They had followed him and his life and now they were gone—too soon.

At the wake, Martino received sympathy from all quarters. His parents' friends—Bianca, Roberto and Gilda; Tazia; Lisa, Cappi and Amelia; and Lena and Rico with their two daughters Vittoria and Elisa, now grown women aged in their thirties— gathered around him. They were clearly overcome by the tragedy and had few words of comfort to offer. They were hurting too.

Martino held Donna's hand, wanting her close. She gave him strength.

Nardo came over with his wife, Rose.

'Any chance we can find something stronger than coffee?' Martino asked his brother.

'I'll go see if the bar is open.'

Nardo returned with a flask of wine and two glasses. He

and Martino and their wives sat at a table. Taddeo, Isabella and Marietta, looking exhausted and red-eyed, wandered over with their partners. They all kissed and embraced and pulled up chairs.

'Well, it seems the house can be saved,' Nardo began, knowing he was surrounded by his siblings. 'But it will take a lot of repairing.'

There was silence, then Martino spoke. 'It won't be the same without them.'

'I think the house should be put to rest too,' Marietta declared, leaning against Elmo for support.

Isabella nodded tearfully.

'All right. We'll have it demolished,' Nardo agreed. 'Looks like all is lost then. Not much survived the flames. Even Pa's life savings—remember he didn't believe in banks? He kept everything in the house and he never told us where. It will be impossible to find it among the rubble.'

Their father had saved tens of thousands of dollars. It seemed a waste to have it go up in flames, after all that work panel beating.

'No, wait,' said Isabella. 'Nonna told me. She told me that if ever anything should happen ...' She stopped and wiped at her tears. 'The money is in a tin in the storage room under the house. It's in a tin and I know where.'

It was decided then to make one last trip to the house as a family and recover what they could, including the tin.

The Saforo siblings visited the house. Martino did not go inside. He remained in the yard where so many memories came tumbling back to him. He remembered the primary school toughs hanging off the fence, weeding and watering the damned garden, push-starting the old Dodge, kicking his soccer ball against the wall—left foot, right foot, left foot—Nonna handing him a chocolate ...

The tin was found. A few items were recovered. And then Martino drove away, knowing he was traversing that street for the final time. He didn't look back.

Epilogue

Later that year, Martino and Donna and their two daughters made the trip to Italy.

As well as seeing the marvellous tourist destinations of Rome, Florence and Venice, they travelled north to Trieste and crossed the border into Yugoslavia to see Rijeka, formerly known as Fiume.

Martino had only been a young boy when he had left Trieste, but still his feet retraced his old steps, finding where the refugee camp had been, the train station, and where he had followed the cleaner on his rounds. He proudly showed his family all he could remember, telling them about the American soldiers and how kind they had been to the Italians.

He had no memory of Fiume, being too young when his family had fled the city. Still, he walked Fiume's cobbled streets and around its magnificent port, trying to get a sense of the place. But it belonged to Yugoslavia and no longer felt Italian. It did not feel like his place of origin. Before he took his leave, he approached the harbour and tossed a penny into its waters. The coin with a kangaroo on its face sank rapidly—a piece of Australia finding its way to the bottom of the faraway port. It felt right to bring something back and leave it behind. For his parents, who hadn't returned.

After months of grieving, Martino sought out Nardo and, with both of them struggling with their loss, made plans to immerse themselves in soccer. They wanted to keep busy, to keep their minds occupied.

Together they approached a club, and bringing financial backing with them the two heavyweight coaches were appointed.

Nardo was made head coach and Martino his assistant. In their first year in first division, they won the premiership and grand final, seeing the team promoted to state league.

They had done it again—together. Their success had the Italian-based club at Spencer Park asking Nardo to return. Of course, he went.

Marietta and Elmo moved to Perth in Western Australia, chasing work. They had two children. Taddeo and Daniela soon followed them, placing half the Saforo family on the other side of Australia. The couple also had two children.

Isabella settled with her husband in Brisbane's New Farm and they raised two boys.

As for Monte … Trialled and convicted of his father's murder, he was later found dead in his cell under suspicious circumstances. Martino wondered if perhaps Francois had somehow had a hand in it. For Francois always knew a guy, who knew a guy, who could do a favour …

Many, many years later, Nardo would be named a 'legend' at the football club that he had served during the 1960s and 1970s, being described as the principle architect of the greatest era in the club's history as coach, presiding over a period in which the club had won twenty-two trophies. A photo of him as coach with his team resides on the club's wall, a permanent tribute to the impact he had there.

Martino also enjoyed a long and successful coaching career, spanning many clubs and winning multiple premierships in high divisions, but there came a day when he finally hung up the soccer boots. His electrical contracting business had also been successful. His father had been right. A trade had served him well. He put through many apprentices of his own and, when it came time to retire, he handed the thriving business over to his son-in-law.

In more recent times, during the soccer seasons, he has been seen in the stands at Spencer Park, supporting the outfit that began as Azzurri, but became known as the Brisbane City Football Club. It is easy to imagine he sits there with the ghosts of those Italians, who set up the club in the 1950s, motivated by a love of the game with the round ball.

And he knows those Italians brought so much more than that.

They came with a suitcase and their dreams and finally bought a house. And in the land of kangaroos, amongst the hard work, the learning of a language and the sharing of cultures, they established a home. That's what it was all about.

Acknowledgments

This acknowledgment contains spoilers.

I would like to acknowledge my father and his siblings for their support. Their experiences in coming out from Italy and settling in Australia in the 1950s inspired the writing of this novel.

While based on many true events, fictional licence was taken for dramatic purposes. However, I want to acknowledge that my father's family was among the first Italian families to settle in Stafford, Brisbane, and that their Stafford house was gutted by fire on 3 July 1978. The fire tragically took the lives of my father's parents, grandmother and sister, leaving Brisbane's large Italian-Australian community in mourning. At the time of their passing, his father was aged 66, mother aged 64, Nonna was 86 and his sister was just 26. My greatest wish is that this story honours their memory and all they achieved.

The soccer achievements featured are based on victories that occurred during the golden years at Brisbane City Soccer Club, once known as Azzurri. My father's older brother played a significant part in that success and has been named a Club Legend. However, it must be said that the character, Reggi, is purely fictional and the soccer events surrounding him are not based on any truth whatsoever.

A sincere thank you to my husband, Rene, who has only ever had support and encouragement for my writing.

I would also like to thank the Museo Italiano in Melbourne for hosting the official launch of my debut novel, *Port of No Return*.

I am forever grateful to my publisher Michelle Lovi at Odyssey Books for putting into print *Port of No Return*, and then continuing their belief and trust in my work to publish its sequel, *Wanderers No More*. Thank you to my editor Jenna O'Connell, whose expertise helped to shape and strengthen both works.

Lastly, and most sincerely, I thank my readers for following my characters on their journey from Italy to Australia, a journey I hope you've found inspiring.

Refugees are people. They are families. They seek peace and a place to call home. They want jobs, education, hope. Wanderers No More? What a wonderful world it would be.

About the Author

Michelle Saftich resides in Brisbane, Australia, with her husband and two children. She holds a Bachelor of Business/ Communications Degree majoring in journalism from the Queensland University of Technology (QUT). For the past twenty years, she has worked in communications, including print journalism, sub-editing, communications management and media relations. In 1999, she was named National Winner for Best News Story in the ASNA (Australian Suburban Newspaper Awards). Born and raised in Brisbane, she spent ten years living in Sydney, and two years in Osaka, Japan, where she taught English.

Connect with Michelle at www.michellesaftich.com